MR. DARCY'S CIPHER

SPIES AND PREJUDICE BOOK 1

VIOLET KING

ABOUT THIS BOOK

A secret letter brings them together. Will an assassin tear them apart?

For Miss Elizabeth Bennet, love is the cipher she cannot crack.

Outside the Longbourn house, Elizabeth Bennet is an ordinary country miss. But in secret, she and her father crack codes to foil Napoleon's schemes against England. More than anything, Elizabeth wants to be loved for herself, but how can she when she lives a double life?

For Mr. Fitzwilliam Darcy, a coded letter hides the key to his heart.

After Fitzwilliam Darcy's brother is killed in France, a coded letter carries his final words and a dangerous secret. Mr. Darcy brings the letter to the

Bennets for answers. But soon the code is the least of Mr. Darcy's conundrums as he finds himself falling for Elizabeth Bennet. Caught between an assassin and an old enemy, can Mr. Darcy accept his feelings and win Miss Elizabeth's heart before it is too late?

Find out in Mr. Darcy's Cipher, Book 1 of the Spies and Prejudice series. Mr. Darcy's Cipher is a *Pride and Prejudice* variation novel of 65,000 words with heaps of romance, humor, suspense, code-cracking, and two sometimes bullheaded but lovable leads who struggle to save a nation while falling in love.

If you love *Pride and Prejudice* variations with a twist of espionage, start reading Mr. Darcy's Cipher now!

CONTENTS

Acknowledgments   vii

Chapter 1   1
Chapter 2   11
Chapter 3   21
Chapter 4   33
Chapter 5   47
Chapter 6   65
Chapter 7   77
Chapter 8   93
Chapter 9   107
Chapter 10   117
Chapter 11   131
Chapter 12   145
Chapter 13   161
Chapter 14   173
Chapter 15   191
Chapter 16   197
Chapter 17   211
Chapter 18   219
Chapter 19   229
Chapter 20   239
Chapter 21   251
Chapter 22   261
Chapter 23   265
Chapter 24   275
Chapter 25   293
Chapter 26   305

Chapter 27   315
Chapter 28   337
Chapter 29   349
Chapter 30   361
Epilogue   371

Author's Note   377
About the Author   383

ACKNOWLEDGMENTS

First, I give thanks to God and my mom for supporting me even on my grumpiest writing days. I am also grateful to my editor Jersey Devil Editing who fixed all of the problems in the manuscript I couldn't see. I wrote this dedication after the edit was done, so if you see errors here, they are mine.

Next, a HUGE THANK YOU to author Elizabeth Ann West who encouraged me to try my hand at writing a novel in the world of Pride and Prejudice. And so much love and gratitude to the whole writing productivity gang, including Pat, Mr. Sparkle, Bella, Susannah, Dana and Echo who kept me getting words on the page at least five days a week!

I am also indebted to the wonderful readers and

reviewers on FFnet , including but not limited to Gaskellian, MerytonMiss, EightYearsandaHalf, Twilight Reader Too, Liysyl, Wermeth, Lynned13, EnglishLitLover, Ashiana and countless others who encouraged me and let me know when my Regency (and overall story) went awry. You have my heartfelt gratitude.

And a massive thank you to Sonya, Steph, Kenny B, Gretchen, and the other fine folks at Rueban's Rockin' Roof Deck Weekly Salon this past summer who listened to me read out the first five chapters of this book said they wanted more. You rock!

Lastly, for everyone who may not be mentioned by name in this dedication, that is my fault. Know I hold you in my heart.

1
———

*I*t was a truth universally acknowledged within the Longbourn House that of Mr. Bennet's five daughters, Lizzie was the only one who had inherited her father's love of puzzles.

At first, humoring Elizabeth was a matter of pride. One autumn afternoon when Elizabeth was nine years of age, she slipped beside him on the chaise and pointed at a large stack of papers from a missive he had received that morning from London.

"What an odd script!" Elizabeth exclaimed at the seemingly nonsensical symbols. "Is it Greek?"

"It is a cipher." Mr. Bennet leaned closer to his daughter, and the ghost of a smile teased his lips. "A secret."

"What kind of secret?"

"To discover that, one must unwind the code."

Lizzie nodded, her dark eyes shining. "Show me!"

Mr. Bennet put in front of her a sheet of paper and explained to her how to go about decoding a simple Caesar cipher. He expected Lizzie to grow weary of the exercise, as her older sister Jane had done a year before, but Elizabeth was tenacious. Before half an hour had passed, she handed back the code, deciphered in small, precise script.

And so father and daughter began a lifelong pattern of instruction. And as Mr. Bennet's eyesight failed him, it was Lizzie who read the missives sent from the prime minister's office to foil Bonaparte's designs on conquering England.

Had Elizabeth been born a man, Mr. Bennet might have informed others of her skills, but code-breaking wasn't an appropriate vocation for a young lady. Worse, he had grown dependent on her abilities as his eyesight rendered the world around him a cipher that became increasingly difficult to navigate. So he kept Lizzie's abilities, and his own deficiencies, from being discovered outside the walls of his own home.

The relationship between father and daughter at points quite irritated Mrs. Bennet, who had no interest in puzzles nor the faculties for solving them. But she humored her husband while at the same time entreating her daughter to stay silent with potential suitors about her oddities. And Lizzie, being a good-natured, lighthearted, and dutiful young woman of twenty years, yielded to her mother in this, not wanting her own eccentricities to stand in the way of her finding a loving match.

Father and daughter sat, head bowed over what appeared to be a Caesar cipher when Mrs. Bennet noisily entered her husband's study.

"My dear Mr. Bennet," said the lady to him. She bustled across the room to the window and flung it open. "How long have the pair of you been cooped up in this room without even the slightest hint of a breeze to liven the air?" The papers on Mr. Bennet's desk fluttered beneath twin paper-weights as a damp autumn breeze blew over the room.

Mr. Bennet leaned back in his chair. The clock said half three, too early for luncheon or tea. His wife rarely ventured into his domain at this point of the day. "It is half three," returned Mr. Bennet. "What is the matter?"

Mrs. Bennet glanced over at Elizabeth, who despite her best efforts had speckles of black ink on her fingers and speckling the dull walnut colored fabric of her linen mitts, as, lips moving, she tapped at a paper scrawled all over in code with the back of her pen.

"Lizzie! Your hands! My heavens, you must wash these immediately and change into something more suitable!"

Elizabeth looked up. "Mother?"

"Suitable for what?" Mr. Bennet asked. "She hasn't any balls or visits planned at this time of the day, has she?"

"No! It is even better." Mrs. Bennet brought her hands up to her chest with a delighted intake of breath. "Your guest, a young, handsome and unmarried gentleman by the name of Mr. Darcy is here in our parlor! Why did you not inform me he was calling? He is in every manner proper, from his waistcoat to his Hessians. I would have had the cook prepare a special lunch so he might feel more welcome and have a more pleasant opportunity to meet and converse with our daughters."

"Mr. Darcy..." Mr. Bennet mused. "Mr. Fitzwilliam Darcy. Yes. I had quite forgotten the date. Mr. Darcy is not here for lunch. His deceased brother sent a letter, presumably in code, and he wished it deciphered. As the younger Mr. Darcy was stationed in France, I felt it imperative to assess the cipher myself to make certain it had nothing to do with our affairs abroad. Now, why have you abandoned the elder Mr. Darcy in our parlor?"

"For Lizzie's sake!" Mrs. Bennet responded. "Elizabeth, my nerves cannot bear the thought of your bluestocking tendencies being revealed to such esteemed company. You may never marry! I fear I might faint. Mr. Bennet, how is it you allowed your daughter to come to such a state? Have you no eyes?"

"I fear I still am in possession of both, however poorly they serve me."

"Well, my dear," Mrs. Bennet said, skimming over the distasteful fact of her husband's failing eyesight as it, to some extent, negated his periodic compliments of her remaining beauty. "It would behoove you both for Lizzie to scrub her hands at the very least. We may not have time to change her into a more flattering dress, but—"

"Lizzie, stay put," Mr. Bennet said. "My dear," he continued. "This gentleman is here to converse with me?"

"His manners are exquisite, and with such a serious air, and elder Mr. Darcy you say? Perhaps eldest," Mrs. Bennet added hopefully. "He is certainly of fine breeding. I had thought he might be but a second or third son commissioned with the militia or army though he gave no rank and he does not wear regimentals—"

"Elder? Eldest? It does not answer the question of why he remains idling in our parlor."

"Lizzie must be made suitable. It is wonderful news. First Mr. Bingley taking possession of Netherfield house, and now—"

"Mr. Bingley? What has any of this to do with Mr. Bingley?"

"You do not listen at all." Mrs. Bennet let out a weary sigh. "How painful is your disregard! We discussed Mr. Bingley a week ago. He is likely arrived at this point. Oh! What if this Mr. Darcy is a guest of Mr. Bingley?"

"Suppose—"

"And Mr. Bingley has taken possession of Netherfield Park. Such a fine thing for our girls, or it would be if you called upon him before some other man's daughter snaps the young gentleman up! If you were to tear your attention for one moment from the war to tend to your duties at home—"

"It will do no good to our daughters to be settled if Bonaparte storms over the breadth of

England and seizes from them anything which they might have gained through marriage."

"Again with Bonaparte!" Mrs. Bennet stomped her foot. "We are all doing as we ought to support our men on the front. Have not myself and the other ladies sewn blankets and knitted warm items to send to our fighting men?

"But one must also accept that the concerns of our lives amount to more than opposing that vile man of the Continent who declares himself an emperor. I could not wish to believe you, my dear Mr. Bennet, spared no care for your daughters beyond how our Lizzie's keen eyes assist you in your deciphering.

"This Mr. Darcy, a handsome, young gentleman who is currently lacking a wife. I have no sense yet of his assets—"

"A difficult thing to determine in a few moments of conversation, though I do not doubt you gave a valiant effort," Mr. Bennet said with no small amount of sarcasm in his tone.

Mrs. Bennet ignored it. "This Mr. Darcy might provide an excellent match for one of our daughters. You understand this is of greater import than mere scribblings, as amusing as you both may find them. Now Lizzie, scrub your hands. Your father will be able to engage in idle conversation until you return—"

It was the wrong thing to say. Mr. Bennet's face flushed, and his voice was low and furious as he stated, "Bonaparte may invade at any moment, and you natter on about our daughter's hands? This gentleman, whether or not he is wed, will leave post-haste as soon as his brother's correspondence is deciphered; and in either case, if he cannot see past a pair of ink-dappled hands, he is of no use to us."

"No use!" Mrs. Bennet exclaimed. "In case you have forgotten, all five of your daughters are as yet unwed. And at the moment of your death, our house and all we own is entailed to your cousin."

"I am well aware of our difficulties, more so because you see fit to remind me of them daily."

"Already you refuse to call upon Mr. Bingley, stating now you do not remember the conversation we had on just this subject in this room a mere week ago. Oh, my nerves! It is as though a thousand spiders are skittering over my skin, and I cannot breathe for the fear. Oh Mr. Bennet!"

Mr. Bennet was unmoved.

"I can wash them," Elizabeth said to mollify her mother. She hated it when her parents fought, especially when she was the cause. No matter the state of her hands though, Elizabeth doubted a talent for deciphering code would offer her entry into a young gentleman's heart. It hardly mattered. If this Mr. Darcy was here about a code, he would depart quickly enough with his questions answered.

"No, Lizzie. We have kept Mr. Darcy waiting long enough. Send him in, Mrs. Bennet," Mr. Bennet ordered. "The quicker we handle it, the quicker he can be on his way."

"The point of this discussion is not to send an available young gentleman on his way—"

"Either send him in, or you will force me to go myself to receive him."

"No! Do not stir yourself on my behalf. I will have him brought here. Elizabeth, if you don't wash that ink away, at least take care to hide your fingers." Mrs. Bennet turned abruptly to the door, her skirts flaring out with the force of her spin as she strode with well-choreographed indignation from the room.

2

*M*rs. Bennet, a middle-aged blonde woman, her hair threaded silver, features touched with a remembered handsomeness and clothes clinging to youthful frivolity, guided Mr. Darcy into a small, well-cared for if not extravagant parlor area. "And Mrs. Darcy, how is she enjoying our fair town?"

For a moment, Darcy considered telling a falsehood, but even if he had been inclined towards lying, which he decidedly was not, an imaginary wife would be quickly disproven as he intended to stay an extended time in Hertfordshire. Still, it irked him to see the pointed curiosity and catlike hunger in Mrs. Bennet's gaze as she fished to find out if he was wed. "I am not as yet married," Mr. Darcy said after a pause.

"Oh! A regretful state for a man such as yourself!" Mrs. Bennet exclaimed with ill-hidden delight. "A wife brings tranquility and joy to a home. I trust you will be allowed leave enough to enjoy the hospitality of our town. There are many young ladies about who might capture your interest..."

Like her daughter, or however many daughters occupied this house, which now through acquaintanceship with their father he might be obligated to offer his attention. "If I might speak with Mr. Bennet," Darcy interjected. "I wrote to arrange this visit. It is business of the utmost urgency."

"Yes," Mrs. Bennet said. "I will let him know you have arrived." And with that, she swept out.

It was odd and not at all pleasant to be abandoned in the parlor of a stranger. Though compared to Mrs. Bennet's inquiries, Darcy's own dark thoughts were an improvement. His brother Reginald's final correspondence, much of it pages and pages of nonsense Latin, some blurred by water, weighed on his heart.

Reginald Darcy had died in France five months ago. The letter, water-stained and crushed at the corners where the envelope had been battered about for some time, was a voice whispering from the grave. Not that Darcy had seen his brother's actual resting place. Water and time had too ravaged his body for transport, especially considering the relations between England and France.

Reggie, lighthearted and at points irreverent Reggie, had lost his life not by an enemy bullet or sword, but instead to a knife in the dark. Murdered by a cutpurse, stripped of his valuables, and left putrefying in the sewer until only his watch remained to identify him.

Why the thief hadn't stolen that and his purse was another mystery Darcy found himself ill-equipped to solve.

Darcy took the watch from his pocket and flipped it open. Half three. What was taking Mrs. Bennet so long?

Darcy wondered again if accompanying Bingley to guest at his new estate was a good decision. Mr. Erasmus Bennet was reputed to be one of the finest codebreakers in England, though if that were the case, it made little sense for him to hole himself up so far from London.

It hardly mattered. The code would have been something Georgiana could decipher. It shouldn't have required a master codebreaker, and it quite annoyed Darcy that he hadn't worked it out on his own.

Of all the times for Reggie to be obscure in his presentation.

Reggie, like Wickham, possessed an easy charm, though unlike Wickham, Reggie's interests lay beyond gambling and tupping unsuspecting young women. Reggie had been intelligent, kind, and daring to a fault.

He had also, apparently by the multiple pages of Latin in the letter, been eager to convince Georgiana he found solace in religion on the Continent. Or converted to Catholicism, heaven forbid! Knowing his younger brother, Darcy doubted a sudden turn towards the devout. Reggie had always been more inclined to the flesh than spirit, mischievous with an easy grin, even as a babe in swaddling clothes.

It was difficult to accept he would never see his brother smile, or frown, or throw himself with reckless abandon into the boxing ring again.

Reggie's letter was addressed to Georgiana, but Darcy could not bear to give it to her without understanding it. First their father's death, then Wickham's betrayal, and now Reggie's senseless murder. Darcy was not a man inclined towards light humor, and the crushing weight of tragedy and crisis had weighted his already serious nature.

Georgiana was fragile, though she hid it behind her manners and a brave smile. Georgiana had loved Reggie, and her mourning of his passing set her mood as black as her clothing these past five months. Reggie and Georgie, as they called each other, were close in temperament, while Darcy, aware of his responsibilities from a young age, had always felt an obligation to watch out for them and ensure they understood and followed the rules.

Darcy's own protectiveness had led him to read his brother's letter to Georgiana. Protectiveness and some hidden vein of jealousy he refused to acknowledge even to himself. Georgiana looked towards Darcy for protection, but there had always been a barrier between them. This was the same barrier that kept Darcy apart from the world.

The lady of the house, Mrs. Bennet, finally returned. "This way, Mr. Darcy," she said. "How long will you be with us in Meryton? Not too short a visit, I hope?"

"A month at the least," Mr. Darcy admitted. "I was invited to stay as a guest of Mr. Bingley."

"Of Netherfield Park! How wonderful!"

They had arrived just yesterday evening, but the local rumor mill had likely been churning about Bingley since the news of his having leased the place reached the ears of the local solicitor's wife. A young, single man of good fortune was always prized. Darcy was lucky in that as a late addition to Bingley's party, the locals did not yet know of his ten thousand pounds.

Mrs. Bennet led Mr. Darcy into a small, chilly study. The windows were wide, letting in a fair amount of sunlight, and one was open, letting in a cold, unpleasant breeze. On a chaise diagonally set from the window, behind a low wooden table scattered with various papers, sat a stocky, older man. His thick, gray hair receded at the temples, and a pair of thick spectacles balanced on his nose. Presumably, this was Mr. Bennet, and beside him, the young, unmarried daughter of the house who Mrs. Bennet had likely insisted dress and rush into the study to sit as though she often spent time there.

Mr. Darcy was having none of it.

The young woman was admittedly handsome with black, lustrous curls tied up in a knot at the nape of her neck and dark eyes that were her best feature, hinting at least some intelligence as her gaze met his. Her hands, partially encased in dull-brown fingerless mitts, bunched in the skirts of her dress in her lap. It was an odd, nervous habit that Darcy did not admire.

"Mr. Bennet, our guest, Mr. Fitzwilliam Darcy, is arrived. Mr. Darcy, may I introduce you to my husband, Mr. Bennet, and our daughter, Elizabeth."

Mr. Bennet and his daughter stood and Mr. Darcy bowed to both. As Miss Elizabeth grasped her skirts to curtsy, Mr. Darcy looked more closely at her hands and noted a speckled discoloration on the fabric above the knuckle of her index finger.

Perhaps her presence here wasn't a pure fabrication. Likely she performed clerical tasks for her father, though why he could not hire a secretary of his own Mr. Darcy could not determine. Was the Bennet family in such dire straits that Mr. Bennet could not afford one? Or perhaps, or likely, Mr. Bennet was cautious, considering the sensitive materials he was rumored to handle on behalf of the prime minister.

It hardly mattered. Mr. Bennet could not intend for his daughter to remain here for the entirety of their meeting.

"A pleasure, Miss Bennet," Mr. Darcy said. "I wouldn't expect you to bore yourself this fine afternoon entangling yourself in the complications of your father's deciphering."

"While I enjoy a brisk walk on an afternoon such as this one, it would be better if I remain at my father's side, Mr. Darcy."

Well, wasn't Miss Bennet forward? Though she didn't act in the slightest bit coquettish. More annoyed. Mr. Darcy was taken aback. "Surely the intricacies of codes and ciphers are not the domain of a properly raised young lady," he protested.

"Lizzie," Mrs. Bennet interrupted, stepping over to her daughter's side and grabbing her by the arm. "Perhaps we should leave Mr. Bennet and Mr. Darcy to their conversation."

Mrs. Bennet gave her daughter's arm a none too subtle tug, but the younger Bennet stood firm. "If I could look over the code you have brought, we might determine the capabilities of a woman of my upbringing."

Mr. Darcy was overcome by the sudden realization he had erred. Severely.

Miss Bennet's dark eyes shone with indignation. "If I may," Miss Bennet held out her hand, palm up. Having a clear view of the appendage, Mr. Darcy realized the mitts contained not merely a single discoloration, but an accumulation of ink speckles and stains that had seeped into the fabric over a long period of time.

"Are you studied in liturgical Latin?" Mr. Darcy asked with an attempt at greater politeness. Judging by the lady's expression, the attempt was unsuccessful.

Miss Bennet's lips tightened to a pale line that only highlighted the high color in her cheeks and flush over her forehead. She said, "I am studied enough."

"If we might take a look," Mr. Bennet added, the corners of his lips twitching with something like amusement. It was a more welcoming expression than his daughter's, who was still furious. Ultimately, whatever jest the elder Bennet was enjoying, Mr. Darcy was clearly the butt of it.

"Mr. Bennet?" Mrs. Bennet tried to meet her husband's gaze, but Mr. Bennet kept his attention fixed on Mr. Darcy.

Having no other polite option, Mr. Darcy handed the letter over.

A soft knock sounded at the door. "That must be Mrs. Hill about refreshments," Mrs. Bennet said, referring to the housekeeper with exaggerated cheer. "I'll just step outside to speak with her. How do you take your tea, Mr. Darcy?"

3

Mr. Darcy might be possessed of handsome features and fine manners, but little else recommended him. Elizabeth Bennet could not and did not wish to contain her fury as she took Mr. Darcy's letter and opened it.

The letter began: *My dearest Georgiana...*

"This letter is not addressed to you," Elizabeth remarked.

"My late brother. Reginald Darcy, sent this to our younger sister."

Elizabeth knew she ought to feel some charitable sentiment for a man who had recently lost a brother, but considering how dismissive Mr. Darcy had been of her and her capabilities—just the slightest hair of being outright rude—Elizabeth could not muster the emotion. "My condolences," she said stiffly.

"Thank you," Mr. Darcy said, his voice as flat as her own.

If this were a young man in mourning, he took care to hide such emotions from those around him. More likely, he did not possess much familial regard at all.

No. That was unfair. She hardly knew the man. Still, however Mr. Darcy mourned, or did not, stealing away his own sister's correspondence did not incline Elizabeth to think well of him.

"If your late brother sent your sister a message in some form of code, would it not make sense to assume she had the tools to decipher it?" Elizabeth asked.

Mr. Darcy's expression froze for the briefest moment. "It is because my sister might decipher it that I have brought it to your father's attention first. My sister Georgiana and my brother Reginald were close. It has been five months since his passing, and she is only beginning to step out of her deep mourning. For the first month, she did not smile, and she hardly ate. As her guardian, I must see to her well-being of the body, mind, and spirit."

Elizabeth weighed Mr. Darcy's explanation. Devotion to family, to especially a beloved sister, was something Elizabeth understood all too well. Though her own sister was the elder, Elizabeth had always been protective of Jane's happiness. Jane had a sweetness of temperament that brought joy to every room, but there was also a fragility to it. Like the bloom of a prize rose, subtle alterations to the soil and air could harm its petals or keep it held tight in bud until it withered and fell.

"And if this letter's contents are something innocuous?" Elizabeth asked.

"Then I will seal it and pass along it with your father's translations to Georgiana immediately. I do not intend to hide our brother's last words from her, but to ensure that they do not add to her grief."

And yet, while Elizabeth understood the urge to protect, she did not, in her heart, agree that Mr. Darcy had the right of it. Did not Georgiana have a right to her own grief?

A difficult tangle and one Elizabeth was not charged to decipher.

Thankfully, Mr. Bennet interrupted her musings with a practical question. "Is the entire letter in code?"

"No," Mr. Darcy said. "The first page is ordinary pleasantries, and Reggie shares—" Mr. Darcy swallowed. It was the only concession in his manner to what Elizabeth was beginning to just to suspect was a far deeper grief than his general demeanor suggested. "He shared small ordinary details of his life in the French capital. Nothing, as far as I can ascertain, relating to the Emperor's designs or movements. And the latter pages were wet. Some words are almost indecipherable even if they made sense before."

Elizabeth skimmed over those pages, trying hard not to feel like a voyeur picking over the silhouette of another man's remains. Nothing immediately caught her eye as a code key. No letters were oddly capitalized or written in a different style. Nor were other simple tricks used. The first letter of each paragraph spelled nothing; neither did the last.

Still, for Mr. Darcy's brother to be in the French capital at all suggested something deeper at play. Through assisting her father, Elizabeth well knew that both Bonaparte and the prime minister employed at points less than honorable means of getting information about their opponents. War was far messier than what the officers in their sharp regimentals shared when flirting with young ladies. But if Reginald Darcy was doing special, secret work for the crown, it would do no good for Elizabeth to suggest such a thing to his grieving and overly constrained older brother. Not without more than a suspicion. The letter continued.

Admittedly, my dearest sister, there is more to life here than the acquisition of pastry. I have found points only the comfort of the Almighty can offer a degree of solace. Sometimes it is only the hand of the Lord who can comfort and protect us in times of trouble.

After that, it was as Mr. Darcy described. Two pages of neatly scribed Latin, formatted as though it was a prayer.

It began:

> Piissimus dominus
> Illustrator iudex
> Auctor magnus
> Incompraehensibilis pacificus
> Optimus iudex
> Omnipotens redemptor
> Gloriosus immortalis
> Imperator fabricator
> Opifex conditor
> Misericors sempiternus
> Rex iudex…

The words were nonsense. At first, Elizabeth thought it might be a Latin Gibberish cipher, but nothing was spelled backwards with false Latin suffixes. Maybe it was an Ave Maria cipher with each letter a faux Latin word, Elizabeth surmised. But lacking the key, deciphering it would take work, not even considering the later water-damaged sections.

Elizabeth handed the letter to her father and outlined for the pair of them what she had seen, suggesting only at the end she believed it was likely there was a cipher at work, but not one easily unraveled in an afternoon.

A knock sounded at the study door. "Mr. Bennet?" Before any of the room's occupants could respond, the door opened, and Mrs. Bennet stepped inside. "A light dinner is ready if Mr. Darcy would like to join us when you have finished your business."

Elizabeth glanced at the clock. It was a quarter to four. They took dinner at four thirty and tea after. Mrs. Hill must have been working like a dervish to have a dinner together so early for the Bennet household.

"I could not impose," Mr. Darcy said stiffly. They took dinner at six thirty in the city. Was Mr.

Darcy looking down his nose at the Bennets for having such country hours?

Mr. Bennet nodded. "You may leave the letter in our care, Mr. Darcy, and I shall write to you when the translation is complete. I will fit it in between my other work as Bonaparte and his disciples do not wait for our convenience to make their moves."

"Yes. I have heard your skills are in great demand from many sources. And my brother is long passed. This is for my peace, and my sister's peace, entirely."

"Shall I direct my missive to the address from which you wrote before?"

"For the duration of the holidays, I will stay as a guest with Mr. Charles Bingley, who has recently leased the nearby estate at Netherfield Park." Mr. Darcy looked resigned. "It should be a simple thing to send any necessary correspondence there."

"But that is such a short distance!" Mrs. Bennet exclaimed. "You must return here to discuss the contents of your brother's correspondence when my husband has finished his work."

Another knock, and Lydia, her voice pitched higher in an attempt at flirtation, said through the door, "Mother! Are you there?"

"Yes, my dear," Mrs. Bennet went to the door and opened it. "Lydia," she admonished with no especial fervor in her tone. "You know better than to interrupt your father while he is working."

Lydia had dressed speedily but with obvious attention to flirting with a young gentleman. Her hair was arranged in perfect ringlets peeking from beneath her bonnet, and her dress was a pale yellow that highlighted her light blue eyes. Unlike Elizabeth, whose mitts were dark beige speckled with ink, Lydia's were the same white silk she wore when attending a local assembly. She smiled at Mr. Darcy and looked up at him through her lashes. "Papa, I apologize for disturbing you. And your guest."

"We had just asked Mr. Darcy to enjoy his luncheon with us," Mrs. Bennet said brightly. "Mr. Darcy, how do you take your tea?"

Mr. Darcy did not acknowledge Mrs. Bennet's invitation the second time. Instead, he inclined his head towards each of them and said, "I must take my leave. Thank you, again."

"Lydia!" Mrs. Bennet called to her daughter. "Will you show Mr. Darcy to the door?"

"Yes, Mother!" Lydia said with delight. She managed to get ahead of the taciturn gentleman. "This way. Are you fond of dancing, Mr. Darcy?"

Mrs. Bennet rubbed the thumb of her right hand along the ridge of the other as she left to follow the pair at enough of a distance as to maintain the illusion of propriety.

After they had gone, Elizabeth muttered. "I wish Lydia the best with him."

Mr. Bennet smiled. "So you, like my wife, would wish Mr. Darcy to become a member of our family?"

"I'd rather marry his horse!" Elizabeth stated with vehemence. "And you know how I despise riding."

"A horse can be led by the reins. A man..." Mr. Bennet laughed, and after a moment, Elizabeth joined him.

Still, Elizabeth's mirth felt hollow. It disturbed her to have been so affected by the man. Granted, her primary emotion concerning Mr. Darcy had been dislike. She tried to tell herself it spurred from his disdain for her abilities. But others had disbelieved her skills in cracking ciphers. None had spurred such instant fury.

As the laughter died, Elizabeth took a second piece of paper and a pen for notes, but her mind was occupied with the first mystery of why Mr. Darcy had affected her so.

"Will you read that out for me?" Mr. Bennet asked.

"Yes, Father." Elizabeth started to read, but her mind wasn't on the code.

Mr. Darcy's handsome features had tricked Elizabeth into expecting more from him, she concluded. That was her mistake, not his. At least his rational desire to flee had spared them all an awkward meal.

That night, in their shared bedroom, Jane sat down on the edge of Elizabeth's bed. "So is Mr. Darcy as terrible as Lydia says?" she asked in a hushed tone.

Elizabeth initial thought was to give a quick yes, but in only the company of her favorite sister, she could not state the man had been wholly terrible. "He was cold, and at points short-tempered, and he dismissed my abilities, but…"

"Usually you are not so restrained in your opinions, Elizabeth. Did you find him handsome?" Jane added, "Lydia found him very handsome. And rude. And generally awful."

"He was handsome." Not that it mattered, considering the nature of their meeting and his temperament. "Like a marble statue and with about as much warmth. I doubt his lips have experienced a smile in all of his years of life. His face would likely shatter into a dozen pieces if he tried."

"You are incorrigible," Jane said with a laugh.

Elizabeth joined her sister in laughing. But even in her shared levity, Elizabeth could not help wondering why she couldn't erase the intensity of Mr. Darcy's gaze from her mind and how it might soften his features if he smiled.

4

_I_t was not Mr. Wickham's first evening at the gambling hell known as "the Danny house," but it had been, by far, his best. An excellent supper filled his belly, and his skin hummed with the pleasant warmth of first-rate whiskey while the taste of an outstanding cigar settled comfortably at the back of his tongue.

"You ought to try one of these," Mr. Wickham said, inhaling another puff of his cigar.

"I prefer to enjoy my drink unencumbered," Mr. Smith, a wide-eyed, self-proclaimed country gentleman in well-kept clothing that was a decade out of fashion, stared at his hand and tapped nervously with his index finger on his cheekbone. "We are not so fond of the pipe in Monogan."

"More's the pity," Mr. Wickham responded absently. Though Mr. Smith did a fair job of hiding his northern accent, there was an odd tone to his vowels that betrayed he was not a Londoner. Better for Wickham. He'd spent enough time in the gambling hells that most knew to give him a wide berth, both because he was a fierce player and his ability to pay his debts shifted with the capriciousness of his own luck.

Commerce was a simple game and one where Mr. Wickham excelled. Three cards were dealt, and one tried to get cards of a kind or runs with the cards in order. He stared down at his hand: ten of clubs, jack of clubs and a four of hearts. One card away from his third straight of the night.

If Mr. Wickham was inclined towards crises of conscience, he might have felt badly about how he'd spent the past two days cleaning out the other man's purse, but luck was a fickle mistress. More often than not, she took from Wickham more than she gave.

Mr. Smith fiddled with his cards before taking two of them and placing them facedown on the table. "*Deux*," he said, with a remarkably smooth French accent.

Mr. Wickham smiled, "You must have had an

excellent tutor," he said and slid two cards across the table.

"*Oui*," Mr. Smith smiled. Beneath his bushy mustache, his teeth were white and straight. "She was like a mother to me."

A stab of jealousy passed through Mr. Wickham. He'd never been able to forge as close a relationship to the nannies or governesses as Darcy. Probably because Darcy had been the young master of the house, while Wickham only a hanger-on, or as whispered in the servant's quarters, a by blow. Thoughts of Darcy fanned an inner core of rage inside Wickham that never eased. Simply by an accident of birth, proper, stick up his bum, Darcy had stolen from Wickham what ought to have rightfully been his.

Mr. Wickham discarded the jack and took another card from the top of the pile. A queen of hearts. He was experienced enough cards not to let his delight show on his face. Though they were not of the same suit, it was a lovely straight, and that would allow him to make enough of a payment to keep his creditors off of his back for at least a few more weeks. If he didn't instead spend the bulk on whores, like he had last night after Mr. Smith had retired.

Mr. Smith looked at his cards. His finger paused at tapping on his cheek for a brief second, then resumed. He had pulled something good, but Mr. Wickham had confidence in his own hand.

Mr. Smith started the betting. "One hundred pounds."

Mr. Wickham made a show of squinting at his cards, but he knew he had the other man. It was only a matter of how much money he wished to take. And Mr. Wickham planned to take it all.

The bets went back and forth until a staggeringly large sum was promised on the table. Then, they agreed to show their cards. Mr. Wickham triumphantly bared his straight. Mr. Smith, his hands trembling, put his cards down with a sudden bright smile. "I got this, old man," he said. In front of him was the queen, king, and ace of diamonds.

Mr. Wickham cursed his own luck. Calculating the sum on the table against his previous winnings, much of which he had won over the past two days had gone to whiskey and loose women, Mr. Wickham realized he lacked the funds to pay. Nor would any of the local moneylenders extend his credit. In fact, he had taken to avoiding them as their requests for repayment grew increasingly insistent.

Mr. Wickham forced a smile. It was bad luck, pure and simple. The same bad luck that had plagued him throughout his entire life. Luck was a fickle whore who displayed her wares and then after allowing a man the briefest touch, snatched them away and left him holding the bag.

Wickham would have to play another hand and win his money back. He was the better card player, and that, more than luck, would win out.

"You wounded me!" Mr. Wickham said with an exaggerated expression. "At least offer me a chance to win a little of my money back."

Mr. Smith, who had been nursing the same glass of brandy for most of the evening, raised it to his lips and said, "It was mostly my money, Mr. Wickham, and I think it might be best for me to take my leave at this point."

"The night is young," Mr. Wickham said, and though he did his best to feign a casual manner, he heard in his own tone a hint of desperation. "I must have at least one more hand to redeem my honor."

"Your ability at cards gives me pause," Mr. Smith said with a laugh. "You have claimed the bulk of the winnings every day since we have met."

"And it seems your luck is turned," Mr. Wickham said. "It is I who should ask to the ending things, as another game will force me to pay a visit to my home vault."

The vault was as imaginary as Mr. Wickham's country estate, but Mr. Smith had no way of knowing that. And the tension in Mr. Wickham's chest eased as he noted the gleam of interest in Mr. Smith's gaze at the mention of the vault.

"Just one more hand," Mr. Wickham said. "For your honor and mine."

"As you wish," Mr. Smith said. "But if we are to play, it should be for more substantial stakes, don't you think?"

Mr. Wickham, with reckless confidence, downed the last of his whiskey and waved for another glass. "Certainly," he said. "I am not one to brag of what I possess," as he possessed nothing of value, "but of my lands, I do have a small country estate. I've spoken of it to you before. Pemberley. Such a small country house may not interest someone of your means, and it is not the most ostentatious country homes, but…" Mr. Wickham described his child-hood home.

Mr. Wickham would never have dared to make such an assertion had he been playing cards with someone local, but Mr. Smith had only been in London for a short time, and as Mr. Wickham described the French and Christian influences as well as the natural elegance of the estate's gardens, he fell into his own tale. What made Fitzwilliam Darcy more worthy of inheriting this estate and the rest of his father's lands than Wickham himself?

They had both grown up together, they had had the same tutors, and hadn't Wickham also excelled? At least in so far as one could excel at impressing an instructor who only required one regurgitate a simple series of facts and opinions as similarly as possible to the instructor's own thoughts? Wickham had as much right to Pemberley as Mr. Darcy himself! Only an accident of birth, of luck, that fickle whore, led Mr. Darcy to have everything while Mr. Wickham gnawed at the scraps.

At the least Darcy could have allowed him Georgiana's dowry.

Mr. Smith leaned forward on his elbows, his chin on his palm as he listened to Wickham's description of the estate. Mr. Wickham was struck again at the unfortunate mix of features that made Mr. Smith appear at first glance far older and less handsome than his smooth skin and bright, brown eyes suggested. Set beneath heavy brows, the eyes were sharp and almond-shaped. His brows and bushy, unfashionable mustache were a slightly darker color than his thick, sandy-brown hair, which receded at his temples.

When Wickham finished, Mr. Smith said, "I am uncertain I have any lands of equal value. All I can offer is a small sum," Mr. Smith stated an amount that made Mr. Wickham's breath catch in his throat.

"Thirty thousand pounds!" Mr. Wickham exclaimed. It was the price of Georgiana's dowry without the burden of a wife. With that amount of money, he could pay his creditors and live comfortably for the rest of his life. It had been his original plan with Georgiana, if only Darcy had capitulated instead of snatching the girl out from under his nose. Restraining his glee, Mr. Wickham added, "Yes, thirty thousand is acceptable."

It was a pittance compared to the value of Pemberley, but Mr. Wickham did not care. Pemberley was a mirage. Thirty thousand pounds, earned cleanly at the gambling table, would be enough to pay off Wickham's creditors, lease a small home, and still have enough set aside to slake his desires for women, wine, and a lifetime's friendly games of cards.

As the pair engaged in negotiations, some of the

other gentleman, officers mostly, had begun to gather around the table.

"Shall we begin?" Mr. Wickham asked.

"Yes."

They asked for paper to write down what they were offering for the bet.

From his purse, Mr. Wickham took out his most valuable and dangerous possession, a copy of his late father's seal. The elder Mr. Darcy had been foolish enough to trust Mr. Wickham, his unacknowledged progeny, with free range of his office and papers. Mr. Wickham had stolen and copied the seal after the old man's death. He didn't use it often. Possessing such an item could see him jailed or possibly hung. But for special occasions, such as now, it was warranted.

This paper confers upon the bearer the ownership of Pemberley estate.

Mr. Wickham wrote out the relevant information about the estate and pressing the seal to a lump of hot wax at the bottom of the page, sealed the bet.

The cards were dealt.

Wickham looked over his hand. A pair of nines and the two of clubs. It took all of his willpower to keep his fear from showing on his face. If he lost this game, he would have to leave London for good. He might even have to leave England altogether and flee to Scotland.

Mr. Smith stroked his mustache. "If you wish to end this, we can call it a draw and—"

"I'll see it through." It was an insult to Wickham's courage to imply that he should forfeit before the game had even begun. More importantly, he didn't have the money to pay Mr. Smith his winnings for the last game.

Mr. Smith nodded. He took two cards.

Mr. Wickham discarded the two of clubs and took a new card. He hesitated and then picked it up. Queen of diamonds. A middling hand, but it was unlikely Mr. Smith had much better since he had discarded two of his three cards.

"Shall we?" Mr. Smith asked. As always, his "sh" vibrated a touch too long and pronounced almost near the back of his teeth.

Mr. Wickham laid down his cards. Then he looked across the table at his partner. A pair of nines and the ace of hearts.

Mr. Wickham felt like he was made of wax. His skin was thick and numb, and the surrounding noise was officers clapping Mr. Smith on the shoulder while others avoided looking at Mr. Wickham as they murmured what felt like condolences whispered over his own grave. Mr. Smith took the paper with Wickham's seal, the rights to an estate Wickham did not own, and folded it into precise quarters.

Luck was a fickle whore, but Mr. Wickham had expected more than this. Perhaps it was galling because the game had been so close. The difference between a queen and an ace.

Mr. Wickham threw back the rest of his whiskey. The buzz was gone, leaving Wickham cold and empty. The faster he got out of here, the better. He stood. "I will leave you to your victory. I would be a fool to tempt fate again for a third time."

Mr. Smith, in a far more authoritative tone than Mr. Wickham had ever heard from the northerner's mouth, said, "We will need a private room."

"No need," Mr. Wickham demurred.

Mr. Smith stood and walked around the table, extending his hand. Mr. Wickham, having no polite way to avoid his opponent, clasped it. This close, the slight twitch at the corners of Mr. Smith's lips and the glitter in his once soft brown eyes seemed sinister. The edge of his mustache seemed to curl up from his skin as though it was pasted on and not grown from his own flesh.

What in the devil?

In a low tone, Mr. Smith said, "We have much to discuss."

The accent, which Mr. Wickham had mistaken for some ill-disguised northern brogue, had thickened. Now, it sounded almost Continental. That perfect French pronunciation he had used earlier in the game.

"You're a—"

"A man of means," Mr. Smith said. "One who has much to offer and much he can take away from an ambitious man. Or shall we instead leave now so I might claim my estate of...what was the name...Pemberley?"

Mr. Wickham's mouth was dry. Stealing away a dead man's seal and using it to give away an estate one did not own was enough of a crime to see him hanged. And Darcy, already against him, would be vengeful in his rage at the discovery of Wickham's audacity.

"We can talk," Mr. Wickham said.

Mr. Smith grinned. "Excellent."

Stepping away from Mr. Wickham, but not letting go of his man's hand, Mr. Smith called out again for a private room.

The edge of Mr. Smith's mustache was definitely peeling. It was subtle, and Wickham doubted anyone else would notice, but the mustache, like everything else about this man bothered him. Who was Mr. Smith?

As he followed Mr. Smith up the stairs to the private room he had requested, Mr. Wickham feared his question would be answered all too soon.

5

Despite Mr. Bennet's initial recalcitrance, he called on Mr. Bingley almost immediately, and Mr. Bingley returned his call with a visit of his own a few days later. Though Mrs. Bennet tried to have Elizabeth stay in the study, the visit had nothing to do with code craft and so Mr. Bennet sent Lizzie to wait with her sisters.

"Once Mr. Bingley has left must get your father to tell us everything about the young gentleman," Mrs. Bennet insisted. "Mr. Bennet can hide nothing from you, nor does he wish to."

Elizabeth was less certain of that supposition. Nor did she have any desire to learn more about Mr. Bingley, who she had determined must have a similar temperament to his close and irritating friend, Mr. Darcy.

An hour after Mr. Bingley had left, with arms linked and Mrs. Bennet's hand atop her daughter's arm to keep her daughter from attempting to flee, Mrs. Bennet led Elizabeth into the study. "Lizzie, you must help your father complete that cipher. No dawdling."

"I can walk on my own," Elizabeth said.

Mrs. Bennet ignored her.

When they entered, Mr. Bennet stood in front of the window by his desk with his cane in his right hand.

"My dear! How delightful it must have been for you to receive company!"

"I suppose you wish to ask about Mr. Bingley."

"Why, Mr. Bennet, I would never presume, but as you have brought up the subject—"

"He is a fine young man with pleasant manners."

"And handsome?"

"I could hardly be trusted to give such an opinion, now could I?"

"My dear Mr. Bennet! Your eyes are not failing so much as that! Was he fair or dark? Large or thin?

He appeared from the window to have wide shoulders and an easy gait."

"Are you wishing our daughters to marry the young stallion or race him?"

Elizabeth smothered a laugh.

"Mr. Bennet!"

"He is young enough and fit enough I suspect for both endeavors."

"Must you always reduce things to jest?" Mrs. Bennet coughed furiously. "This conversation is not fit for a young lady's ears."

"Then I will spare you further humor, my dear," Mr. Bennet said. "For you are as fair as the day I married you, and I would not ask you to age a day."

"Well!" Mrs. Bennet clasped her hands at her throat. "Oh, my dear Mr. Bennet."

Elizabeth averted her gaze. Her father was never needlessly cruel, but she sensed some manipulation in his compliments. Perhaps it was because of the traits he valued, beauty had become—with the deterioration of his eyesight—the least important to him.

Still, it made Mrs. Bennet happy, and that happiness eased some of the tension between mother and daughter. For that, Elizabeth was relieved.

Mrs. Bennet attempted to pull a few more details about the gentleman from her husband, but it was in vain. Eventually, in a flurry of movement and chatter, she left again.

Elizabeth went to the shelf and took down some of her and her father's notes on previously solved and common keys for substitution ciphers. She dropped the books on the desk with a satisfying thump before beginning to page through them.

"And you, Lizzie, did you have questions about young Mr. Bingley?"

"He is a friend of Mr. Darcy's, is he not?"

"Mr. Darcy is staying at Netherfield Park as Mr. Bingley's guest."

"Then there is nothing more I need to know."

"You should not let this Mr. Darcy irritate you so," Mr. Bennet said.

"It is fortunate I dislike him. If he were a gentleman in manner as well as inheritance, then for fear of breaking my mother's heart at the possibility of a good match, I would feel badly for letting him learn of my eccentricities," Elizabeth said bitterly.

"Eccentricities?"

"Most men do not search for ciphering in a wife." Even if Mrs. Bennet had not insisted on telling Elizabeth such at every available opportunity, Mr. John Dunn, her first suitor, had taught her how damaging to her prospects sharing her love of codes and ciphers could be.

"A woman may play with puzzles, but for heaven's sake, no more talk of war. Such missives are not appropriate for a lady or a wife."

Jane had grabbed and held Elizabeth's arm before she could smack him, and then later that evening, Jane held Elizabeth as she cried.

It was fortunate then, that Elizabeth despised Mr. Darcy. His dismissal of her had been irritating, but since she had no hope or interest of a match with him, she was free to prove herself and, without physical violence, remove that expression of smug coldness from his face.

Mr. Bennet said, "Lizzie, you are a diamond of the first order. If a man cannot recognize that, it is his failing, not yours."

Elizabeth swallowed. Her father was sometimes selfish in his jests, but he loved her, and, almost as importantly, he understood her.

Unfortunately, he was also wrong.

To secure a husband, Elizabeth would have to play the fool and hide her own abilities. It didn't preclude a love match, which was her true desire.

After she had achieved her husband's regard in other areas, she would reveal her ciphering. Society expected a man and woman to marry knowing little about each other. Every person had their secrets. Love was born of an instinctive understanding of another's character. She would do better to abandon the foolish hope of finding a husband who encouraged her less acceptable interests. It was foolishness, plain and simple.

"Papa, would you have chosen a wife who could decipher as well as you?"

Mr. Bennet laughed. "Dear Lizzie, I doubt any woman could decipher as well as myself, excepting you, who are a part of my flesh and blessed with a youngster's eyes."

Definitely impossible.

Elizabeth flipped through the books quickly. None of the standard keys had yielded results or inspiration, a surprise to neither her nor her father.

Over the following week, Elizabeth split her time between a slew of decoding requests from Sir Drake's office and Mr. Darcy's cipher.

Though the afternoons held the brisk, watery sunlight that Elizabeth found ideal for walking, even during those sabbaticals, Mr. Darcy's letter dominated her every sense. She would solve it and prove to the prig that she was not merely an ornament, but a capable and intelligent if not a proper woman.

Latin substitution ciphers were relatively simple, each word a replacement for a letter in the alphabet. Of course, it depended on the alphabet. This letter had been addressed to Mr. Darcy's younger sister. An educated young lady of her age was likely to know French, Latin, and English at the least. Considering the letter had come from France and was written in mock Latin, English was the most likely language for the message to be written in.

Elizabeth first determined which words in the Latin "prayer" appeared most frequently, and assigned them a common letter: S, R, E, L, O, and T. Then through various iterations, tried to get a sense of what the message might be. It was complicated by a lack of punctuation or sign of spaces between words, not to mention the splotches of water on the final two pages.

Every day, after they finished their official work, Elizabeth read out each trial to her father, and they discussed the possibilities for the message's content until Mr. Bennet dozed off. Then Elizabeth continued on her own, and, through brute force, she managed to make sense of the first half.

Piissimus dominus

Illustrator iudex

Auctor magnus

Incompraehensibilis pacificus

Optimus iudex

Omnipotens redemptor

Gloriosus immortalis

Imperator fabricator

Opifex conditor

Misericors sempiternus

Rex iudex

Sempiternus maximus

Optimus clemens

Aeternus deus

Sempiternus opifex

Fabricator magnus

Aeternus dominus

Rector clementissimus

Dominus fabricator

Redemptor optimus

Dominus clementissimus

Misericors redemptor

Redemptor dominus

Incompraehensibilis dominator

Illustrator sapientissimus

Magnus conseruator...

DELIUERTHISTOLORDCUNNING-
HAMANDREMEMBERTHEBUTTERFLIES

From there it was lines and lines of gibberish, further confused by an increasing number of water-stained words on the final two pages, rendericng the last few lines illegible.

UUPBMOAKERZYFOLRACDBUKPLD-
ABOUILALBOUAILTIBATOHUETTELIKE-
POUBAMAKELEAUSSUIFRE

Elizabeth penned out a letter outlining her initial progress. It was frustrating to have to take so long with it. The codes used by their own agents were more regular, and perhaps Elizabeth had grown complacent with the ease of solving them. Worse, the second half of this cipher looked like a different code altogether. Whoever Lord Cunningham was likely had the key on hand. Elizabeth doubted it concerned Miss Darcy at all, but she had promised herself she would decipher the entire thing, and giving up halfway felt like admitting defeat.

She tried running the remaining text through various shift and substitution ciphers, but without a hint as to the method of encoding, it was a like throwing horseshoes blind. Frequency yielded little insight. Elizabeth's eyes were burning when Jane stepped into Mr. Bennet's study and called the pair for dinner.

"Huh?" Mr. Bennet sat up suddenly. His glasses sat askew on his nose, and he adjusted them. "What time is it?"

"Dinner, father," Jane said. "You worked through tea. How goes Mr. Darcy's puzzle?"

Elizabeth looked down at her scrawled notes. "Soon," she said. "The first half is done."

Jane smiled. "That is good news. I gave you and Papa as much time as possible, but our mother and sisters await us."

Elizabeth stood and stretched her arms over her head as her joints cracked. Outside the window, the rosy orange of sunset kissed the horizon. Now Elizabeth was not caught up in the cipher, she realized she had become quite chilly.

"Go ahead with your sister," Mr. Bennet said. "I will straighten up in here."

Which was Mr. Bennet's excuse to forestall sitting at the table and being subjected to his wife and daughters' girlish chatter for as long as possible.

"Yes, Father," Elizabeth said, and linking arms with her sister, they walked together from the study.

As they entered the dining room, Lydia and Kitty were both flushed with excitement, their voices high and fast as they spoke to Mrs. Bennet, who leaned forward with interest, and Mary, who sat back ramrod-straight with her hands folded on her lap.

"Madame Godiva said my future husband has hair like the sun, and that I would meet him soon."

"She said your fate was entwined with a man with bright blond hair—" Kitty interrupted.

"Of course!" Lydia exclaimed, tapping her palm on the table. The china rattled. "That gentleman is my future husband. Why else would my fate be entwined with a strange and handsome man?"

Mrs. Bennet nodded eagerly. "I have heard from some of the ladies in the village that Madame Godiva has some Gypsy blood, and this allows her these visions."

"She did not say. But—"

"I think you should be more cautious, sister," Mary interrupted. "Does not the Bible warn us of becoming enamored of false idols?"

"I do not intend to worship the woman," Lydia retorted with exasperation. "I merely state she has a gift. I told you about the buggy accident."

Elizabeth glanced at Jane, who gave a minute shake of her head.

Lydia, seeing that her two oldest sisters had joined them, exclaimed, "Good and finally, you are here. I am famished. Where is Father?"

"Coming."

Lydia breathed out sharply through her nose. "I wish he would hurry. We are having Cornish hens with blackberry sauce."

"You were telling us about Madame Godiva," Mrs. Bennet said.

"Yes! Yes! Kitty and I, as has become our custom, went to pay a visit to the soldiers in town, and that is where we met Madame Godiva. She has a gift!"

The door to the dining room opened again, and Mr. Bennet entered. He stood straight and tall, barely leaning on the ornate wooden cane in his right hand. It was an unacknowledged truth in the household that Mr. Bennet used the cane more to ensure he did not trip over any small objects in the halls rather than to steady his gait. He glared in Lydia's general direction and said, "What is this ruckus? I thought we were having dinner."

"Mr. Bennet!" Mrs. Bennet crossed the room and linked her arm through her husband's free one. "It is a joy to see you up and about."

"I am often up and about as there is nothing wrong with my legs," Mr. Bennet responded crossly.

"Or your stomach, I suspect. Girls, say good evening to your father. I will have the first course brought in."

Elizabeth and Jane took their seats at the table while Lydia explained again in a rush about her discovery of Madame Godiva and what the fortune teller had shared about Lydia's future prospects."

Mr. Bennet asked, "How much did she charge you?"

"Nothing, Father! Madame Godiva stepped out of her shop, and when her gaze met mine, I was transfixed. Her eyes are two different shades of green, one bright and the other dark. And when her eyes caught mine, a curious sensation passed over me, as though the fierceness of her gaze had tickled something in my soul."

"I should hope you didn't laugh too hard," Mr. Bennet said, his lips twitching with amusement at his own joke. "A tickling of the soul can be over-whelming."

"Papa!"

Mrs. Bennet asked, "What did this Madame Godiva tell you?"

"She said an inner revelation had compelled her

to step out from her wagon, and that same impulse drew her to me. Me! She said she should like to read my palm, and I told her I had no extra coin, but she insisted. She said for one with her gifts, the compulsion to right a wrong sometimes took over her limbs and she had no choice but to do as her gift demanded."

Now Elizabeth was intrigued. "Which wrong did she need to correct?"

"I could only imagine it was that horrible Mr. Darcy and how abysmally he treated me when he called on us. I hope Mr. Bingley is of a better temperament! Papa says he is a gentleman, but there are different types of gentlemen."

Elizabeth nodded.

Lydia sighed, and then resting her fork on her plate, continued. "But Madame Godiva led me into her wagon, and it was the most remarkable place, with bright red and gold curtains and a sweet incense that made me almost feel lightheaded."

"You went with her on your own?" Mr. Bennet asked.

"What harm could she do? I had no money, and she was alone. Just one small, old woman and her wagon with all of her worldly possessions."

"One small woman who you saw, and who knew

how many other compatriots!" Mr. Bennet inter-jected. "I do not approve of you and Kitty going so far on your own. Not if you refuse to exercise such basic caution as to not throw yourself willy-nilly into a stranger's wagon."

"Oh, Mr. Bennet! Your fatherly regard and care for your daughters is without bound," Mrs. Bennet said in a vain attempt to soothe her husband's ire. "But two young ladies cannot be forced to spend all of their time indoors, constrained to the bounds of our estate."

"I should think it would be easier on your nerves to know with confidence that all of your daughters are safe," Mr. Bennet said dryly.

"Oh! And now you remind me of my nerves. Mr. Bennet, will nothing satisfy you beyond my accompanying Lydia and Kitty on their next excur-sion into town?" Before Mr. Bennet could respond, Mrs. Bennet continued, "Of course, nothing would satisfy you. I must accompany my daughters and witness this woman's gifts for myself. Tomorrow. The assembly is in a fortnight, and we will have much in small essentials to acquire in any case. Mary will also join us."

Mary's head shot up. "Mother! I do not wish to consort with false idols."

"Oh, calm yourself, Mary. She is a fortune teller, not a Biblical plague. We will stop at the music shop after she has told you something useful about your future and you can look over the sheet music."

"Yes, Mother," Mary pressed her lips together and stabbed her half-eaten meat with her fork.

"And Lizzie and Jane as well."

Elizabeth looked up from her plate. She was not to be so easily persuaded by sheet music and platitudes. "I am satisfied with my existing gowns and bonnets for the Saturday assembly."

"Satisfied! Well, that is hardly enough. All five of you, unmarried, and you will present only a satisfying appearance to Mr. Bingley. Should we play our hand correctly, he will certainly choose one of you as his wife."

"If Mr. Bingley has hair like the sun," Lydia said, "perhaps he is the man my fate is entwined with."

"A man with hair like the sun is neither specific nor unique," Mr. Bennet said. "How is it you are so convinced of this woman's gifts?"

"Because of the cart. She said an unexpected calamity would slow our journey from town, but that all would work out by the evening. And our cart... the wheel was caught in the mud as we left town. I feared it was a broken axle, as did the driver, but a young officer—"

"And a handsome one," Kitty interjected.

"His hair was brown," Lydia said dismissively. "He helped extricate our cart, and we were able from that point to return home. So you understand, this was a sign of Madame Godiva's power. She can see the future, and I believe I will soon meet the man I will marry."

Mr. Bennet said, "So long as you are properly supervised and expect only your allowance to spend on her services, I suppose it's no more of a frippery than another bonnet or dress."

"Oh, Mr. Bennet!" Mrs. Bennet clutched her hands to her chest. "We must use all methods at our disposal before a woman of lesser quality than our daughters snatches this fine, available young gentleman away from us."

"And if this Mr. Bingley is of a similar character to Mr. Darcy?"

"Impossible," Lydia said, placing her knife in the joint of the hen's wing and cutting viciously. "That stiff and insufferable man is one of a kind."

Elizabeth was inclined to agree.

6

-----

*I*n Mr. Bingley's small but cozy library, Mr. Darcy and Miss Bingley occupied armchairs at a polite remove. They were technically chaperoned, though Miss. Caroline's maid sat on the other side of the room with a book in her lap. She stared intently at the pages, even venturing to flip one every couple of minutes.

Mr. Darcy wished he had some way to eject her, as the library was where he went for peace and quiet, but he was a guest in her brother's house and he could not ask her to leave without being rude.

Even at home, Miss Bingley dressed for company. Her morning dress was French silk trimmed with velvet, the color a rich blue. Though she was in the country, on most mornings she received callers through luncheon. Mr. Darcy hoped she would soon be called away again, not that he could, as the Bingley's guest, ask her to leave him in peace while he worked through his correspondence.

Two letters today. One from the Bennet household, and the second from Percy Bragg, an acquaintance from his time at Eton. Mr. Bragg was always chasing the next invention or scheme, and once again, he was likely seeking Mr. Darcy's financing. Not that Mr. Darcy had ever agreed to take part in any of Bragg's endeavors before.

Mr. Darcy opened E. Bennet's letter and began to read. *Lord Cunningham? Butterflies?* Perhaps Mr. Bennet wasn't as excellent a decipherer as reputed.

"You seem awfully serious," Miss Bingley said, fingering her embroidery. "No troubles at Pemberley I hope?"

Mr. Darcy shook his head. He had explained nothing about Georgiana's letter to Miss Bingley. She was a gossip, and he did not wish his personal business to become fodder of bowers and receiving rooms.

"And your business?"

"All is well." Mr. Darcy folded the letter closed

and stood. His thoughts were whirring about so, he could not stay seated. Who was Lord Cunningham? Had Georgiana a suitor? If she did, she would have spoken of it to Reggie before she broached the subject with Darcy, especially after Wickham. With a channel and a part of the continent between them, Georgiana and Reginald were closer than she and Fitzwilliam.

It hurt. Mr. Darcy hated being resentful of a dead man, but he could not deny the truth to himself. When they were children, he would rather have been exploring the countryside or playing games with his younger siblings, but duty compelled. The summer with the butterflies, Georgiana had attempted to tell him over dinner, her face flushed with excitement about the secret she and Georgie had discovered. But their father had disapproved of excitement at the table, and Darcy felt obligated to support him in dampening Georgiana's enthusiasm.

Though Darcy was only two years his brother Reginald's elder, Reggie had often referred to him as grandfather Fitz. "Grandfather Fitz, his tongue like a switch."

Mr. Darcy swallowed. Wickham had taken up that mantra, and while Reggie's admonition had been more in humor, Wickham's was cruel. If only Darcy had seen it at the time.

"Is it about the letter you are having deciphered? May I see it?"

Darcy stopped. "Did your brother tell you of this?" Bingley was a good friend, but he trusted too easily. Especially his sister, who had tended to his scrapes as a child and broken hearts as an adult.

"Charles said something of a deciphering," Miss Bingley stood and crossed the space between them. They were standing face to face, uncomfortably close. He smelled lavender. He put his hands, still holding E. Bennet's letter, behind his back as she said, "For your sister. You took it to Mr. Bennet, is that right?"

"Yes."

"Who knows if this deciphering is even accurate? It may as well be a ruse."

"To what purpose?"

"It is well known in Meryton that the Bennet family has five unwed daughters of marriageable age, and their estate is entailed. They have reason to capture your interest through any means." Miss Bingley's voice was calm. She stared up at him through her lashes, her fingers resting on the gentle swell of her bosom.

Darcy averted his gaze. Perhaps Miss Bingley was right. What did he know about this Bennet family besides they had one headstrong daughter who was forward, brash, and at points hostile? The mother had certainly been ambitious enough about getting him to spend time with any or all of her daughters.

Caroline added, with a laugh, "My brother suspected another young lady might be 'assisting' their father on the occasion when he called, but I suppose the family felt it unwise to be so brazen on a second occasion."

Mr. Darcy shook his head. "I believe Miss Elizabeth was sincerely assisting her father."

"Perhaps she was. But women rarely take action for one reason alone."

That much was true of Miss Bingley. Even now her perfume and the placement of her hand was a planned temptation. One Mr. Darcy had little interest in, though he could not shrug her off. It would be impolite.

His mind flashed toMiss Elizabeth, standing and taking a letter from him, her dark eyes glinting. That had not been a seduction, but he could not escape the memory of it.

The letter was signed E. Bennet. What was Mr.

Bennet's given name? Edmund? Erasmus? Or had Miss Elizabeth had penned this? A lady's correspondence often had a lingering impression of her scent: lavender, honeysuckle, or rose. Mr. Darcy resisted the temptation to bring the pages to his nose to check.

Foolishness! He hadn't even liked the woman. She had been too forward, and the entire conversation had been an embarrassment.

Mr. Darcy had put the first letter aside and picked up the second just as the door to the library was flung open, and Mr. Bingley strode in. "Darcy! There you are!

Miss. Bingley took a quick step back and turned to the door. She walked to her brother, hands extended. "Charles! Why are you in such a stir?"

"Caroline, if Darcy and I might have a moment. I have news for his ears alone."

"Nothing trying, I hope?"

"Please, Caroline."

"Meredith!" Caroline looked back at her maid. "This way, come along."

Caroline did not bother to remember the names of her servants. She addressed her male servants as John, except for Mr. Bingley's valet, and called the maids Mary. Except for her personal maid, who was

Meredith. As it was the rule of her house, Mr. Darcy followed it, but he did not institute such a tradition at Pemberley.

When Miss Bingley and her maid had left, Mr. Bingley closed the door to the library and said, "There is a rumor in the gambling hells that a young gentleman made a bet with your estate at Pemberley. Bragg wrote it out in detail."

"Bragg is a fool." Mr. Darcy held up the unread letter. "Is that what this says?"

"Likely, and I would give rumor little credence, except he says he witnessed it himself. At Danny's."

"Are you certain?" Mr. Darcy opened the letter and skimmed over the contents. "He says there was a seal involved."

"A forgery. It must have been. And everyone knows you do not gamble."

No, Darcy did not. Gambling was Wickham's vice. A slow, burning anger settled in Mr. Darcy's gut. "Wickham."

"Your foster brother? I know you two had a falling out but—"

"Wickham grew up at Pemberley. And he knows how to spin a tale." He also knew where Darcy's father had kept his seal. "I must write to my solicitor." If Mr. Wickham had his father's seal, there was no end to the damage he could do. But if Wickham had been in possession of the seal, why had he seduced Georgiana? He could have at least attempted to take it to a bank and make a withdrawal in Darcy's father's name. Or used it to establish credit for another endeavor. Perhaps he already had. Or perhaps, until now, Wickham had been too careful and too craven to start such a ruse.

Mr. Darcy did not know, but he intended to find out.

"Darcy, relax," Mr. Bingley said. "I know this is a serious situation, but talking with your solicitor should clear things up. That and a report to the constabulary. If he is using a seal in such a way, he risks hanging or exile."

That he did. And Darcy would be glad to watch him swing. Mr. Wickham's seduction and attempt to ruin Georgiana had been disgraceful, and Darcy would have forced the man to pistols at dawn if he had not been intimately familiar with how good a shot Wickham was, and how broken Georgiana would be if her oldest brother died on her behalf. But now, this theft and attempt to defraud was not only immoral but also illegal.

Darcy would make sure Wickham paid to the full extent the law allowed. He quickly penned an explanation to his solicitor, a second to the housekeeper at Pemberley estate, and a third to Georgiana, asking her in the most general terms to take caution. She would resent him for the warning, still having some regard for Wickham even after all he had done, but it could not be helped.

Only when Mr. Darcy had finished this essential correspondence did he return to E. Bennet's letter. Hand aching, he penned out a quick reply. "I know of no Lord Cunningham, nor does he have any acquaintanceship with my sister or myself."

Mr. Darcy stood.

"Are you finished then?" Mr. Bingley, who had taken a seat on the armchair Caroline had occupied, asked. A writing desk sat over his lap, and on it, a game of solitaire was spread.

"Yes." Mr. Darcy wanted to tear off to London this instant, hunt Wickham down, and throttle him.

"Good. It is fortunate tomorrow we have the Assembly to distract us."

"I wish to go to London."

"And skulk through gambling hells until you run the villain off to practice his villainy in another place?" Mr. Bingley shook his head. "It is better you leave this to your solicitor and the law, Darcy."

Mr. Bingley was right, but it did not make

admitting that to either himself or his friend any easier. "This is Wickham. I know it in my guts."

"And your solicitor knows of Mr. Wickham's description and tendencies?"

Mr. Darcy nodded.

"Good then. I had promised your dear sister I would show you a fine time and I will not shirk this duty."

"You spoke with Georgiana?"

"Miss Georgiana wrote. She cares for you deeply."

Mr. Darcy swallowed. He should not allow himself to becomes so emotional about simple filial affection, but Georgiana was all he had left. He would do anything necessary to ensure her safety and happiness, and if that meant he stayed here a while longer and engage in frivolity, then he would grit his teeth and see it done. "Miss Georgiana... What is it you were telling me?"

"There are many opportunities to acquaint ourselves with fine, local ladies, including Saturday's Assembly. You have already set sight on one of the Bennet sisters, have you not?"

"Miss Elizabeth."

"And she is handsome?" Mr. Bingley put the writing tray aside. His cards slid to the base in an unruly pile. He stood and stretched his arms in front of him. "You have been remarkably circumspect in speaking of her virtues, which is not how one friend should behave towards another."

Mr. Darcy sighed. Bingley was always falling in and out of love, caught between shallow infatuations and even shallower miseries. If he hadn't been so good-natured in temperament, Mr. Darcy would not have handled the shifts in emotion. But Mr. Bingley was like a stone who gleefully skipped over the surface of a lake to the opposite shore. He might experience love as a brief tap of liquid against his soul, but it vanished when he caught flight again.

"She was handsome enough," Mr. Darcy continued. "But unremarkable." Except for her eyes. And the way she had challenged him, making him feel like a cad while also wanting to prove himself more.

Mr. Bingley walked to his friend and gave Mr. Darcy an affectionate punch on the shoulder. "Then perhaps you will find another, more attractive lady to occupy your interest over the course of your stay?"

"I have no interest in balls or finding a wife."

"Who said anything of finding a wife? One can

converse with a lady and enjoy her company without seeking to wife."

Or so Mr. Bingley told himself. Mr. Darcy wondered what it would be like to have such an uncomplicated view of the world as his friend. For Mr. Bingley, every person was a delight and every gathering an opportunity to find convivial friends and conversation. He enjoyed dancing and flirting, though never to excess. He excelled at shooting and other sport, but not so much as to cause others consternation. He fluttered through the world. A good friend. A good confidant. A good man.

Mr. Darcy did not flutter. He did not soar. If pressed, he might call himself a still lake, deep and cold, sustaining the surrounding land with little fanfare. When he took a wife, as with everything else in his life, it would be for duty. The bonds of love he had to his sister, to his late brother, were already, at points, too tight. With time, affection would grow in his future marriage, slowly and with calm dedication. That was for the best. A lake was not well served by a tempest at its core.

7

The morning dawned gray with dripping skies. Elizabeth crept out of the house early. The weather offered a fine opportunity to work on Mr. Darcy's code, and an even finer opportunity to tromp through puddles beneath dripping leaves as her mind worked, untangling some of the more troubling pieces while the hems of her skirts grew waterlogged.

Inspiration hit her suddenly, like a beam through the breaking clouds. The water spots on the letter had seemed odd to her. Why would they start on the second and third page? And why in the page's middle but not the edges, where water had damaged the envelope?

What if they were a part of the code? The

letters were not oddly capitalized, but the water damage marked a clear differentiation. It might mean something!

Elizabeth hurried back, shaking off droplets from her shawl before sneaking through the servant's entrance into the kitchen. Mrs. Hill had a bowl full of apples prepared to cut for the afternoon's tarts. Elizabeth grabbed one and took a large bite.

"Miss Elizabeth!" the cook admonished, but there was no heat in it. Elizabeth had been stealing fruit and bread ends from the kitchen after her walks for many years. The cook added, "Hang your shawl by the stove to dry it out, and pray you wipe the mud from those boots!"

In that, Elizabeth did as she was told. She spread the shawl out on the stool next to the stove and gave her thanks again before stepping into the main house. If she worked at it through the afternoon, she'd be able to have the cipher decoded before dinner. That would show the odious Mr. Darcy!

When Elizabeth stepped into the hallway, Mary slipped out from behind one of the curtains "Come here," she whispered, beckoning Elizabeth to her side.

Elizabeth was so shocked by her staid younger sister's behavior, she hurried over. Mary pulled the thick velvet drape over both of them as Mrs. Bennet's voice echoed from the main hallway. "The carriage is here but where is Lizzie!"

The sound of footsteps moving towards them. Elizabeth held her breath. Dust tickled her nose, and she pinched it, trying to hold off a sneeze. She could not see through the drape, and the thick fabric caused the voices to sound off-pitch and strange. Hopefully neither would see her or Mary's feet poking out from beneath the velvet.

"Lizzie does not need another bonnet, Mama," Lydia said pointedly. "She is more concerned with her codes than fashion anyhow."

"But Lizzie ought to have her fortune told. I must learn if there is hope for her."

"And if there isn't? Lizzie has no care for marriage."

Elizabeth knew why her relationship with her mother was strained, but Lydia was a mystery. As a child, she'd been sweet, following Elizabeth out for walks on fair days. Lydia has always been fastidious about her clothing and concerned about her own beauty, but the past two years as she'd grown into a womanly form, Lydia has become difficult, uncommunicative, and prone to outbursts of meanness. Jane assured Elizabeth their sister would grow past these fits of temper, but Jane always saw the best in everyone. It was a virtue of the highest order. It also blinded her to people's faults.

Lydia begged. "Please, Mama, Lizzie's walks can take *hours*. We want to get back home before the rain starts again."

"And our dear Mary."

"You can ask Mme. Godiva about her. Do you *really* think Mary's entreaties to the Lord against wickedness and false worship will please Madame Godiva?"

Mrs. Bennet sighed. "There is some truth to your words."

"We should leave. If they want to join us, they can come along on our next visit to town."

"Yes, quite right. It will be Kitty, Jane, you and I. That may serve better. We do not wish to overtax the Madame's powers."

Or her patience, most like, Elizabeth thought.

Their voices faded. Elizabeth and Mary hid behind the curtain until after the others had left the house and then for a few minutes longer, just to be certain Lydia or Kitty hadn't forgotten a parasol.

Finally, Elizabeth pushed the curtain aside. "Achoo!"

"God Bless you," Mary said.

Lizzie looked up and gave her sister a bright smile. Who would have known staid Mary had such mischief in her? "Thank you. The curtain was inspired."

But Mary was not at all pleased with her own cleverness. "I know it was wrong of me to hide." Mary clutched her hands together. "It is wrong to deceive one's parents who we are supposed to love and obey, but it is also wrong to engage in witch-craft. Perhaps we should have gone to entreat them against such wickedness."

"No, Mary," Lizzie reassured her sister. "Nothing we said would have altered their inten-tions. Perhaps... umm...you should go upstairs and pray for them a while. That would be enough, I think."

Mary nodded. "Yes. I will do that. Thank you, Lizzie." She took Lizzie's hands and squeezed them. Her eyes were shining. "Yes, and I will not amuse myself with the pianoforte, but instead immerse myself in dutiful study and reflection."

No, alas, Mary was, even in this, completely herself. If she'd been born a man, they might have sent her to the priesthood for study. Though, despite her avowed piety, Mary had never claimed to have any special vocation.

Elizabeth shook her head as her sister left. Some ciphers, like her sister, were too challenging to solve.

That afternoon, to Elizabeth's delight, the water-damaged sections yielded fruit. She marked the water damaged words, not counting the last two lines which were wholly illegible.

DELIUERTHISTOLORDCUNNINGHAMAND
REMEMBER

Separating them from the rest of the text yielded: THEUORLDUILLUAILTHEELIKEA-MAKELESSUIFE

Elizabeth nibbled at her bottom lip. Latin didnot distinguish U, V, or W.

She sounded it out to herself. "The world will wail thee like a makeless wife."

"Huh?" Mr. Bennet looked up from his encoding. "What is that?"

Elizabeth explained how she had separated out the water damaged sections of the code. "This is what it says. 'The world will wail thee like a makeless wife.'"

Mr. Bennet laughed. "Brilliant, Lizzie. And threaded with seeds of truth."

"What does it mean?"

"Sounds like the Bard. Perhaps it is from one of his plays."

A soft knock sounded at the door. The housekeeper, Mrs. Adams, said, "Mr. Bennet, a letter for you from Netherfield Park."

"Is it from Mr. Darcy? Come in, Mrs. Adams."

The housekeeper bustled in. She was a round, gray-haired woman with a large, bulbous nose and bright blue eyes. Her apron was well starched, and she walked with the posture of a militiaman. "Mr. Bennet, Miss Elizabeth." She handed the letter over. "I trust you will have return correspondence. Shall I let the boy know when to expect it?"

"A moment," Mr. Bennet held his hand up. "Read it out, Lizzie."

Mrs. Adams handed it over, and Elizabeth skimmed it. "Mr. Darcy knows nothing of a Lord Cunningham," she read. "That is odd, is it not?"

"Perhaps Miss Darcy is looking to take a husband, and her brother was warning her off?" Mr. Bennet suggested, and then shook his head. "The younger Darcy put a lot of work into disguising a second code within the first. Try adding the letters up and see if they could be a part of shift cipher."

Elizabeth did as she was bid, but she had little confidence it would be helpful. Mr. Reginald Darcy used those specific words for a reason. Perhaps Miss Darcy was serving as a conduit between her brother and someone doing ciphering work for the Navy or Wellington. The thought filled Elizabeth with excitement.

If Reginald Darcy had been doing work of a more clandestine nature in France, his sister would be someone he could trust and who he could write to without raising suspicions. She would not even need to understand how to decipher either code if he had given her a key for the primary one and the second was for Lord Cunningham's eyes only. But even if she wasn't a decipherer, by decoding and passing the letters along, she was more than she appeared. Perhaps she was a kindred spirit.

After about fifteen minutes of fiddling with permutations, Elizabeth pushed the paper aside. If anyone knew what work of Shakespeare this sentence came from, it was Mary. Instead of beating her head against permutations, she might make more progress simply to ask. "Excuse me, Papa," Elizabeth said.

"Taking another walk?" Mr. Bennet said, looking up. He knew his daughter's habit of walking through her thoughts.

"I need to speak with Mary."

"Mary? I thought she was out with your mother."

"She did not wish her fortune told."

"I am glad to see her exhibiting some sense," Mr. Bennet waved her off. "Go. See if you cannot get Mary away from that pianoforte and into the fresh air."

Elizabeth doubted she would be successful at that, but hopefully Mary would answer her question. She found her sister at the pianoforte. Mary had her eyes closed and she was playing, as usual, with measured precision. Elizabeth knew how much her sister loved music, but the enthusiasm never made it into Mary's performances. She had technical perfection but little heart. Elizabeth knew this frustrated her sister, which led her to practice more, assuming it was some calculable fault that led to others' disinterest in her performances.

Elizabeth, who practiced infrequently and only had a small selection of pieces she could play with any accomplishment, still drew more applause on the rare occasions she took to the instrument, much to Mary's quiet self-flagellation. Elizabeth had tried to push Mary once to a more extemporaneous attitude in her playing, but Mary had panicked and the composition had fallen apart after less than a minute. From there, Elizabeth did not give her sister further advice but instead tried to support her as best she could.

When Mary had finished, Elizabeth applauded. "That was lovely."

"I missed the third and the seventh note on the second stanza," Mary said. She pulled the lid of the pianoforte over the keys with a light thump. "Had you wished to practice?" she asked.

"No."

"You should practice. Your keying sometimes gets garbled in more complicated passages. Not that I intend to imply a lack of talent or grace, only that practice will serve you in the pursuit of beauty, which is in itself reflects God's grace."

"Yes...er..." Mary could sometimes be difficult to talk to. "I will. But not at this moment. I had hoped you could help me with a literary reference."

Mary turned around on the stool. "Me? Yes I will do my best, but...what is it you wish to know?"

Elizabeth repeated the line of code, "'The world will wail thee like a makeless wife.' Papa believes it might be from one of Shakespeare's plays."

"Sonnets." Mary closed her eyes. "It is the ninth, line three...no, the fourth. It is about the importance of bearing children."

Mary recited, tapping her finger on the stool at the end of each line to punctuate the words:

> *"Is it for fear to wet a widow's eye*
> *"That thou consumest thyself in single life?*
> *"Ah! if thou issueless shalt hap to die.*
> *"The world will wail thee, like a makeless*
>   *wife;*
> *"The world will be thy widow and*
>   *still weep*
> *"That thou no form of thee hast left*
>   *behind,*
> *"When every private widow well may keep*
> *"By children's eyes her husband's shape*
>   *in mind.*
> *"Look, what an unthrift in the world*
>   *doth spend*
> *"Shifts but his place, for still the world*
>   *enjoys it;*
> *"But beauty's waste hath in the world*
>   *an end,*

"And kept unused, the user so destroys it.
"No love toward others in that bosom sits
"That on himself such murderous shame
    commits."

Mary interpreted her readings in as literal a manner as possible, overlooking subtler or more scandalous interpretations, but in this, she seemed to have captured the spirit of the sonnet with some accuracy. Why had Mr. Reginald Darcy hidden this phrase in the cipher text? And so cleverly, marking them with what appeared to be random water droplets?

"Does that help?" Mary asked. "I can write it out for you if you'd wish. Did you wish to study the sonnets? It has been some time since I have memorized them, and I would love to have some serious company with whom to read them. Lydia and Kitty simply laughed and gossiped about some of them. They even claimed some were about his admiring…" Mary looked around, and then leaned in to Elizabeth, her eyes wide. "Another man."

Elizabeth's cheeks warmed. She had little doubt her sisters were correct, which only made discussing such things with Mary more embarrassing.

"I think they were saying it to upset me. Sometimes Lydia's jests can be cruel," Mary added. "I have tried to remind her of the sin of telling falsehoods, but she does not listen. Lydia has always been a frivolous sort, not that she cannot improve herself should she so choose."

"I… Can you write this one out for me? The ninth sonnet? Papa wishes to use it for a code."

"Certainly. Once you have married, you will devote yourself to motherhood and family as you ought, but it is good you are so attentive to his needs now. Is it very difficult?"

"I enjoy it," Elizabeth said, sharply. "I can decipher quite a bit on my own now." Practically all of it, if she were to be honest, which, despite Mary's admonitions about falsehoods, was a truth she would likely ignore.

"I will write this out for you presently. While you are waiting, why not take some time to practice your fingering. It is important, when attracting a husband, to show all manner of womanly accomplishments. That is what Mother says, and she did succeed in attracting a husband."

Elizabeth would never look at her parents as an example of her concept of marital bliss, but there was truth in Mary's words. She practiced until Mary returned. Taking the sonnet in hand, she went back to her father's study. Why this line? Why these words?

The night before the Assembly, Elizabeth woke from her sleep. Mr. Darcy's voice echoed in her head. "A makeless wife."

Elizabeth rubbed her eyes. Of course Mr. Darcy would accuse her in her dreams. Why had his brother chosen to send such a sonnet to their little sister? Threatening her with a childless existence?

Ninth sonnet. Fourth line. The line contained nine words in total. Four began with W.

Nine. Four.

Elizabeth sat straight up in her bed. An Affine cipher! It depended on a new form of modular math pioneered by Carl Friedrich Gauss's *Disquisitiones Arithmeticae*. The book had been published in Germany in1801. Mr. Bennet had acquired a translated edition in 1807 and both Bennets had puzzled through it, creating and cracking codes for each other.

If this was an Affine cipher, and the A coefficient was nine and the B coefficient was four, then it was a simple piece of reverse math to decipher the rest. Elizabeth's fingers itched. She could not sleep now. Not with the answer so close.

Elizabeth put on her dressing gown and lighting

a candle at her bedside, crept out of her bedroom, down the stairs, and into the study.

Assuming the nonsense letters between the watermarks were the second code, not counting the ones which were a part of the first section, then the letters to be deciphered were:

WPBMKEZYFOARACBKPABOJBA-TOWTTPOWBAUR

Elizabeth took the text from the shelf again and flipped through it until she found the relevant section. Each letter would originally have been assigned a value of A=1, B =2 through Z=26. An Affine cipher was a simple shift, using the equation, $f(x) \equiv ax+b$ (mod 26). Assuming A as nine and B as four, yielded $f(x) \equiv 9x+4$ (mod 26). From there, all she needed was to do the reverse: x = inverse (9) (y − 4) (mod 26).

Elizabeth whipped through the equation, her heart pounding as she wrote out each letter and then double checked her work.

CHRYSALIDEONOURSHOREPROTECT-THECROWN

Chrysalide on our shore. Protect the Crown.

A chill passed over Elizabeth, and she hugged her dressing gown around herself. Was the Regent in danger?

Chrysalide. Chrysalis.

Remember the butterflies.

She folded up the letter and her translation, placing them each in two separate drawers in her father's desk. She would check it again tomorrow, but she was certain her deciphering was correct.

Who were you Reginald Darcy, and what work were you really doing for the army? Whatever it was, he had died to send this message, and Elizabeth would have to make certain his death was not in vain.

8

On the morning of the Assembly, heavy rain pattered against the roof, making the day as gray and troubling as Elizabeth's mood. She rechecked her deciphering with her father and penned an urgent letter to the prime minister's office.

"This is good work," Mr. Bennet said. "But we cannot share this with anyone else until we are certain they have acted upon our warning. If it is acted upon."

"Why would they ignore us?"

"Not us, but Mr. Reginald Darcy. If he was even one of ours."

"Of course he is one of ours! He died for this! And Mr. Darcy—" He was a cad, but not a traitor.

"This letter may well be a sham. Something to have us running about in circles chasing our own tails. We shall see. In any sense, we must be cautious and keep these revelations to ourselves."

As much as it galled her to have to play the fool with Mr. Darcy, Elizabeth agreed. Nervous energy captured her as she went through her morning activities and preparing for the Assembly. It was out of her hands, Elizabeth reminded herself. The letter was at least five months old. Perhaps the danger to the Regent had passed. Or perhaps it had never been.

"Lizzie, are you well?" Jane remarked when Lizzie returned to her room to change into her morning dress."

"I did not sleep well," Elizabeth said. She could not bear to lie outright to her sister, and even this skirting of the truth made her feel ill.

"Oh, poor Lizzie!" Jane said, capturing Elizabeth in an embrace. "We shall have tea brewed with chamomile and mint! You will be right as rain for the Assembly and to meet Mr. Bingley. We will see!"

Elizabeth nodded. Her guilt hung over her like a shroud. She drank the tea, which helped, and then with vigorous intent, gave her attention to her family obligations. Elizabeth could do no more to decipher the code now, and she would not allow her diffuse fears to spoil Jane's fun.

It was still raining at noon, and Mrs. Bennet despaired the evening would be a disaster. "Our first impressions will be as drowned hens, and how is Mr. Bingley to appreciate a half dozen drowned hens? Oh! The dear Lord gives us trials such as he sees fit and says we must rise to them, but my nerves! I cannot stand it, but I must!"

Mary, stiff and proper at the cleared-away dining table, looked up from her book, and from memory quoted, "Cast thy burden upon the Lord, and He shall sustain thee: He shall never suffer the righteous to be moved."

Mrs. Bennet sighed. "Perhaps, dear child, you might wish to spend time on the pianoforte. I'm certain you will be called on at some soon point to display your skills."

Mary nodded solemnly and took herself away. Elizabeth attempted the same, but Mrs. Bennet refused to give her leave to return to her cipher. Instead, she spoke of the fortune teller, Madame Godiva, and how Elizabeth and Mary, but especially Elizabeth would have to make herself available for their next excursion into town.

"Oh, Madame Godiva spoke such a wondrous

fortune for our dear Lydia and Kitty. Jane refused to share what the fortune teller had said to her, but she was pleased. A mother can tell, you understand. A mother always knows."

Jane had said little of the experience the previous evening, stating only, "I love you more than life, Lizzie, but I fear you would tear the Madame's words to shreds, whether or not they were true."

"You do not believe she can see the future, do you?" Elizabeth asked.

Jane said, "Her words lifted my heart. She saw love in my future."

"Then she is not completely without her wits. Anyone could see a future for you with love because you are, above all things, good."

"You think too highly of me, Lizzie."

"Never." Elizabeth put her arms around her sister. Few things were as wonderful as they appeared, but Jane was one. Elizabeth loved her sister's steadiness, honesty, and most of all her kindness.

Still, it did not mean Elizabeth needed her fortune told. She would see through the entire charade and ruin everyone's fun.

"Lizzie, are you listening? It is bad enough your

father woolgathers when I am trying to tell him something, but it is also to some extent to be expected. He is but a man. A good man, and one we must ensure stays alive lest... I cannot bear to think of losing Mr. Bennet!" Mrs. Bennet grabbed Elizabeth by both hands in a grip that made Elizabeth breathe in sharply through her teeth. "Dear Lizzie, tell me you will marry! I cannot bear the thought of you as a spinster aunt living upon our Jane's back."

Nobody ever doubted Jane would marry. If only Elizabeth had been born a man. Even if her deciphering might even gain her an income. As it was, her best options were as a wife or governess. The former held a much greater possibility of love than the latter, Elizabeth had determined years ago. "Yes, Mother," she said, making sure to meet Mrs. Bennet's eyes. "I plan to marry. I will."

Mrs. Bennet breathed in a large sigh. She pulled her hands away. "Good. It is such an ease to my nerves to hear your vow. Now I only have to fear for our Mary and myself if I am unfortunate enough to outlive your father."

When the family arrived at the Assembly, it was sparsely populated. Mrs. Bennet considered this all for the best, but as the hall filled and none of the new arrivals appeared to be Mr. Bingley or his reported seven bachelors, her discomfiture grew more pronounced.

Worse, Mr. Bingley's party, when they finally entered the Assembly hall, was comprised of only five altogether. Mr. Bingley, his two sisters, the husband of his eldest, and Mr. Darcy.

Elizabeth's attention swept to the latter. Mr. Darcy was as stiff and cool as he had been when he arrived at their home with his brother's letter in hand. Had the letter been a plant? If so, wouldn't Mr. Darcy have put in more effort to give over a good impression of himself?

As the other young ladies whispered behind their fans about his fine, tall person, handsome features, and noble mien, and of the most import, his having ten thousand a year, poor Mr. Bingley was quickly overshadowed.

Fools, all of them!

Mr. Darcy's noble mien was him looking down his nose at Meryton, Hertfordshire, and all before him. In this, he seemed perfectly suited to the woman on Mr. Bingley's arm, who shared Mr. Bingley's bright blue eyes and honey-brown hair, now piled high in a graceful sweep of curls punctuated by glittering jeweled hairpins. Mr. Bingley's sister, presumably. Her face was pinched, and she unfurled her fan over her nose and lips as though its stiff feathers would provide a firm barrier between herself and all that was beneath her.

Detaching herself from her brother, she went to Mr. Darcy and whispered something to him. Her fan lowered as she smiled, her teeth ivory perfection.

Mr. Darcy nodded once with stiff formality. If the letter was a ruse, Mr. Darcy could not have any knowledge of it. He was too proper to engage in spycraft, let alone treason.

Jane hooked arms with Elizabeth and, placing her palm just below Elizabeth's shoulder, whispered, "My, he is handsome, is he not?"

"Mr. Darcy!" Elizabeth breathed in sharply. By heaven, Jane could not have been compromised by Mr. Darcy's fair looks!

But Jane laughed. "No silly! Mr. Bingley. It is not merely his countenance, but in his smile. One senses a certain kindness."

Elizabeth turned her gaze back towards Mr. Bingley. He did have a pleasant countenance, and unlike his sister or Mr. Darcy, he met those in his path with easy, unaffected manners. His brother-in-law, Mr. Hurst, and older sister also appeared of a more grounded nature, though Mrs. Hurst dressed as stylishly as her younger sister, Caroline.

"Mr. Bingley appears to be handsome and well-mannered," Elizabeth said. Though she could not help adding, out of a sense of protectiveness towards her sister, "But he and Mr. Darcy are close I would assume, and close friends often have a similar nature."

Jane was undeterred. "Then perhaps it is Mr. Darcy who was softened by Mr. Bingley and not the reverse."

"Then I fear, before his acquaintanceship with Mr. Bingley, Mr. Darcy must have been as cutting as a diamond and about as warm."

Elizabeth couldn't help but note the contrast between Mr. Darcy and his friend. Mr. Darcy deigned only to dance twice, once with Mrs. Hurst and once with Miss Bingley. He spent the rest of his time stalking about, speaking only occasionally to one of his own party.

The tide of opinion quickly turned against him.

Lydia found herself the gleeful center of attention as she shared her own earlier experience with Mr. Darcy. "He was the proudest and most disagreeable man in the world!"

If Elizabeth had felt any inclination towards

defending Mr. Darcy, his slight of her immediately dashed it. Due to the scarcity of gentlemen, Elizabeth had been obliged to sit down for two dances. Mr. Bingley, having danced prettily and with much enthusiasm with Elizabeth's sister Jane, stepped away from the floor for two minutes to entreat Mr. Darcy to join him.

"I certainly shall not. You know how I detest dancing unless I am particularly acquainted with my partner. Besides, you are dancing with the only handsome girl in the room." Mr. Darcy looked at the eldest Miss Bennet.

Elizabeth stood, the horror of Mr. Darcy's regard being aimed at Elizabeth's eldest and most beloved sister, forcing her into motion before she could stop herself.

Mr. Bingley, being of an open and generous nature, at once extolled Jane's virtues, of which he had only made acquaintance, and added, "But there is one of her sisters, standing just behind you. She is very pretty, and I dare say agreeable."

Elizabeth stepped back, hoping to place herself in the shelter of a large potted plant, but it was too late. Mr. Darcy turned, and for a chilling and miserable moment, the full weight of his disregard rested on Elizabeth. "Miss Elizabeth."

"So this is Miss Elizabeth," Mr. Bingley said, cocking his head. "She is quite handsome!"

"Passably."

Elizabeth's hands clenched. She forced herself to take a breath. A man might engage in a tantrum, but a lady must always hold her temper. "My father has been working diligently on your project since our last correspondence."

"Of butterflies and imaginary lords."

"Of Chrysalide." It was a risk, bringing the subject up in a crowded ballroom, especially if Mr. Darcy had planted it with some ulterior motive. Elizabeth studied his expression for some recognition of the word.

But Mr. Darcy only furrowed his brow. "A French cocoon. What nonsense is this?"

At that moment, the attention of everyone in the room was caught up by two new arrivals. Both were most gentlemanlike in officers' regimentals. The first, Mr. Denny, was stocky and dark with excellent posture and a pleasing face. But he was outshone in an instant by his partner, who was a stranger to all but his friend.

Stranger as he was, he possessed all the best part of beauty, a fine countenance, a good figure, a fine smile, and a pleasing address. Both men immediately took pains to confront the disparity of gentlemen to ladies by entreating the two ladies closest to them to dance.

Mr. Darcy's attention was suddenly arrested by the sight of the stranger who, upon noting Mr. Darcy's gaze, lost all color in his face. Mr. Darcy, in contrast, flushed bright red.

After a moment, the stranger inclined his head at Darcy. He then held his hand out to one of the ladies he had been speaking with and directed her to the dance floor where another dance was beginning.

Mr. Darcy clenched his hands, and he took a step towards the stranger. The tendons in his neck stood out in sharp relief, and Elizabeth wondered with a thrill if Mr. Darcy was planning to strike the man. Elizabeth added a point in the stranger's favor.

"Darcy!" Mr. Bingley took Mr. Darcy's arm. "Not here," he added in a harsh whisper.

Mr. Darcy whispered something to his friend too softly for Elizabeth to hear.

Mr. Bingley asked in a more regular voice, "Do you wish to leave?"

"No."

"I can speak with Caroline. And Miss Bennet.

We do not know if he is even involved with the rumors—"

"Go. Dance."

"You cannot confront him. Not without evidence."

Evidence of what? Now Elizabeth was intrigued. Whether this strife had anything to do with Mr. Darcy's letter, Elizabeth could never resist a mystery.

"I do not wish to speak of this further. I will not embarrass you, Bingley. You have my word."

Mr. Bingley clapped Mr. Darcy on the shoulder. "Good man."

Mr. Darcy nodded stiffly, and Mr. Bingley returned to the dance floor with Jane.

"Are you still here?" Mr. Darcy asked, looking down his nose at her. "I will not dance with you. I am in no humor at present to give consequence to unsuitable young ladies, especially those who have been slighted by other men."

Elizabeth saw red. "Then I shall take myself from your esteemed presence and beg a dance from your acquaintance. Would you say he has hair like the sun?"

"No." His neck pulsed, and Elizabeth smiled.

"Gold then. Or perhaps some cheerful flower."

"Mr. Wickham is not to be trusted."

Elizabeth laughed. "And you, Mr. Darcy, are not to be believed." She curtsied. "I take my leave."

As she walked away, she heard him call out, "Miss Elizabeth," but Elizabeth pretended she did not hear. Not to be trusted! Mr. Darcy was just the sort of arrogant cad to assume himself worthy of trust without making the slightest effort to prove himself. Elizabeth dearly wished to take Mr. Darcy down a notch. Perhaps Mr. Wickham, more than the code, would provide a means to do this. What about the man got Mr. Darcy's back up so?

9

*J*ust when Mr. Darcy determined this evening could not get worse, it had. He should never have attended this blasted Assembly. If he had been able to refuse with any degree of politeness, but...

Wickham. Here. Mr. Wickham was as charming as ever, and the country ladies, young and old, peasant and gentry, all bent to him like flowers in the sun.

Or perhaps some cheerful flower.

To the devil with Wickham, and blast Miss Elizabeth Bennet as well! How had she gotten under his skin?

Mr. Darcy stood by the refreshments table clutching a glass of negus. It was too sweet, and the flavor of mulled wine, lemon, and sugar cloyed at the back of his throat. He emptied the glass anyway and quickly spooned himself a second serving.

Wickham had wagered Pemberley as if he owned it, and now he was here, pretending ignorance even as he rubbed the affront of his presence in Mr. Darcy's face.

Blast him! Blast them all.

Miss Bingley approached him with a concerned expression. "Mr. Darcy, it's not like you to take so heavily of the punch. Are you well?"

"Well enough."

"Charles admonished me not to speak to Mr. Denny's acquaintance, and as a dutiful sister, I will not. What is his name again?"

"Wickham. George Wickham. Avoid his company. He is a charlatan and a fool." And a criminal, though Darcy could not make such an accusation in this place, to the sister of his host, without evidence.

"I would never!" Miss Bingley assured him. "I set my sights only on those I consider of quality." She gave him a long look. Mr. Darcy took another sip of his drink as she continued, "An Assembly may be diverting, but it is just that, an amusing diversion." Miss Bingley flicked her fan open and looked over it at Mr. Wickham. Miss Elizabeth and another young lady walked towards him, arm in arm. "Miss Elizabeth appears keen to make the young Wickham's acquaintance."

A surge of anger passed through Mr. Darcy. The other young woman, Miss Lucas, who Mr. Bingley had danced with earlier this evening, said something and Miss Elizabeth laughed. The expression lit her entire face, and Mr. Darcy's breath caught in his throat. She was passably handsome when she scowled, but when she smiled…

"Mr. Darcy, you seem to have a greater interest in the dance floor than these refreshments." She fluttered her fan again. "Perhaps you wish to engage in another dance?"

"A second dance gives an improper impression," Mr. Darcy said.

"Nonsense! My brother has already danced with that eldest Bennet sister twice. A sweet young lady, but we all know nothing will come of that."

Mr. Wickham made some remark, and Miss Elizabeth inclined her head, smiling again. Had the cad asked Miss Bennet to dance? Mr. Darcy would not accept that.

Mr. Darcy bowed. "Excuse me," he said.

Mr. Darcy made a straight line the towards the

group. Now Mr. Denny and Miss Elizabeth were exchanging was pleasantries, which was at least more tolerable. Mr. Darcy came up to Miss Elizabeth's side. He nodded to Mr. Denny and more grudgingly to Mr. Wickham before holding out his hand, "Miss Elizabeth, the next dance is soon to begin."

Miss Elizabeth smelled of apricot and mint. She looked up at him. Her cheeks were flushed. She quirked her lips and glanced down at his hand before folding her own together in front of her. "I believe you might be correct," she said.

"I am asking for your next dance," Mr. Darcy said. He avoided looking at Mr. Wickham, knowing the sight of his nemesis would snap his already fragile hold on his temper. "If you would please," he added.

"I daresay I would not please, as I have promised my next dance to Mr. Denny, who has, to this point, been perfectly amiable."

Mr. Denny blinked and then grinned. "I… Yes, it is my honor, Miss Elizabeth."

"So there you have it then," Miss Elizabeth said. "You need not trouble yourself with dancing, as you made it plain in our earlier conversation you have no interest in such pursuits."

"I believe Miss Elizabeth has you pegged to the pound," Mr. Wickham interjected.

Mr. Darcy's hands clenched, and he put them behind his back for fear he might strike his once-foster brother. "Miss Elizabeth and I are hardly acquainted. Neither of us can make a fair judgment of the other's character."

The first notes of the next dance began, and Miss Elizabeth took Mr. Denny's hand. Mr. Wickham bowed to Miss Lucas and with a nod to Mr. Darcy, escorted her on the floor.

Mr. Darcy stared. How had Wickham bought himself a commission? Perhaps he had traded away "Pemberley" and fled London before his dupe could discover how uneven the stakes had truly been. If nothing else, Mr. Wickham put up the appearance of a stable income. Mr. Wickham was excellent at putting up appearances, a skill Mr. Darcy had never mastered.

Mr. Denny and Miss Elizabeth met at the center, her hand resting atop his as the dance began. Mr. Darcy swallowed. His mouth was dry, and he found his anger twinned between Mr. Wickham, who was laying his sunshine charm upon Miss Elizabeth's unsuspecting companion, and Mr.

Denny, who likely did not deserve Mr. Darcy's disapprobation.

Not that Mr. Darcy could help himself.

Passably handsome? For the second time in as many weeks, Mr. Darcy realized he had once again erred. Miss Elizabeth was passably handsome when she scowled, but when she danced...

The scent of lavender heralded Miss Bingley's nearness even before she spoke, "Mr. Darcy? I had thought such country dances held no appeal for you."

"I only wished a word with Miss Elizabeth."

"The word is you gave Miss Elizabeth the cut direct."

"I would hope you were not the sort to engage in gossip," Mr. Darcy said, which was about as close to a skirting of the truth as he could manage. He might *hope* that Miss Bingley did not engage in gossip, but it was clear from their acquaintanceship she most definitely did. And between young ladies, gossip could be as deadly as a sword or well-placed dagger.

"So do you have an interest in the young lady?"

"Insofar as she does not deserve Mr. Wickham's attentions. Beyond that, any connection between us must at most be cordial."

Miss Bingley placed her hand on Mr. Darcy's forearm. "Then perhaps, in the interests of geniality, you ought not glare such daggers at her."

Was he glaring?

Mr. Darcy turned his attention back to Mr. Wickham. He projected the image of gentlemanly ease, but on the rare moments his gaze rested on Mr. Darcy, his shoulders stiffened, and his expression seemed to freeze. Whether this had anything to do with the rumor of him gambling with Mr. Darcy's estate or was merely a result of their already troubled history, Mr. Darcy had no way to determine.

The dance ended. As Mr. Wickham led Miss Lucas back to Miss Elizabeth and Mr. Denny, Mr. Darcy made certain to cross their path.

"Mr. Wickham," he said. "If I might have a word."

"I would be pleased, except the next dance is set to begin, and I have promised it to Miss Elizabeth."

"This is about Pemberley."

Mr. Wickham laughed, a bit too forcefully. "I have not set foot in our childhood home for at least a year, as I am certain you are well aware."

"And your commission has brought an end to your nights of commerce and whist?"

"Any debts I may have incurred are now paid, and if you insist upon dredging up such unseemly things here, with ladies present, I pray I must take leave of this conversation."

"I only wished to tell you Miss Darcy is faring well."

"She has suffered too many losses, Mr. Darcy. My condolences to you both."

Mr. Darcy, having no polite alternative but to end the conversation, simply nodded. At that moment, Mr. Denny and Miss Elizabeth returned. Both were laughing.

"My, Miss Elizabeth, you do offer a clever jest!" Mr. Denny laughed again, and Mr. Darcy wanted to hit him.

"Miss Elizabeth is quite handsome, is she not? And spirited," Mr. Wickham said.

Mr. Darcy could not speak through his anger. He had made a right hash of things, and now Wickham was here to loot the spoils.

MissElizabeth said, "Charlotte, Mr. Denny is quite a pleasant dance partner, both in demeanor and conversation."

"Pleasant," Mr. Denny retorted, his lips still twitching with mirth. "I hope to have made more of an impression than merely pleasant."

"Oh but Mr. Denny, for a lady of a practical bent such as myself and Miss Lucas, pleasant offers far greater pleasures than brooding or enigmatic. I will also add that you are possessed of fine features and a finer sense of humor. That, in and of itself, is beyond compare."

"Then I shall take such compliments and hold them in my heart as precious jewels."

Mr. Denny flirted too much.

Mr. Wickham said, "Miss Elizabeth, any man would be fortunate to be given such precious jewels from a beautiful woman's lips."

"Scandalous!" Miss Bingley remarked, fluttering her fan.

Mr. Wickham took Miss Elizabeth's hand. When the dancers had taken their places on the floor, Miss Bingley murmured, "They are lovely together. Dark and light, sun and shadow. A fine contrast."

Anything he said would be a lie, so Mr. Darcy remained silent. He had warned her. It should have been enough. But he watched them as they started their dance, and a low, seething rage mingled with protectiveness in his belly.

They stepped away from each other, moving in precise steps through the dance, crossing, and meeting again. As they circled, backs to each other, Mr. Wickham caught Mr. Darcy's gaze and smiled.

As children, Wickham had always coveted Darcy's toys. And when he could not claim them, more often than not, those toys were found in corners and under the beds, broken.

For a moment, he saw Miss Elizabeth as a doll, her dark eyes like shiny stones, her face cracked, staring up from the floor, arms and legs askew as the others danced in measured steps past her small and broken form.

Mr. Darcy swallowed. This excess of emotion he felt around her did neither he nor Miss Elizabeth any service.

Mr. Darcy nodded once and turned on his heel, returning to the refreshments.

10

———————

*T*he following morning, the post came with troubling news.

Mr. Bennet went white as his daughter read out the letter. "Mr. Dowding passed on?"

"He appears to have suffered a sudden apoplexy," Elizabeth explained.

"We were at Eton together. He was always in vigorous health."

Those boyhood days were at some remove from the present for Mr. Bennet, though Elizabeth would not be forward enough to say it outright. Before his eyes had begun to fail, Mr. Bennet had been an excellent marksman.

Mr. Bennet sighed. "I suppose the funeral has already passed."

"It has. This missive concerns Mr. Dowding's work. They are worried his keys may have been compromised." Mr. Dowding was more than merely an old friend—he was also one of the chief encoders for the navy. He created the keys that Lord Nelson and others less famous used to hide the coordination of overall fleet movements. Rumor had it Lord Wellington had pressed the navy to use Mr. Dowding's services. Now, with Dowding dead, another encoder would be needed. "They are asking we create a series of codes and keys to aid our work on the peninsula!"

"This is a challenging request..." Mr. Bennet mused. He tapped the pad of his index finger over his lips. "We will have to create something unique, but accessible. And it will not simply be one request. They will want new keys periodically."

"It is our duty to accept," Elizabeth said, relishing the opportunity.

After some thought, Mr. Bennet agreed.

"Lizzie! By heavens, where is that girl?" Mrs. Bennet pushed opened the study door and strode in. "Mrs. Lucas is here. Mr. Bennet, you simply will have to find yourself another assistant for the next hour or so. Lizzie, we need you."

Elizabeth gave her father a helpless look and

stood. She did wish to see Charlotte and share her experience both with Mr. Darcy and with Mr. Wickham in the confidence of her best friend, but it felt like a betrayal to leave important work undone. "I will return as soon as I'm able."

"I am not such an invalid as that. Encoding is more a matter of the mind than the eyes, so be assured, progress will be made by the time you have returned."

Elizabeth nodded, though his assurance stung. She had hoped to be of more value than a pair of eyes to her father, and believed herself a capable decipherer, but in many ways, Mr. Bennet saw Elizabeth as an extension of himself. And perhaps there was truth to it. When she married, her work with him would take a distant second to her family and responsibilities as lady of household.

When Elizabeth and Mrs. Bennet returned to the sitting room, Lady Lucas and her daughter, Elizabeth's best friend Charlotte, were seated. Charlotte sipped a cup of morning cocoa. "Lizzie!"

Elizabeth crossed the room and sat beside her friend. They exchanged excited pleasantries while their mothers went over the previous night's Assembly in immense detail.

"You began the evening well, Charlotte," Mrs.

Bennet said. She was not speaking to Charlotte but instead to Mrs. Lucas, and because of that did not await an answer from Charlotte and instead continued on. "You were Mr. Bingley's first choice."

Charlotte hesitated, glancing at her mother, before responding. "Yes, but he seemed to like his second better."

It was a dance of pleasantry and domination, one Mrs. Bennet excelled at. Elizabeth, in contrast, found the whole thing tedious. Everyone realized Mr. Bingley's preference was for Jane, and the conflict between Mr. Darcy and Mr. Wickham had been far more interesting.

"Oh! You mean Jane, I suppose—" Mrs. Bennet artfully stumbled in her speech.

"How do you think Mr. Darcy and Mr. Wickham are acquainted?" Elizabeth cut in.

Charlotte leaned towards Elizabeth. "Mr. Darcy and Mr. Wickham, acquainted?"

Mrs. Bennet laughed. "Two more different gentlemen I cannot scarcely imagine! Mr. Wickham is the sun and Mr. Darcy an angry cloud."

Charlotte whispered, "Had you a special interest in Mr. Wickham?"

"No! Certainly not. I just wondered at Mr. Darcy's expression when he and Mr. Denny entered." Elizabeth kept Mr. Darcy's warning about Mr. Wickham to herself. Having no true grounds to trust Mr. Darcy and no acquaintanceship beyond a pleasant dance with Mr. Wickham, Elizabeth would not endanger either man's reputation. But she hadn't imagined the reaction either. She distinctly recalled Mr. Darcy's flush and Mr. Wickham's eyes widening as his skin grew most pale.

"Expression?" Mrs. Bennet said. "I saw no expression! What expression are you speaking of Lizzie? Out with it."

Elizabeth shook her head. She had no desire to give her mother further ammunition for her gossip. "I just… I am probably mistaken."

"Perhaps Mr. Darcy had a spell of gas," Mrs. Bennet suggested.

Kitty raised her handkerchief to her mouth and smothered a cough that sounded suspiciously like a laugh. "He was paying special court to the negus and pastry throughout the entire affair! And his manners, so formal and unwelcoming! Why, he spent close to a half hour with Mrs. Long and did not say a word!"

"Are you certain, mother?" Jane interjected. "I saw Mr. Darcy speaking to her."

"Aye, because she asked him at last how he liked

Netherfield, and he could not help answering her, but she said he seemed very angry at being spoken to."

"Miss Bingley told me," said Jane, "that he never speaks much unless among his intimate acquaintances. With *them* he is remarkably agreeable."

Jane truly saw the best in everyone. And perhaps there was something to it. Mr. Bingley had been perfectly amiable, and somehow he and Mr. Darcy maintained a close enough friendship for Mr. Bingley to invite Mr. Darcy to Netherfield as his guest.

"I just wish Mr. Darcy hadn't slighted you so, Eliza," Charlotte said, using the nickname she had agreed suited Elizabeth best when both were twelve. "And then, not five minutes later, he asks you to dance again. It makes no sense."

"He was jealous," Mary said, looking up from her book. "Jealousy is a sin and a fire in the blood."

Elizabeth doubted Mr. Darcy could muster a fire in his blood, no matter his sins. Especially after his cruel rejection of her when he said, "I have no interest in a woman who is slighted by other men."

No, jealousy had not played into his reversal. It had been something else, some history between him and Mr. Wickham. The same history that led him, inexplicably, to warn Elizabeth off of the man even as he stomped on her womanly pride.

"Mr. Wickham asked you to dance, once and properly," Miss Charlotte said.

"Him and Mr. Denny," Elizabeth said. She studied her friend carefully at the suggestion of Mr. Denny. He had seemed a solid sort, but possessed of a sense of humor. Perhaps Charlotte might discover some deeper affection for him?

"Oh, but that odious Mr. Darcy," Lydia said with a bit too much relish. "To be considered merely passable, I do not know how you could bear it."

"None of us here place any stock in Mr. Darcy's words." Mrs. Bennet said, the high pitch of her voice hardening a little as she glared at her youngest daughter.

Lydia, not used to her mother's disapprobation, shrank in on herself, staring down at her hands. "I only meant to remark that Mr. Wickham was the more discerning of the two."

"Was he?"

"And Mr. Wickham is so very handsome. Far more so than Mr. Darcy," Lydia said. "Mr. Wickham has hair like the sun! We had the loveliest dance, he and I, and he made the kindliest remarks about my dress and bonnet! I had hoped he would ask me again, but it would have been improper, considering he had not yet been introduced to our father. You are so lucky Jane, to be danced with *twice*!"

Mrs. Bennet said, "We do not know of Mr. Wickham's situation, Lydia. He may look fine in his regimentals but possess only a pauper's income. Now Mr. Bingley—he is a fine and responsible young gentleman!—seemed to have some admiration for Jane. Indeed, I rather believe he did. I heard something about it—"

"Perhaps you mean what I overheard between him and Mr. Robinson?" Charlotte interjected.

Elizabeth squeezed Charlotte's hand. The rightful topic of this conversation was Jane and her prospects, and Elizabeth herself had forgotten it in her curiosity about Mr. Wickham and Mr. Darcy. That did not speak well for Elizabeth's sisterly affection, which was shameful. "What did you hear, dear Charlotte? Tell us."

"Yes, do tell us," Mrs. Bennet said, her voice syrup sweetness again.

Charlotte explained that Mr. Robinson had asked Mr. Bingley how he was enjoying the

Meryton assembly, and which of the ladies he thought was the prettiest, and Mr. Bingley's immediate answer to the last question had been, "Oh! The eldest Bennet beyond a doubt. There cannot be two opinions on that point."

As Mrs. Bennet attempted, with little fervor, to demur, Jane's eyes brightened, and the corners of her lips rose. Of the Bennet sisters, Jane had always been the most astute at maintaining her composure, and even in this moment of glorious happiness, she still kept her reaction within the bounds of propriety. Elizabeth envied that.

Elizabeth was too sharp in her emotions and insights to rein herself in so well. As the conversation continued, Elizabeth found her thoughts drifting back to the mystery of Mr. Wickham.

Elizabeth should have enjoyed his company, but something in his demeanor had put her on edge. Maybe it was Mr. Darcy's warning, though a warning for Mr. Darcy ought not have held much weight with her. Or perhaps it was the ease with which he bestowed compliments. Elizabeth had a certain wariness of easily won praise.

True, she preferred them to Mr. Darcy's scorn and insult, but his words were pleasantries, nothing more. The only moment he had exhibited a true interest in what Elizabeth had to say was when he asked her, with all casualness, how long she had been acquainted with Mr. Darcy.

It was all very troubling. And with the letter, its code and warning, Elizabeth couldn't let the subtle animosity between the two men alone. Had Mr. Darcy taken the letter to protect his sister? And how did Mr. Wickham figure into it all?

Elizabeth resolved to discuss it with Charlotte. Her best friend did not think through things swiftly, but she was thorough, and she often noticed things that Elizabeth overlooked.

They gossiped a while longer, and Elizabeth, seeing both their mothers were well occupied with their analysis of events, begged a moment with Charlotte alone. "I should like to show her my new bonnet," she offered as an excuse.

"New bonnet? Is that the one you purchased a fortnight ago before Mr. Bingley's arrival?"

"I have not seen it," Miss Charlotte interjected. "I would very much like to, Mother,"

"Go on," Mrs. Lucas waved them both off.

When Elizabeth and Charlotte were in Elizabeth and Jane's room, Charlotte asked, "So what is really troubling you, Lizzie? I should not have thought you would allow Mr. Darcy's behavior to weigh so heavily on your person."

"It hasn't. Mr. Darcy has been a prat since he first stepped into my father's study with his letter."

"Letter? What letter?"

Elizabeth explained about Mr. Darcy and his sister's letter, avoiding all mention of the second cipher and the danger posed to the Regent.

"Remember the butterflies? Lord Cunningham? That is so odd!"

"Yes. And Mr. Darcy does not believe it to be an accurate deciphering at all! But these were Mr. Reginald Darcy's last words to his beloved sister, and I fear Mr. Darcy will not allow Miss Darcy to read her brother's letter at all."

"He is awfully cold," Charlotte said. "Though as her guardian, he has the right to keep such things from her. Especially if he fears Miss Darcy having an improper relationship with this Lord Cunningham."

"Why would Miss Darcy's own brother ask her to deliver a letter to someone who was pushing an improper suit?" Elizabeth shook her head. "That would make little sense."

"You should write to Miss Georgiana," Charlotte suggested.

"Write her? I cannot just pen the entire story out in the letter."

"It does not seem much of a story, but if you insist upon secrecy, then write to her in the code you deciphered. You will learn if she can understand it and what her response will be."

Elizabeth bit her bottom lip. It might work. She could at least test the initial code and explain to her the first cipher. If nothing else, Elizabeth could get some hint as to the identity of this Lord Cunningham."

"Charlotte, you are brilliant!" Elizabeth exclaimed.

Charlotte laughed. "Hardly brilliant. It just seemed the simplest solution. After all, if Mr. Darcy had not interfered, then Miss Georgiana Darcy would have had the letter in hand, and all would be well."

Elizabeth nodded. The letter had indeed been addressed to Miss Georgiana Darcy. It was not a betrayal to ensure the intended recipient learned something of the contents, especially not with so much at stake. She would say nothing of the threat to the Regent. If this Lord Cunningham had been the intended recipient of the original letter, then Elizabeth would have her father correspond with

Lord Cunningham and gain insight as to how, or if, he was serving the crown.

Decided, Elizabeth walked to the foot of her bed and opened the chest. "You should at least take a brief look at this bonnet, Charlotte, in case somebody asks. And more importantly, what did you think of Mr. Denny?"

Miss Charlotte's cheeks flushed, and she said, "Put the bonnet on, so I might see how fetching it looks."

After the Lucases left, Elizabeth made her way down to the study and penned a letter in Reginald Darcy's code to Miss Darcy. Though Elizabeth knew she was in the right, it still felt improper writing a young lady without even making her acquaintance. Yet the sooner she opened the conversation, the sooner she could learn how best to handle the younger Mr. Darcy's warning.

It was for the good of the country, and also for the good of Mr. Reginald Darcy's memory. The apparently random nature of his death, considering the warning he had mailed out prior to it, seemed implausible. Perhaps it would help assuage Miss Georgiana's grief to know her brother's death had not been due to some cool capriciousness of fate, but instead, a sacrifice to preserve everything they held dear. Their home. Their nation's sovereignty.

When Elizabeth had finished, she signed the letter *Miss Elizabeth Bennet* and added it to the pile to post, slipping the letter between three other envelopes.

From there, she looked over her father's notes for encoding. His hand was smooth, considering his failing eyesight, though some of the lines of script ran together or off the page, depending on how well he had judged the remaining space. Elizabeth went through the papers, making suggestions and notations of her own.

Only when the post had been taken up to mail did Elizabeth's sense of guilt and nervousness begin to ease.

11

Two days later, Jane cornered Elizabeth in the stairwell. "I know you do not wish to do this," Jane started. "But do it anyway, for me."

"You know I would do anything for you, Jane," Elizabeth said. Still, the vague nature of Jane's request made Elizabeth nervous. "What do you ask of me?"

"Miss Caroline Bingley wishes to meet with me in town and do some shopping."

Elizabeth winced. "Miss Bingley, that popinjay with her nose so high in the air? Why would you wish to spend an afternoon with her?"

"She is Mr. Bingley's sister, and not so terrible once you speak with her."

Jane could make pleasant conversation with a

rooster attempting to peck her to death. Though to be fair, Miss Bingley was more taciturn peacock than anything so common as a rooster. "You can manage Miss Bingley," Elizabeth said. "Why would you need me?"

"Miss Bingley and Mrs. Hurst. Together, they are rather intimidating. And you are so witty. I had thought it might be easier managed if I were not alone."

Elizabeth could think of more salubrious ways to spend an afternoon, but Jane was her sister, so reluctantly she agreed.

Jane's face blossomed with a full, beauteous smile. She rocked forward on her toes and took both of Elizabeth's hands. "You will!"

"She will what?"

Both sisters looked up the stairs to where their youngest, Lydia, was walking towards them with a parasol in hand. "What will you do?" Lydia was dressed prettily in pale yellow trimmed with lace. She looked at Elizabeth suspiciously. "I thought Lizzie was to coop herself up with father in the study for the day."

"We are to meet with Miss Bingley in town," Jane said before Elizabeth could stop her.

"Not dressed in that dusty skirt, you cannot,"

Lydia lectured, pointing at the hems of Elizabeth's dress, which had taken on a grayish cast at the lower hem from Elizabeth's late morning walk. "Miss Bingley is so fashionable!"

"I was preparing to change."

"Good. And we shall walk with you. Kitty and I had wanted to visit the town and pay respect to our fighting men. Kitty!" Lydia called back over her shoulder. "Jane and Lizzie are walking with us to town!"

Kitty, dressed in salmon and lace, joined her sister at the top of the stairs. "Wonderful! Mrs. Forester revealed a new group of soldiers is coming. I should like to meet them."

"Do you think we might cross paths with Mr. Wickham? I was so hoping!" Lydia's eyes were wide and shining as she said the handsome soldier's name.

Elizabeth did not like her sister's obvious infatuation. Lydia was like a hummingbird, darting from flower to flower, but while flirting was not a cause for ruination, Mr. Wickham was a stranger and far too handsome. And Lydia was young, pretty, and irreverent.

Elizabeth changed. When she returned, their

mother and Mary, with a Bible in hand, had also agreed to go, and the carriage was called.

Lydia and Mrs. Bennet chattered on about fashion, town gossip, and Miss Bingley's fashion.

Lydia said, "I should like to speak with Miss Bingley. Her dress, her fan, her bonnet—it was all so very London and so beautiful."

"If that is what you wish, you must stay with us for the entire afternoon," Jane said. Elizabeth was struck again with admiration for her sister. Elizabeth had wanted to warn Lydia from engaging in a flirtation with Mr. Wickham, but anything she said would be taken poorly. Jane, without even a mention of Mr. Wickham, had distracted Lydia from her plan of meeting with him.

Jane and Miss Bingley had agreed to meet at the haberdashery, and Miss Bingley stood in front of the building with two wrapped packages. She handed them to a servant as the Bennets' carriage drove towards her. Miss Bingley was striking in her cream walking dress with a layered collar up to her chin, bodice crossed with golden ribbon and a golden shawl embroidered with black. Her boots, a soft calfskin, were hardly dirtied from walking about.

Elizabeth found it remarkable she would wear a

color so easily stained for a walk about town, but likely her plans included stepping from the carriage into a shop, then back out of the shop and into another indoor enclosure.

As they pulled up, Mary said, "I would like to visit the music store. And perhaps look at some books."

"Later!" Mrs. Bennet said, throwing both of her hands up in the air. "We must do all we can to make the very best impression on Miss Bingley, for Jane's sake. And then we shall have Madame Godiva tell us your future, Mary. It has already worked out so wonderfully for Jane."

Elizabeth glanced at the well-worn, leather-bound Bible cradled in Mary's lap. She had armored herself before entering the lion's den. Elizabeth's lips quirked.

"Miss. Bingley!" Jane said, alighting first. "I hope we did not keep you waiting."

"I was enjoying the air. It is lovely to see sunshine." Miss Bingley's eyes narrowed as Elizabeth alighted from the carriage followed by her sisters and mother.

"Oh Miss Bingley, it is a delight to see you! Is Mr. Bingley also in town? It would be a wonderful coincidence if we were to cross paths, would it not Jane?" Mrs. Bennet said.

Elizabeth's face grew warm in sympathetic embarrassment for her sister. But Jane took it in stride. "Miss Bingley and I had arranged to meet, not something to her brother's interest. She was also interested in seeing Madame Godiva."

Jane had not mentioned this to Elizabeth, though Miss Bingley nodded at the suggestion. "Miss Bennet has told me wonderful things about Madame Godiva's abilities."

"A truly talented woman," Mrs. Bennet cut in. "My daughters Mary and Elizabeth have yet to experience her powers, but I found her so refreshing. Why, Jane was so pleased when she had her future told!"

"Miss Bingley, allow me to introduce you formally to my mother and sisters." Jane introduced each and the daughters curtsied.

Lydia said, "Forgive my forwardness, Miss Bingley, but the layering of your skirts and the color of your ribbon is so lovely. Is this the style of London?"

"Last season," Miss Bingley said. Her tone was dismissive, but Elizabeth recognized more than a hint of pride in her manner. It reminded Elizabeth unfavorably of Mr. Darcy. Miss Bingley looked down upon the Bennets as though their relative stations were separated by the width of the English Channel. "That is a lovely frock too," Miss Bingley added, waving her hand towards Lydia's best walking dress. "Did you do the embroidery yourself? The work is so very detailed, one can hardly notice an occasionally misplaced stitch."

Lydia's face flushed as she brushed her fingers over her stitching.

Elizabeth often found Lydia irritating, especially in recent years, but she was Elizabeth's sister and did not deserve Miss Bingley's prettily disguised insult. Elizabeth glanced over Miss Bingley's appearance, searching for something with which to find fault. "Is that hanging thread?" she asked, peering at Miss Bingley's neckline.

There was no hanging thread, but Miss Bingley looked down anyway. With her chin in that position, the layered neck ruff made her look like a rooster covered in flour. Elizabeth's lips quirked even as she attempted to maintain a serious expression. Jane gave Elizabeth a warning glare even her own lips twitched.

Elizabeth tried to catch Lydia's gaze to bring her in on the joke, but Lydia focused on Miss Bingley's neckline. "What thread? I see no thread. Lizzie, what are you on about?"

Elizabeth shook her head. "It must have been a trick of the light," she said. "My apologies, Miss Bingley."

"Hmmph."

"Our Lizzie is often prone to fits of vision," Mrs. Bennet cut in. "It fails her at the most inopportune times. Sometimes I wake in the middle of the night, my heart fluttering at the thought of what will happen to her if her eyesight fails in its entirety!"

"It can be very distressing," Elizabeth said dryly.

"Madame Godiva's home is just a street over," Mrs. Bennet explained. "She is leasing a small home for the winter."

"Well, that is a relief. I admit I was not sure of the propriety of visiting a woman who lived in a wagon. Is she a Gypsy?"

"Not precisely, though her ways are odd, and she must have some foreign blood to see the future as she does. Peering into ethereal planes is not exactly civilized, is it?" Mrs. Bennet said.

Miss Bingley said, "I have heard Gypsies can become violent. Why the *Morning Chronicle* had an article last month about a woman and child abducted by Gypsies, and they were not seen again. We might have been murdered!"

"All of us? Together in broad daylight?" Elizabeth laughed. Whether in a wagon or a leased home, it seemed unlikely. "If this Madame Godiva were the murderous type, I suspect we would have heard rumor of missing persons and mangled bodies by this point."

"Lizzie!" Mrs. Bennet gasped. "Such talk is not fit for proper conversation!"

"It is not I who brought up the subject of murder."

Jane said. "Madame Godiva is a widow. She is sweet and kind. I believe she has some perception for understanding the future and takes joy in sharing her observations with others. Perhaps she is lonely, and if our company eases her pain and gives her purpose, what harm can come from that?"

A great deal of harm, Elizabeth suspected, if she could bring herself to believe Madame Godiva had any of the abilities she claimed to possess.

As they walked, Lydia caught a glimpse of Mr. Denny walking towards their direction on the opposite side of the road.

Lydia exclaimed, "Why, that is Mr. Denny. Mr. Wickham's friend?"

Elizabeth wished Charlotte had joined them this afternoon.

Mrs. Bennet whispered, "Mr. Denny has an income of two hundred a year."

Mrs. Bennet's tone and manner were dismissive, but Elizabeth thought a woman could live comfortably in a small household with an income of two hundred a year, provided she was allowed her own freedoms. While Elizabeth had no particular regard for Mr. Denny, and if Charlotte and Mr. Denny both developed a fondness for each other, perhaps something could grow from it. Even if Sir Lucas considered two hundred yearly too miserly for his eldest daughter.

"Mr. Denny!" Lydia called out.

Mr. Denny returned their wave and crossed to meet them.

Elizabeth was confident Lydia, with her attentions purely on appearance, had no interest in Mr. Denny himself. At the same time, Elizabeth also wished to learn more about Mr. Wickham, and Lydia's questioning, which was certain to occur, along with Miss Bingley's longer acquaintanceship with Mr. Darcy, might yield some insight.

Mr. Denny smiled in return and walked towards them. "Beautiful afternoon, is it not?"

"Yes. Glorious. One could hardly count it as nearing winter." Lydia flashed her most dazzling smile. "It is a delight to see you, Mr. Denny. And your friend, Mr. Wickham? He is not given leave to walk about the town today?"

"Mr. Wickham has… umm… taken on some extra duties for himself at the barracks."

"Oh," Lydia remarked. "He is so very diligent, isn't he?"

"Very," Mr. Denny said in an oddly flat tone.

Elizabeth asked, "How long have you and Mr. Wickham been acquainted?"

"We were assigned together to the same unit."

So they had not been acquainted long, and Mr. Denny had a certain reserve when speaking of Mr. Wickham.

Interesting.

"Mr. Wickham, you say," Miss Bingley interjected. "He and Mr. Darcy were raised together, though I fear they had some falling out."

Raised together? How had Mr. Darcy seen no need to remark on that when issuing a blanket warning against Mr. Wickham's character?

"Do you know what happened?" Elizabeth

asked.

"I would say it was a lady, but Mr. Darcy is so reserved in his expression of affection one would hardly discover such a thing through ordinary word of mouth."

"If there was a falling out, I hope such ill temper will be eased by their seeing each other again," Jane said. "Childhood bonds are often the strongest, especially amongst family."

"Mr. Darcy and Mr. Wickham are not related." Miss Bingley said firmly.

"I had not meant to imply that they might be," Jane said, her cheeks reddening with a faint blush. "Merely that two young boys who are raised together might have formed a strong bond. Such a bond is difficult to break. It may be damaged, but not broken…" Jane shook her head. "One would have to do something truly unforgivable. And I refuse to believe such a thing of either man, having had only the faintest interaction with both."

Perhaps Jane was correct. Or perhaps Mr. Darcy's standards being so unbending, he had viewed some action of Mr. Wickham's as being unforgivable and acted accordingly. That, in Elizabeth's mind, seemed the most likely.

But since neither Mr. Bingley nor Mr. Denny

had any further insight into the matter, Elizabeth saw no need to press it further.

Lydia pressed it further. "Does Mr. Wickham often take on extra duties?"

Mr. Denny shrugged. "When it is necessary." He turned to Elizabeth, "Miss Elizabeth, that bonnet is very fetching on you. If you don't mind my remarking."

It was better Charlotte was not here. Elizabeth had no interest in Mr. Denny, and it upset Elizabeth to receive such a clear expression of preference from him.

"Well, Mr. Denny," Mrs. Bennet cut in, rather shortly. "We must be on our way."

"Where to? Perhaps I can offer an escort."

"It is women's business."

Mr. Denny glanced behind him. "You too?"

"Excuse me?" Mrs. Bennet asked.

"Many ladies are visiting that spiritualist. What is her name, Godiva?"

"Be that as it may, we must be on our way."

"Yes, of course. Ladies." Mr. Denny bowed.

When Mr. Denny was well behind them, Mrs. Bennet whispered, "Two hundred a year. Lizzie, you must set your expectations higher than that, my dear."

12

*M*adame Godiva's leased home was at the edge of the main thorough-fare. The house was small, eighteen feet in front with a small yard in the back where her wagon was presumably settled. As they approached the door, it opened, and a small, simply dressed young house-maid answered. "I will inform Madame her guests have arrived."

"Remarkable," Mrs. Bennet said after the young woman had led them into the parlor. "Jane, had you made an appointment to see her?"

"No," Jane said. "She said I would be welcomed at any time."

As Jane spoke, the housemaid straightened up items about the room. She was slight in frame, but

Elizabeth suspected older than she first appeared. She had mousy brown hair and a snub nose. Her eyes were sharp as she moved about. "I will bring you refreshments, and the Madame will be with you presently," she said with a heavy Cockney accent.

A thick, red velvet curtain separated the receiving room from the rest of the house. The maid pushed it aside as she bustled out.

The others continued to converse as refreshments were brought. Some ten minutes after that, the curtain was pushed aside again, and a stooped woman in a layered, brightly colored frock stepped into the room. She held an ornately carved cane with vines and flowers running up the base to a wide knob, which Elizabeth realized was the head of the snake.

Madame Godiva's hunched-over frame and layers of fabric gave the impression of her being quite old, but she did not possess the sagging wrinkles of someone who was truly elderly. She was likely no older than Elizabeth's mother. Her eyes, however, were quite startling. Two shades of green as Lydia had described.

Madame Godiva said, "Mrs. Bennet, Miss Bennet, Miss Lydia, Miss Kitty, and you must be Miss Mary and Miss Elizabeth," she said, nodding to each in turn. Elizabeth curtsied, and after a pause, Mary did the same. It was an awkward motion for Mary, who was still clutching her leather-bound Bible. "Mother wishes me to speak with you, and it is my duty to obey my parents, but I have no interest in having my fortune explained," Mary said.

Mme. Godiva smiled. "Certainly not. As it says in Leviticus, 19:31, 'Do not turn to mediums or necromancers; do not seek them out, and so make yourselves unclean by them: I am the Lord your God.' We can have a cup of tea and discuss music. You are quite fond of music, are you not?"

Mary's eyes widened, and she looked at Mme. Godiva with newfound interest. "I am fond of the pianoforte and the compositions of Ignaz Pleyel. Mary rubbed her thumb over the cover of her Bible and then said, "I suppose, if it is just a conversation, then we can converse."

Mme. Godiva said, "And yet, I believe this fashionable young lady of London style also has questions for me." Mme. Godiva turned to Miss Bingley. The fortune teller's stillness, in combination with her two-tone eyes, struck Elizabeth as an interesting note of drama. She hoped it unsettled Miss Bingley. "Miss Bingley is it?"

Miss Bingley's eyes widened. "Yes. Did you tell her I would be joining you, Miss Bennet?"

Jane shook her head.

Elizabeth was less impressed, as the housemaid had certainly heard their mother refer to Miss Bingley by name and relayed such information to her mistress.

Madame Godiva continued, "You are playing court to a certain young gentleman and are concerned he may not recognize your advances?"

Miss Bingley nodded. "What do you see?"

"Perhaps this discussion is best held in private. Will you come first?"

"Yes, I am interested in your thoughts." Miss Bingley agreed. With that, all concerns about murder forgotten, Miss Bingley followed Madame Godiva further into her house.

"How remarkable," Mrs. Bennet gushed, gesturing with her hand towards the curtain, which had shivered to stillness. "Madame Godiva has a gift! To know Miss Bingley's name without having laid eyes upon her!"

"Yes! It is exactly the same as I felt when she first sought me out," Lydia remarked. "She says she gets visions and sometimes is compelled to take action."

Compelled by the sight of a lady of means, Elizabeth mused. Still, the fortune teller's powers of observation did her credit. Her calming of Mary's nerves was inspired, first with the quotation from the Bible and then the bit about music, which Mrs. Bennet would have shared almost immediately upon being asked about her family on the previous visit. Predicting Miss Bingley's designs had also been a good exercise in deduction. What young, fashionable woman of wealth would consult with a soothsayer except for in pursuit of a husband?"

After some ten minutes, Miss Bingley returned, and Mrs. Bennet was called in next, which only made sense as she would give the soothsayer all the information she needed to guess at all of her daughter's futures.

Yes, Madame Godiva was very intelligent indeed.

While the young ladies waited, they interrogated Miss Bingley on what she had been told, but she kept the details of the conversation to her herself, claiming she did not want to disturb the possibilities that had been outlined in their talk.

After Miss Bingley came Mary, who returned with a pamphlet of Psalms, and then Kitty was called in.

"Now, may I visit the music store?" Mary asked. "Mme. Godiva said I might find new sheet music today. Something to stir the heart of one who might admire me. It was not telling of the future, more an explanation of the possibilities," she added defensively.

Mrs. Bennet agreed, and extracting a promise for all to meet again at the carriage in an hour to return for dinner, they left.

After Kitty came Lydia, and then Jane. Lydia and Kitty left soon after Kitty's fortune was told, leaving Elizabeth and Miss Bingley alone together in the sitting room.

Miss Bingley took a sip of her tea and said, "Madame Godiva says Mr. Darcy will be tempted by someone unsuitable."

Elizabeth said, "That seems unfortunate." And confusing. What business did Miss Bingley have discussing Mr. Darcy with Elizabeth?

"He will not succumb. Mr. Darcy has always been the picture of propriety."

Elizabeth nodded and took a biscuit from the tray.

"Lady Catherine de Bourgh, his aunt, claims he is engaged to her niece, but Mr. Darcy never speaks of it. Anne is a sweet girl, but not particularly robust in body or spirit. Mr. Darcy needs someone who will challenge him and offset his serious nature. I believe if he found such a lady, then he would marry her."

"And you intend to be that woman?" Elizabeth asked.

"I cannot predict the ultimate object of his affections," Miss Bingley said primly. "But I believe he would find a woman of his station more suitable than a country miss."

Miss Bingley saw Elizabeth as competition for Mr. Darcy? Elizabeth almost laughed but managed to disguise the emotion as a cough.

"Miss Elizabeth?" Miss Bingley leaned towards Elizabeth.

"Yes. Yes. I should not have swallowed my biscuit just then." Elizabeth managed. She took up the dregs of her tea and swallowed.

The curtain opened again, and Jane returned. "Oh, Miss Bingley, I feel so much lighter now."

"Do you? What did she say?"

"Oh, I cannot share it. The future is too fragile, and my hopes too deep."

"Miss Elizabeth," the housemaid came through the curtain. "Madame Godiva will receive you now."

"I cannot sit here any longer," Miss Bingley said. "Do you mind if we step outside, just for some air?"

"Lizzie?" Jane gave Elizabeth a beseeching look. "We will step outside and enjoy the sunlight if that suits you, Lizzie."

Elizabeth agreed. Best someone enjoyed the sunshine.

The housemaid led Elizabeth down a dark, narrow hallway to another thickly curtained door. She pushed it aside, and Elizabeth stepped inside. A sharp, smoky sweetness filled the air. An incense of some kind. The curtains were drawn, and oil lanterns were placed on tables at either side of the room. Layers of fabric hung from the walls. A second, translucent curtain separated the front from the back of the room. Behind it sat the silhouette of Mme. Godiva, rendered ghostly through the gauzy fabric. She called out, "This way, child."

It was a wonder Mary hadn't immediately turned on her heel and fled. Or more likely, Madame Godiva had met with Mary in a different room.

Elizabeth, not fearful of idolatry and demons, strode towards Madame Godiva. When Elizabeth passed through the gauzy curtain, Mme. Godiva said, "Sit." She waved a hand towards a cushioned chair that had also been draped in a length of pale white fabric.

Elizabeth sat. The chair was surprisingly comfortable, and Elizabeth settled herself to wait. In the dim light, she could not get a good look at Mme. Godiva's face, though her two-toned eyes shone eerily in the lantern light. Madame Godiva had streaks in her hair, which Elizabeth expected was to some extent powder as it gathered at the roots. She squinted at Elizabeth and said, "You are not the sort who wishes to have your fortune told."

"Did my mother tell you this?"

"She shared that you had doubts, and those doubts are written on your face. It is difficult for you, seeing more than others do, and because of your sex, having those observations dismissed."

"I do not pretend to see the future," Elizabeth responded sharply.

"Then in that, we are of an accord. You see the present, as do I. Tell me, Miss Elizabeth Bennet, what do you see of me?"

"Am I not here to have you read my possibilities in the smoke or something of that persuasion?"

"You see me as a Gypsy charlatan with designs upon some piece of your family's fortune."

"I cannot believe you are a Gypsy. Gypsies travel together. They stay for a few days, a week at most, and then they leave. You have leased a home, and your accent is Cockney. You are also not as old as you pretend."

"No, but it is easier to speak truth and have it believed when one is perceived to be old and strange. We all wear masks to make our way in this world. Give me your palm," she said.

Despite herself, Elizabeth wanted to see what the woman would do next. Elizabeth pulled her glove from her left hand and extended it. Madame Godiva flipped her palm up and held the hand with a firm grip. She squinted and pulled Elizabeth's hand closer to the lantern light. Her own hands were bare, and her skin was warm and dry.

"You are the sort who makes her own destiny. Be cautious of judging too quickly. You are often correct, but a quick glance over something does not yield the same insight as a slower, more measured approach."

"No vision of true love or a settled future?"

"I could offer you a more in-depth prognostication, but you would only shrug it aside."

Elizabeth sighed. Madame Godiva was not wrong.

While she might not see the future, she had already had occasion to speak with many of the ladies at the village, and perhaps she might have learned something that could apply to Elizabeth's own problem.

"You have spoken with others about their own fortunes, have you not?"

"What a person shares with me and what the Fates disclose about them is not to share."

"I am not interested in fortunes or fate. Merely your own observations. My sister Lydia seems particularly enamored of a young soldier who we met at Saturday's Assembly, while she was slighted by another young gentleman who was also in attendance."

"You speak of the odious Mr. Darcy?"

Elizabeth's lips twitched. "So Lydia spoke of him?"

Madame Godiva ran her thumb over Elizabeth's palm. "He has slighted you as well."

Elizabeth was surprised Lydia had mentioned that. "Slighted me, warned me, and then attempted awkwardly to regain my regard. He is most troubling."

"A complicated man. Your fates are entwined."

"Not for long, I hope. I dislike him. Mr. Darcy is

unthinking and rude, and yet he seemed sincere in warning me off of Mr. Wickham."

"Perhaps he wanted you for himself?"

Elizabeth laughed. "Hardly that. I am, in his own words, but passably handsome, and even if he held my features in higher regard, he is already too aware of my own eccentricities and far too proper to tolerate them."

"But he asked you to dance."

"After he said he would not dance with me or anyone who had been slighted by other men."

"Did you find Mr. Wickham more convivial?"

"Mr. Wickham smiled with his mouth but not his eyes."

"And Mr. Darcy?"

"Mr. Darcy does not smile at all."

"I will not call this a fortune, merely advice. You are an intelligent, perceptive, and sensitive young lady. Do not shutter it behind airs and small deceptions. Find someone who loves you as you are. Else you will have neither the security nor happiness you desire."

Elizabeth closed her eyes. Being loved for herself was all she wanted, but even a lady like Jane, who was as close to a womanly ideal as Elizabeth could imagine, had to play at small deceptions in the name of propriety. Small deceptions were a woman's way of moving through the world. Madame Godiva herself was almost in her entirety a small deception. Was she then unhappy?

Perhaps.

Mme. Godiva's grip on Elizabeth's hand tightened until it was almost painful. Her body tensed, and she shuddered. The two-toned eyes seemed in that moment to stare into the depths of Elizabeth's soul. Elizabeth shivered.

Madame Godiva said, "I see a letter and betrayal."

"Lydia told you about the letter." Of course she had, and now Madame Godiva was using this information to unsettle Elizabeth and thus inspire belief. Elizabeth would not be moved.

Madame Godiva said, "A ball. A needle. A prince."

"This is ridiculous."

"Mr. Darcy will ask your hand in marriage." Elizabeth wanted to laugh, but something in the light and the play of shadows over Madame Godiva's face and those eyes froze all mirth from Elizabeth's spirit.

"Twice."

Instead of humor, Elizabeth felt the stirrings of

anger. She had already seen through the charlatan, and they had been having a pleasant enough conversation, and now this. "I said I did not believe you. Do not think you can change my mind with exaggerated theatrics."

Madame Godiva slumped forward, her chin knocking against her chest in a way that looked painful.

Elizabeth, who had been trying to pull her hand away, jerked back on the chair and had to steady herself. Once she had, she stood. "We are finished," she said.

The fortune teller lifted her arm and waved back towards the exit of the wagon. "Yes. Go, please."

Elizabeth took a moment to collect herself in the sitting room before returning to Miss Bingley and Jane. How dare that woman! How could she believe Elizabeth would fall for such blatant, overblown theatrics? Mr. Darcy ask her hand in marriage! Twice? Insanity!

When Elizabeth had returned to her sister and Jane, they eagerly asked Elizabeth about her fortune. Elizabeth, still rattled, demurred.

"You seem upset," Jane said, taking Elizabeth's hand. "It was not so terrible as all of that, was it?"

Elizabeth forced a smile. "I fear her skills of observation are greater than those of prognostication. She says Mr. Darcy will ask my hand in marriage." Elizabeth took a breath. In the bright sunlight, away from Mme. Godiva's two-toned eyes and the eerie aura she had engineered in her wagon, the ridiculousness of that declaration finally stirred some of the natural lightness in Elizabeth's spirit.

Miss Bingley's eyes narrowed, and she said, "Foolishness!"

While Elizabeth agreed, Miss Bingley's vehemence was irritating. More irritating however was when Jane, in a far more sympathetic tone, squeezed Elizabeth's hand again and remarked, "How strange. I truly believed Madame Godiva had a gift."

13

----

*A*fter the disastrous Assembly, neither Mr. Bingley nor Miss Bingley objected when Mr. Darcy claimed important business in London kept him from attending Sir Lucas's ball. Instead, he paid a special visit to his solicitor, Mr. Hart, who had not seen nor heard anything about anyone gambling with the Pemberley estate nor any illicit use of a Darcy family seal at all.

"As I explained in my letter, Mr. Darcy, if Mr. Wickham is in possession of your father's seal, your father, rest his soul, is five years gone and any contracts made with that bit of wood and wax will not survive the light of truth. Be at ease."

"I have had recent occasion to cross paths with Mr. Wickham. He assures me his debts are paid, and he was further able to buy a commission in our militia. Can you look into how this was accomplished?" Mr. Darcy in this request was skirting the edges of propriety. He did not directly ask his solicitor to make inquiries or hire a Bow Street runner to ferret out information, but the request was implied.

Mr. Darcy and Mr. Hart discussed what funds might be dispensed to acquire information, and Mr. Darcy agreed. Mr. Darcy stayed the night in his London townhouse and returned the afternoon after the ball.

Mr. Bingley kept London hours: the dinner served at half six, and after bathing and changing, it surprised Mr. Darcy to discover the eldest Bennet sister seated beside Miss Bingley at the table. Bingley was making his preferences known.

Miss Bingley, Miss Bennet," Mr. Darcy greeted them with a bow. "It is a pleasure to make your acquaintance."

Miss Bennet nodded, but there was a certain coldness to her expression. "Mr. Darcy."

Mrs. Hurst sat at Miss Bennet's opposite side,

with her husband across the table and seated to the right of Mr. Bingley. The seat opposite Miss Bingley had been left empty, and Miss Bingley gave him a proper nod and measured smile as she said, "Mr. Darcy, please, sit."

Servants entered with the first course. Mr. Darcy sat.

Miss Bingley said, "You must be exhausted from your travels. Is there any news?"

What information had Miss Bingley already pried out of her brother about his trip? Mr. Darcy did not like her meddling, and he had no intention of offering her any more fodder for her imagination. "All is well."

"Oh! That is wonderful. I had thought with you having to leave so quickly that there might have been an emergency. But you are already gone and back."

The eldest Bennet, who though not nearly as fashionable as Miss Bingley still held a fresh-faced innocence and warm manner that drew the eye, nodded serenely and said, "I am happy to hear all is well with you and your business." Miss Bennet's nose wrinkled, and a moment later, she sneezed.

"God bless you," Mrs. Hurst said. "Is your gown dried out well enough from being caught in the storm? You should have allowed Caroline to loan you something for this evening."

"I have already imposed enough," Miss Bennet said. "And an hour in front of the fire warmed me to my toes."

Had Miss Bennet been caught out in that downpour? Why hadn't she taken a carriage for her visit? Perhaps the Bennet family was too poor. Another sign of how unsuitable Miss Bennet was for Bingley. Or any Bennet for Darcy, not that he had any interest in Miss Elizabeth or any of the others.

Mr. Bingley turned to Mr. Darcy with a wide smile. "I would say the ladies were disappointed at your absence last night, but as you have no fondness for dancing, it was only I who suffered without your heartening presence."

If it were anyone except Bingley, Mr. Darcy would have assumed the words veiled insults. But Mr. Bingley was too sincere to engage in deliberate slights.

"We missed you, Mr. Darcy," Miss Bingley said. "Many remarked on your absence."

Mr. Darcy suspected that they had remarked upon it, either with joy or relief. "Did Mr. Wickham attend?"

"Elizabeth mentioned that you and Mr.

Wickham are acquainted," Miss Bennet said. The tone of her voice had lowered, and her eyes were wide with what appeared to be concerned interest. "From childhood, is it?"

"We are no longer close," Mr. Darcy said. He had to give credit to the eldest Miss Bennet. She had already ingratiated herself into the household, and her skills at dissembling put Miss Bingley to shame. Mr. Darcy could hardly point out anything in her manner beyond simple concern. It was no surprise Bingley already imagined Miss Bennet an angel.

Miss Bennet said, "In answer to your question, it was disappointing for the ladies to have both you and Mr. Wickham absent. It had seemed towards the end of the Assembly you had warmed to dancing. Or so my sister relayed to me."

"You and your sister are close, are you?"

Miss Bennet nodded. "What hurts her, hurts me."

Mr. Darcy got the distinct impression he was being taken to task, and worse that he deserved it.

"I—" Mr. Darcy hadn't much experience with apologies. His father had always been clear: a gentleman, one tasked with managing a large estate, must never appear weak. If he had done another, especially one of lower station, a wrong, then adequate restitution could be made. But one must never prostrate himself. It was an indignity.

"Mr. Darcy? Are you well?" Miss Bennet asked.

"I should not have spoken so harshly of your sister. She is handsome enough, as are you."

"Well that is a high compliment indeed," Mr. Bingley said, clapping Mr. Darcy a bit too heartily on the back. "As Mr. Darcy claims, quite correctly, you, Miss Bennet, are unusually handsome. Remarkably so."

Jane smiled; it was a measured expression that seemed a touch too serene in contrast to Mr. Bingley's obvious enthusiasm. Miss Bennet was a kind, mannered woman, but she did not appear to hold his friend in any particular regard. Her interest, as with so many others, was likely in his yearly income.

Mr. Darcy did not hold that against her as many would. A lady's business was securing a husband, preferably one who allowed her to maintain a quality of life at least to the degree to which she had become accustomed in childhood. In the same way, it was an eldest son's duty to find a lady of adequate station to continue his own family line. But Mr. Bingley was more idealistic. He wished a love match, and Darcy, as his friend, would not allow him to sacrifice his dreams upon a false altar. Even one as prettily constructed as Miss Bennet.

Eventually, though, Bingley would ask Darcy's advice, and at that point, Darcy could set his friend straight. Until then, Darcy could only hope Bingley didn't allow himself to fall too deeply into infatuation.

"Well, Mr. Darcy," Miss Bennet said, "While I accept your apology, it is my sister who would most benefit from your words." She sneezed again.

"Yes. Yes. I will express my regrets to her in person," Mr. Darcy agreed, and then kicked himself. Now he would have to contrive not only to speak with her again but also to prostrate himself, at least for a moment. It was worse because she had defended her own honor in slighting him, dancing both with Mr. Denny and then Mr. Wickham.

Wickham. All of this was Wickham's fault. Darcy disliked crowds and strangers, but he would not have been so agitated had Wickham's treachery not been a factor. And how had Mr. Wickham paid for his commission? On a gambling hell table on the back of Pemberley?

Mr. Darcy stabbed his knife into his roasted tenderloin, scraping the edge against the plate.

When they had finished eating, Mrs. Hurst said,

"This rain shows no signs of easing. Miss Bennet, you cannot ride back in this weather on horseback."

Miss Bennet blushed and looked down at her plate. "I hate to impose——"

"It is no imposition!" Bingley said. Frankly, he looked delighted. "It is enough you were caught in the shower riding to visit. We will not send you out in the dark in a downpour. I have already asked the housekeeper to prepare a guest room for you."

Miss Bingley looked from her brother back to Miss Bennet. "Yes. It seems we have."

Miss Bennet sneezed again.

"I hope you are not catching cold," Mrs. Hurst said. "An autumn cold is a terrible thing."

"No, it would be too much," Miss Bennet sniffed. "I have always been very healthy."

They stayed up after dinner, conversing and playing games, but it was clear as time passed that Jane's sneezes came more frequently. Eventually, Mrs. Hurst insisted they all go to sleep.

The next morning, Miss Bennet was thoroughly ill. Mr. Bingley insisted she be given time and care to recover, and Miss Bennet had a letter sent to Longbourn updating the family as to her condition.

All seemed settled at noon when they had another visitor, a Miss Elizabeth Bennet, her complexion glowing and eyes brilliant with the warmth of exercise.

All except the elder Miss Bennet were gathered in the breakfast parlor when their visitor was sent in. MissElizabeth's appearance caused a great deal of surprise that she should have walked three miles so early in the day in such foul weather, and by herself. The hems of her skirts were damp and flecked with mud, the same mud which rimmed her boots.

While Mr. Darcy could not help but admire the healthy flush exercise had bestowed upon Miss Elizabeth's complexion, he doubted the need for her to come so far. Yes, this was the country, and the likelihood of Miss Elizabeth getting snatched by highwaymen or stumbling across other disreputable characters was slight, but Mr. Darcy felt an odd protectiveness of her. She had risked her safety, and Mr. Darcy found that intolerable.

He also realized as Mr. Bingley extended a warm greeting in a manner that was somehow better than politeness, Mr. Darcy's promise to Miss Jane Bennet had become imminent. Darcy had promised to apologize to Miss Elizabeth in person, and now, she was here.

"My sister," Elizabeth asked. She gripped her

skirts to keep the damp hems from dragging upon the floor, and her voice rose in pitch as she continued, "Jane said not to worry, but even if there were cause to worry, Jane would admonish us not to. It is her way. She thinks more for the convenience of others than about herself. Is she awake or asleep? Is she too ill to leave her bed?"

Mr. Bingley delivered the news as kindly as he could, but it became apparent that the elder Miss Bennet was doing more poorly than her correspondence had suggested. Though she had awakened and eaten a light repast, she was still feverish and unable to leave her room.

Elizabeth swallowed, and a chill passed over her. "Please, I would like to see her."

Miss Elizabeth's request was granted, and to Mr. Darcy's relief, she was immediately taken from the breakfast parlor to be with her sister.

When they had left, Mr. Hurst resumed his breakfast.

Miss Bingley soon returned, ate a few bites, placed the tines of the fork on the edge of her plate and, looking up at Mr. Darcy, said, "I suppose it speaks well for Miss Elizabeth that she cares so deeply for her sister. But it was ill-advised for her to tromp for three miles—three miles!—through mud and fields. There is something to that exertion that seems almost uncivilized."

While Mr. Darcy had been harboring some of the same concerns and feeling some degree of irritation at Miss Elizabeth making her way here in a lonely, panicked dash, he found Miss Bingley's tone and her use of the word "uncivilized" to be a touch overblown.

He said, "I believe familial regard is something that separates us all from lesser beasts. And it is obvious the sisters are quite close. Miss Elizabeth immediately recognized through Miss Bennet's correspondence an attempt to minimize her illness." If only Darcy and his brother had been so close. Perhaps Darcy would have been able to identify what had caused Reginald not only to buy himself a commission but further to ask, and in fact insist, on being sent far from England's shores.

"I have nothing but the highest regard for Miss Elizabeth's sense of familial duty," Miss Bingley said. "Possibly it is the difference between the country and city. In London, a young lady of consequence would not travel such a distance on her own and in such poor weather."

Mr. Darcy asked, "Have you sent for the apothecary?"

"Yes, and Mr. Jones will be here presently," Mr. Bingley said.

"With rest and fair treatment, the dear lady will become well again." Miss Bingley said, her voice a little too sweet.

Mr. Darcy finished the rest of his breakfast in silence. The food was tasteless and settled poorly in his stomach. His thoughts were also uncomfortable. He disliked apologizing, but he had given his word. Darcy was a man of his word. At least here, he could contrive to make his apology to Miss Elizabeth with some degree of privacy before her sister was well enough to have both return to their home.

14

*E*lizabeth could describe her beginnings at Netherfield Park as discouraging. As she explained her reason for paying such a sudden visit, she was well and truly discomfited by the combined pressure of the Bingleys', Hursts', and Mr. Darcy's attention. Especially Mr. Darcy, whose expression was as cold as ever but somehow made worse by his obvious interest in the state of her soggy hems. Or perhaps it was her face, flushed from the three-mile walk.

Then, upon being guided to Jane's sickbed, Elizabeth's worst fears were brought to life.

Jane was not well. Her skin was pale and shiny with sweat, and her eyes were a pinkish shade, almost as though she had been weeping. She was leaned back on a pile of pillows, and as Elizabeth and Miss Bennet walked into the room, Jane took a deep breath, and with a visible effort lifted her head.

Elizabeth ran to her sister's side and took Jane's hands. "You are far sicker than you told us," Elizabeth said.

"I did not want you to worry. The Bingleys are taking wonderful care of me, and I can only be grateful for their hospitality, especially as I have become a burden. Miss Bingley, you and your family have my gratitude."

"Miss Bennet is too kind," Miss Bingley said. To Elizabeth's surprise, the woman seemed genuine in her praise. "We have sent for the apothecary, and all that is required for you is that you rest and improve."

Miss Bingley's solicitude softened Elizabeth's ill feeling about the woman.

"Lizzie!" Jane took a breath. "I am so glad you are here. I did not wish to worry you, but your visit—" Jane coughed. "It is good to see you."

Mr. Bingley stayed a minute or so longer, and after she had left, Jane was not up to much conversation. She managed "Miss Bingley and Mrs. Hurst have been so kind. And Mr. Darcy—"

"Mr. Darcy has been kind to you?"

"In his way. I suppose. I took him to task for his treatment of you at the Assembly." Jane coughed again, a violent fit that made her wince.

Elizabeth pulled Jane's blanket up to cover her shoulders. "Be quiet and rest."

Jane managed a smile. "But his face—"

"I do not wish to speak of Mr. Darcy.

Jane nodded, and soon after her eyes closed, and she slept again.

When breakfast was over, the sisters returned, and Elizabeth grudgingly began to hold them in some regard as they were so solicitous towards Jane. The apothecary came and examined Jane, advising her to return to bed and promising her some draughts.

Jane had little trouble following that advice. As the afternoon progressed, her fever rose, and she complained of a pounding headache. Elizabeth was too concerned about her sister to leave even for a moment. To her surprise, the other ladies were rarely absent; though perhaps it was because with the gentleman being out, they had in fact nothing to do.

When the clock struck three, Elizabeth was caught between the necessity for politeness, which required she not impose herself too greatly upon the Bingley household, and her own deep worry for her sister. Finally, and through her own reservations, Elizabeth said, "I should go."

"We can send you in our chaise——" Miss Bingley began, but Jane interrupted her, reaching for Elizabeth.

"Please, do not leave just yet," Jane said. Her face was flushed with fever, and her eyes too bright.

"Then stay you must," Mr. Bingley grudgingly agreed. "I will send word to your family and have them bring back a supply of clothes for you and Jane."

Soon after, Jane fell asleep again, and Elizabeth, leaving her sister in the care of Mrs. Hurst and Miss Bingley for a few moments to relieve herself, stole from the room. Elizabeth returned, and a mere few steps from her sister's room, Elizabeth had the sudden and disturbing feeling someone was watching her. She froze and looked up and down the hall.

Mr. Darcy stood in the shadow of an alcove. He took a step towards her and bowed. "Miss Eliza-beth. How fares your sister?"

Was he truly worried about Jane? Elizabeth's initial admonition against stalking about in dark corners like a specter died upon her lips. "Jane's fever persists, but she is sleeping with a bit more ease," Elizabeth explained.

Mr. Darcy nodded.

Why did he stare at her so? His attention was piercing, making her skin flush and tingle. Elizabeth averted her gaze. "I must return to her," she said with a curtsy and fled back towards her sister's room.

"Miss Elizabeth?"

Elizabeth hesitated, her hand on the knob. "Mr. Darcy?"

"I—" He looked almost pained.

"You are not catching ill yourself, are you, Mr. Darcy?"

"I am quite well," Mr. Darcy said. "You are correct. You should tend to your sister." He bowed, and with no further words, turned on his heel and walked rapidly back down the hall in the opposite direction.

Elizabeth shook her head. She could not even manage to feel offended. *What an odd man!*

At half past six, Elizabeth was summoned to dinner. The Bingleys asked after Jane's health, and

Miss Bingley and Mrs. Hurst immediately exclaimed their sympathy for Jane's condition, remarking how miserable it was to be in the grasp of a violent cold. But their sympathy quickly ebbed. They immediately returned to their own affairs as though Jane, in her sickroom, no longer existed.

Mr. Bingley was the only one of them who seemed truly concerned about Jane's condition for Jane's own sake. He and perhaps Mr. Darcy, who though he attended to Miss Bingley's constant, ill-disguised flirtations, kept looking at Elizabeth. Staring. Elizabeth recognized it was uncharitable for her to take such objection to his merely *looking*, but he stared so forcefully. She could hardly look up from her plate without feeling his eyes upon her.

Miss Bingley soon noted Mr. Darcy's attention, and her remarks towards Elizabeth became less sympathetic and more barbed.

Mr. Hurst was indolent and offered little conversation, being far more concerned with his meal and the promise later on of cards and drink, and so Elizabeth mostly conversed with Mr. Bingley, who was at least congenial and interested in Jane's well-being.

As soon as Elizabeth could, she returned to

Jane. Considering Miss Bingley's barely concealed annoyance at Mr. Darcy's inexplicable focus on Elizabeth, she had little doubt Miss Bingley would only grow more open in expressing her disapprobation for Elizabeth in her absence.

Blast Mr. Darcy! Even in his silence, he made trouble for her.

Elizabeth could only hope Miss Bingley's dislike of Elizabeth did not influence her brother with regard to Jane. Dear, sweet Jane, who had not even wished to engage in the ruse of pretending her only option for a visit was on horseback, and now suffered the consequences of their mother's machinations.

To Elizabeth's mixed dismay and relief, the sisters returned to Jane's bedside and sat with her until summoned for coffee. Elizabeth was loath to leave her sister's side until late in the evening when Jane settled into something more like a restful sleep. Then, Elizabeth resigned herself to the necessity, purely out of politeness, of joining the others downstairs for after-dinner entertainment.

Stepping from the room, she looked to either side, fearing Mr. Darcy might be stalking her again, but thankfully the hall was empty. When she reached the drawing room, she found the whole party there and was immediately invited to join them. At the table sat Mr. Darcy, his face unreadable but still staring. Elizabeth declined, making her sister the excuse, and said she would amuse herself for a short time below with a book.

Mr. Hurst, with more energy than he had given any reaction the entire day, breathed in through his teeth and asked, "Do you prefer reading to cards?" as though such a thing was an unimaginable tragedy.

"Miss Eliza Bennet," said Miss Bingley, "despises cards. She is a great reader, and more so, and intricate thinker, as I have heard, occupying herself with little more than mathematics and codes."

From where had she heard such a thing? Elizabeth was careful to keep information about her ciphering work within the walls of her home. It was not rumored in such specificity, which meant Miss Bingley must have "heard" of Elizabeth's deciphering through Mr. Darcy.

Elizabeth shot Mr. Darcy a glare, which was about as effective as giving pointed looks to a sheet of glass for the effect it seemed to have on the dratted man.

"I deserve neither such praise nor such censure," Elizabeth argued. "It is true I sometimes aid my father in penning his correspondence, but that is hardly the same as occupying myself only with coding or literature or any particular interest." Elizabeth's protestation tasted like ashes in her mouth. Why was it she could not take proper credit for her own work?

Of course, such a thing was impossible. She was already at a disadvantage by not having a dowry of substance nor being born of an esteemed family. A woman's only reliable method for advancement was in securing a husband, and a rumor of eccentricity along with Elizabeth's other failings would sink what prospects she had.

"Now Caroline, your words are unfair," said Mr. Bingley, and Elizabeth felt a sharp sense of gratitude and affection for him. "Miss Elizabeth clearly takes great pleasure in caring for her family, and I hope it will be soon increased by seeing Miss Bennet quite well again."

Elizabeth thanked Mr. Bingley with much enthusiasm and walked towards the table where the books were lying.

"If those are not to your satisfaction," Mr. Bingley said, "I can have others fetched from the library. I wish my collection were larger for your benefit in my credit, but I am more for riding than reading, and though my library is small, I have not yet finished working through my collection."

Elizabeth assured him that she could suit herself perfectly with the books in the room. Unfortunately, it was not enough to sit quietly, flip through a book, and have the others leave her be. Miss Bingley, sensing an opportunity to flatter Mr. Darcy and express her own interest in both literature and Mr. Darcy's property, exclaimed, "What a delightful library you have at Pemberley, Mr. Darcy!"

They spoke for a while longer on libraries, Miss Bingley attempting, presumably, to get Elizabeth to make mention of her family's so it could be remarked upon. Finally Elizabeth gave up on reading altogether and set herself between Mr. Bingley and Mrs. Hurst to observe the game.

Elizabeth felt it best she not be dealt into the game as her improper interest in mathematics and codes allowed her a good facility at predicting probabilities and winning more than she lost. She could not hide her skills when playing Mr. Darcy, nor would she want to. Taking Mr. Darcy down a peg would be too satisfying, even if it were only a Pyrrhic victory.

"Is Miss Darcy much grown since the spring?" asked Miss Bingley.

Elizabeth's interest was immediately piqued. Though she had read Miss Darcy's correspondence, and worse, recently written to the young woman herself, she hardly knew anything about Miss Georgiana Darcy beyond the fact that she was the younger sister of Mr. Fitzwilliam and Reginald Darcy.

Miss Bingley continued, "Will she be as tall as I am?"

Mr. Darcy responded, "I think she will. She is about now Miss Elizabeth Bennet's height, or rather taller." Mr. Darcy was staring at Elizabeth again.

Elizabeth, not one to back down, met his gaze squarely. Whatever problems he had with her, she hoped he would express it to her sooner rather than later, else she be subjected to yet more discomfort through his silent regard.

"How I long to see her again!" Miss Bingley fanned out her cards and leaned forward, inclining her body towards Mr. Darcy as she spoke. "I never met with anyone who delighted me so much. Such a countenance, such manners! Her performance on the pianoforte is exquisite."

"Has Miss Darcy expressed much interest in books or codes?" Elizabeth asked.

Miss Bingley pursed her lips. "She reads widely, but of codes, it would not have occurred to me to ask."

"Oh!" Elizabeth exclaimed. "I had assumed you had a special interest in such topics as you had made such an effort to unearth such information concerning myself."

"One hears all sorts of things while conversing with new acquaintances," Miss Bingley said, her tone syrupy sweet. "I did not mean to trouble you."

Elizabeth smiled brightly. "Trouble me? Not at all! I take pride in helping my father, and my family, as best I can."

Five cards were dealt, and glancing over Mr. Bingley's shoulder, Elizabeth saw he had an excellent hand. He stared at the cards, moving on from the left to the center, and Elizabeth realized he did not know it. He moved to lower his arm, as though to abandon the cards, and Elizabeth murmured, "Stay."

"What was that, Miss Bennet?" Miss Bingley asked.

"I believe I shall play this hand," Mr. Bingley interjected.

"Superb," said Mr. Hurst.

Miss Bingley, sensing the conversation was moving away from her, said, "Miss Darcy is so very accomplished for her age!"

"It is amazing to me," said Bingley, "how young ladies can have the patience to be so very accomplished in so many ways, as they all are."

"All young ladies accomplished! My dear Charles, what do you mean?"

"Precisely as I said. They all paint tables, cover screens, and net purses. I scarcely have such skills, and I have never heard of a young lady spoken of, the first time at least, without being informed that she was indeed, very accomplished."

"Your list of the common extent of accomplishments," said Darcy, "has too much truth. Any woman can be trained to accomplish common things, but I am very far from agreeing with your estimation."

Elizabeth, unable and frankly unwilling to hold her tongue, remarked, "Does this mean Mr. Darcy's judge of a lady's accomplishments has more to do with her mastery of the uncommon?"

"Most certainly," said Mr. Darcy. "No one can be esteemed who does not greatly surpass the usual. A woman must have a thorough knowledge of music, singing, drawing, dancing, and the modern languages, and besides all of this, she must possess a certain something in her air and manner of walking, the tone of her voice, her address and expressions, or the word will be little deserved."

It was fortunate Elizabeth felt no need to live up to Mr. Darcy's standards. She doubted he would ever discover a woman who could meet his expectations.

"All of this she must possess," added Darcy, as though all of this was not more than enough, "and to that she must yet add something more substantial in the improvement of her mind."

Elizabeth could not help but laugh. "I am certain it will be delightful when you meet such a paragon."

Miss Bingley, seizing upon Elizabeth's statement with the same gleeful expression of the cat capturing a mouse in its teeth, asked, "Are you so severe upon your own sex as to doubt the possibility of this?"

Outside of a children's tale, for certain.

Elizabeth refused to relent on her perfectly reasonable assertion. "I can only say I have never seen such a woman. But should I meet her, I will endeavor to be suitably impressed."

Mrs. Hurst and Miss Bingley cried out against the injustice of Elizabeth's statement, both protesting that they knew many such women. Elizabeth surmised their insistence came mostly from a high self-opinion. Miss Bingley certainly presented herself as one who believed oneself in every way accomplished.

Miss Bingley turned to Mr. Darcy for support, which in Elizabeth's mind seemed like a terrible idea, and said, "Certainly, you have made acquaintance with such women."

"I have met six," Mr. Darcy said, offering no further elaboration. With that, the conversation came to an end.

Elizabeth soon afterward gratefully returned to her sister's sickbed. Her natural good humor reasserted herself as she imagined her sister's reaction to the entire affair. She only prayed Jane's health would improve quickly enough for her to admonish Elizabeth for her impropriety.

After some time, three firm raps sounded on Jane's door.

"Come in," Elizabeth said, glancing at Jane who thankfully remained asleep.

To her shock, Mr. Darcy opened the door. He

left the door ajar and barely crossed the threshold into the room. "Miss Elizabeth," he said.

Too flummoxed to manage anything intelligent or accomplished, Elizabeth said, "Mr. Darcy?"

"I misspoke. At the Assembly, in my remark about your appearance."

Elizabeth was still too confused to do more than nod.

Mr. Darcy took a breath, his posture and manner as stiff and cold as a granite statue. "You are more than passably handsome. Not that I have any regard whatsoever for your looks. But it is fair to you are near as handsome as your sister. That is all."

Was that all? Yes, he was staring again, silently awaiting—what, a word of thanks? The gall of him. *The unmitigated gall!*

"That is all?" Elizabeth snapped. "This day, every moment you cross my path, you are stalking about and staring like some...ghostly menace! And now you invade my sister's sickroom with declarations of insult, in all manner a self-proclaimed Emperor. 'Not that you have any regard for my looks!' Not that I have ever wished you to have such regard, but now I must narrow down your intention. Am I near as handsome as my sister when she dances? Or is it when she lies abed in the midst of a violent fever?"

Mr. Darcy opened his mouth as though to respond, but Elizabeth was too caught up in her own temper to have any wish to hear him. "You may give yourself accord to declare me unaccomplished, as though winning some measure of your regard, however infinitesimal, is a mark of accomplishment! If you believe so, you are very much mistaken."

"My words were meant as an apology!"

"Apology?" Elizabeth laughed. "If so, you ought to make more effort in the attempt. Was there anything else? Is there a wart on my chin that I have overlooked? Or perhaps my breath is foul?"

"No." Mr. Darcy took a step back, and after a moment, bowed. "I take my leave," he said.

Elizabeth gave him no further acknowledgment, turning her attention to Jane, who had begun to whimper and twitch, perhaps caught in the throes of a fevered nightmare. Elizabeth felt much the same. Her skin was hot, and her body shook with fury.

She prayed at that moment for Jane's health not only out of pure sisterly regard but also with the hope Jane would be well enough to return home before she had to endure another apology from Mr. Darcy.

Mr. Darcy will ask your hand in marriage. Twice.

The fortune teller had clearly been mad. Never mind a proposal. Elizabeth would be glad to live the rest of her life without ever having a single conversation with Mr. Darcy again.

15

*D*arcy's temper, on the rare occasions it flared, ran hot. But good manners, drilled into him since he had taken his first, waddling steps, ensured he did not immediately let loose on that blasted, infuriating woman. He had apologized. And taking a page from Bingley's book, he had even tried to compare Miss Elizabeth to her own beloved and handsome sister. And yet she had taken offense. He who had attempted to bridge the chasm between their stations to express his own regrets.

As Mr. Darcy walked down the hall towards his guest room, he went over his apology word for word to discern what part of it she could have misinterpreted.

Admittedly, the comparison to her sister cast neither lady in the best light, as Miss Bennet was currently feverish and quite ill. Maybe if he had been more specific about the context in which he was making the comparison, Miss Elizabeth would take it in the way Mr. Darcy had intended.

Not that I have any particular regard for your looks.

Perhaps he could have phrased that better. It was not that he had no regard for Miss Elizabeth's looks, more that he did not want another woman attempting to ensnare him, or, more specifically, his income and properties. Miss Bingley was certainly enamored of those two things herself and made no secret of her intentions despite Mr. Darcy's persistent refusal to engage with her flirtations.

Though in Miss Elizabeth's defense, she had not once showed any wish to ensnare him... or even to have a civilized discussion with him on any topic.

If Mr. Darcy was being honest with himself, he should admit some interest in having a civilized conversation with Miss Elizabeth Bennet. She might not be accomplished in the traditional sense, but her intelligence and enthusiasm sparkled, and it extended beyond mere mathematics or codes.

Miss Elizabeth had handled Miss Bingley with true aplomb when the woman had so obviously intended to insult her. And Miss Elizabeth had a certain focus, determination, and, yes, a bravery that could only be admired. At points, it might seem more suited to a man, but there was no mistaking Miss Elizabeth for a man. Her figure, her eyes, and her manner were in no way masculine.

Mr. Darcy sighed. Perhaps there had been truth to her words. His apology had conveyed nothing of those thoughts.

Should he attempt to apologize again?

Visions of a second, even more awkward attempt left him cold. No. He was not well trained in making apologies, but he understood the importance of making restitution to one he had wronged. And if, perhaps, through some small action he could bring forth, for a moment even, Miss Elizabeth's dazzling smile, it would be worth it.

With that thought firmly in mind, he made his way to the kitchens to speak with the cook.

Mr. Darcy had finished the first stage of planning his campaign—as his cousin, Col. Fitzwilliam, would often phrase actions such as these—and returned to the drawing room just before Miss Elizabeth hurried in again to report that her sister has grown worse.

"I cannot leave her," Miss Elizabeth said. She

avoided Mr. Darcy's gaze, instead keeping her attention focused on Mr. Bingley, who urged Mr. Jones be sent for immediately.

"No!" Miss Bingley exclaimed. "No country advice can be of any service. We must send an express to town for one of the most eminent physicians."

"I could not ask you to trouble yourself to that degree," Miss Elizabeth said, but with little heat.

Mr. Darcy, having sat with both his sister and brother through their childhood illnesses, found most often the best cure for a fever was uninter-rupted rest, and he was glad to concur when Mr. Bingley suggested Mr. Jones be called for early in the morning if Miss Bennet was not decidedly better.

To Mr. Darcy's relief, Miss Elizabeth left again immediately thereafter. She made him uncomfort-able, and Mr. Darcy did not court discomfort. Though Mr. Darcy tried to settle himself with listening to the sisters' duets after supper, he found all the interest in the others and their entertain-ments quite vanished with Miss Elizabeth gone.

Mr. Darcy excused himself as soon as he politely could. Miss Bennet had seemed to have congestion, and so Mr. Darcy had suggested to the cook one of his mother's recipes: hot water with sweet almond oil, syrup of violets, saffron, and nutmeg, delivered as steam from a clay pot. He could only hope this remedy would have a more positive effect on the Bennet sisters than his apology.

16

When Elizabeth returned to her sister, to her shock a housemaid at the head of Jane's bed was holding a clay pot to Jane's nose. With a fan, the housemaid waved steam into Jane's face.

"What are you doing?" Elizabeth asked.

"It was Mr. Darcy's orders, miss. My mama did the same when I caught ill as a child. Miss Bennet's breathing a little easier already."

Elizabeth approached the bed. The thought of Mr. Darcy insisting on any form of treatment for Jane was repugnant, but her sister was breathing more evenly, and she had stopped struggling in her sleep against her dreams.

When the steam had faded, the maid stepped

away with the pot and said, "I'll be taking this back down to the kitchen. But you give a ring if needs be, Miss Elizabeth. Your sister has a kindly heart, and we want very much to see her improved again."

Somehow, in her brief stay, Jane had won over the servants. Elizabeth could only admire her sister as usual.

"Thank you, and…" As much is it galled her, Elizabeth could not help but feel gratitude at Mr. Darcy's sudden and inexplicable solicitude. "Thank Mr. Darcy. For Jane."

The maid curtsied again and gathering up implements, left. Elizabeth passed the rest of the night in her sister's room, and by morning, Jane was much improved. The housemaid returned early in the morning with another steam treatment and a cup of chamomile tea with lemon and honey. "Mr. Darcy says it is just the thing for his sister," the housemaid explained.

In addition to the tea, they also delivered a tray with two bowls of honeyed porridge and toast with a boiled egg.

Elizabeth, who had been too worried through the day and night to do more than pick at her food, ate the porridge with relish. Again, she felt unwanted gratitude towards Mr. Darcy. How was that he could be so terrible in person and yet so kind in his absence?

Jane woke and sipped at her tea, even taking a couple of spoonfuls of the porridge before exhaustion overwhelmed her again and she closed her eyes.

Now that Jane was at least somewhat on the mend, Elizabeth requested to have a note sent to Longbourn, desiring her mother to visit and form her own judgment of the situation. Mrs. Bennet, Lydia, and Kitty arrived at Netherfield soon after the family breakfast.

Jane was so well improved, Mrs. Bennet, instead of showing the remorse she ought to have, seemed well satisfied with her daughter's situation.

"Perhaps I can be carried home," Jane suggested, but, much to Elizabeth's dismay, neither Mrs. Bennet nor the apothecary thought this suggestion advisable. The mother and sisters sat together for a while, and then upon Miss Bingley's invitation, Mrs. Bennet and her three daughters attended Miss Bingley in the breakfast parlor.

Miss Bingley said, "Miss Elizabeth says Miss Bennet is much improved, and I hope you have seen the same."

"Indeed I have," was Mrs. Bennet's answer.

"But she is still a great deal too ill to be moved. Mr. Jones says we must not think of moving her, and I agree. We must trespass a little longer on your kindness."

"Removed!" cried Mr. Bingley. "It must not be thought of. My sister, I am sure, will not hear of her removal."

Any hopes Miss Bingley would insist on their leaving were soon dashed. She said with cold civility, "You may depend upon it, madame. Miss Bennet will receive every possible attention while she remains with us."

From there, Elizabeth resigned herself to another day at Netherfield Park. Elizabeth might have found the experience tolerable without having to endure Mr. Darcy and Miss Bingley, especially Mr. Darcy, who had become even more of a conundrum in his solicitude than before with his rudeness. But as difficult as it might be for Elizabeth in her good health, she would not abandon Jane to such capricious mercy.

Mrs. Bennet continued, first extolling Jane's virtues, "… for she has, without exception, the sweetest temper I've ever met with. I often tell my other girls they are nothing to her. You have a sweet room here Mr. Bingley, in a charming prospect over the gravel walk. I do not know a place in the country equal to Netherfield. You will not think of quitting it in a hurry, I hope, though you have but a short lease."

Listening to her mother go on, Elizabeth realized all here, with the exception possibly of Mr. Bingley and herself, were involved in their own machinations. Lydia and Kitty were whispering to each other, Mrs. Bennet was intent on securing a marriage for all five of her daughters, and Mr. Darcy—who knew what he was plotting, only that he was plotting something.

Miss Bingley glanced at Elizabeth and then Mrs. Bennet. She pursed her lips.

"Whatever I do is done in a hurry," replied Mr. Bingley, "and therefore if I should resolve to quit Netherfield, I should probably be off in five minutes. At present, however, I consider myself as quite fixed here."

Perhaps Mr. Bingley and Mr. Darcy had as much in common as Elizabeth had first suspected. Both were capricious. Except Mr. Bingley had seemed genuine in his concern for Jane. Was it only a whim? Elizabeth could not keep some sharpness from her voice as she said, "I should hope your enjoyment of Netherfield is more than a fleeting fancy."

"Fleeting fancy?" Mr. Bingley's expression belied nervousness, and Elizabeth felt some relief. Hopefully Mr. Bingley had only attempted to seem capricious.

Elizabeth said, "While I admit at points I enjoy an intricate conundrum, in the matter of character, one who is clear in his own aspirations and who strives, in the pursuit of them, to neither confuse nor offend is by far preferable."

"Lizzie," cried her mother, "remember where you are, and do not run on in the wild manner that you are suffered to do at home."

"I should hope you saw no intent on my part to confuse or offend?" Mr. Bingley said.

Elizabeth smiled. "Certainly not. Mr. Bingley, in all things, you have offered yourself as the picture of gentlemanly kindness."

Mr. Darcy, to everyone's surprise, said, "I find much to admire in Miss Elizabeth's value for the forthright."

Was Mr. Darcy making a jest at Elizabeth's expense? He seemed no less serious or formal than the usual. Perhaps he meant to give her a genuine compliment? She should expire on the spot!

After an awkward moment, Mrs. Bennet, never one to let silence lie, continued, "Yes, Mr. Darcy, indeed! Our village offers much to admire in regard to the forthright. And so many entertainments! I cannot see that London has any great advantage over the country, except for the shops in public places. The country is a fast deal pleasanter, is it not, Mr. Bingley?"

"When I am in the country," he replied, "I never wish to leave it. When I am in town, it is pretty much the same. They each have their advantages, and I can be equally happy in either."

Again with equal happiness! Was this another attempt at pretend ambivalence? With Mr. Bingley's statements of varying whims, he made himself more of a cipher than Mr. Darcy. Elizabeth had thought Mr. Bingley held a special admiration for Jane, but if he was equally content with one woman as the other, then Jane's particular character hardly mattered. How could Jane be happy on the arm of a man who found her as both ornamental and interchangeable as a well-tied cravat?

Jane had already fallen into a most quiet and intense infatuation. One fueled by a second dance, an invitation by proxy to dinner, and Mr. Bingley's solicitude in her illness. Mr. Bingley had seemed more steady in his concern for Jane's health than the others, but perhaps Elizabeth had only wanted to see him that way. What if Jane were wrong?

A man who held every woman in precisely equal regard admitted no special admiration for any. In that, Charlotte had been quite accurate in stating that if Jane went to secure Mr. Bingley's hand, she had best show more of her own feelings. Mr. Bingley had been effusive in his own praise. Whether that praise had meaning, however, was another thing entirely.

Mrs. Bennet, having no inkling of Elizabeth's worries, continued, "What an agreeable man Sir William Lucas is! So much the man of fashion! So genteel and easy! He had always something to say of everybody to everybody, do you not agree, Mr. Bingley? That is my idea of good breeding; those persons who fancy themselves very important, but never open their mouth, quite mistake the matter." Mrs. Bennet went on, "And the Lucases are very good sort of girls, I assure you. It is a pity they are not handsome! Not that I think Charlotte is very plain—but then she is our particular friend."

Elizabeth hated it when her mother set Charlotte down to raise her own daughters as a comparison. "Mother—" Elizabeth started to say in defense of her friend, but Mr. Darcy cut over them both.

"A woman's beauty can take many forms. Miss Lucas seemed a pleasant enough young woman, in my observation of her."

Who was this man, and what had he done with Mr. Darcy?

Mrs. Bennet, taken aback, stuttered, "Oh—dear yes—she is intelligent and kind and possessed of her own virtues. But Lady Lucas herself has often admitted she envied me Jane's beauty. I do not like to boast of my own child, but to be sure, Jane—one does not often see anybody so better-looking. It is what everybody says. I do not trust my own partiality. When Jane was only fifteen, there was a man at my brother Gardiner's house in town so much in love with Jane that my sister-in-law was sure he would make her an offer before we came away. But he did not. Perhaps he thought her too young."

"Jane was too young, her suitor too old, and of little interest to her," Elizabeth said plainly.

Mrs. Bennet cleared her throat. "Well!" She turned back to Mr. Bingley and began again to praise him for his kindness to Jane with an apology also for troubling him with Lizzie. As they prepared to leave, Lydia, who had been whispering with Kitty through the entire conversation, put herself forward and asked, "I was wondering, before we leave, Mr. Bingley, when did you intend to give your promised ball at Netherfield?"

Elizabeth thought her sister more than brash in her approach, but Mr. Bingley simply smiled and said, "I am perfectly ready, I assure you, to keep my engagement. When your sister is recovered, you shall name the very day of the ball. None of us wish to be dancing while she is ill."

"Of course not. Yes, it will be much better to wait until Jane is well, and at that time, perhaps Mr. Wickham will be able to attend if his duties do not keep him away."

"Absolutely not!" Mr. Darcy said with shocking decisiveness.

"Now Darcy," Mr. Bingley started, turning towards his friend.

"No."

"You have no evidence—"

"Do what you wish. But if you invite him, I shall not attend."

It was the most emotion Elizabeth had seen from Mr. Darcy in... well... ever. Though she was more kindly disposed towards Mr. Darcy after seeing the efforts he had made for Jane's comfort,

Elizabeth was not sure if his absenting himself from another ball constituted much of a problem. At the same time, Mr. Darcy, for all of his numerous faults, did not appear in the slightest inclined towards dishonesty. Whatever issue he had with Mr. Wickham, it was genuine. That did not mean it was deserved. Mr. Darcy found fault with most things, and even at his best, he was not a person with whom one easily got along.

Elizabeth did not know what to think.

"Oh!" Mrs. Bennet exclaimed. "Dear Mr. Bingley, neither I nor my daughters would wish to suggest anything to cause you or your friend discomfort." She refused to address Mr. Darcy directly. "Mr. Wickham and Mr. Darcy were raised together in childhood, and why my darling Jane had been remarking how close such bonds can be and how painful their breaking. Why, she expressed a deep wish, if possible, that both parties might reconcile their differences as—"

"No."

Mrs. Bennet, whose mouth was parted to speak, shut it and then opened it again, giving the impression of a landed fish. She said, "Well... Well! If such is the situation, then that is how it must be."

Mr. Darcy responded, "Do as you wish, Bingley.

But should you open your doors to Mr. Wickham, then be assured I will absent myself that night." On that note, Mr. Darcy bowed, turned on his heel, and left.

Mr. Bingley, looking a little lost, attempted in his amiable manner to resolve the conversation on a more salubrious note. "Mrs. Bennet, your eldest daughter's kindly and forgiving nature does both her and you credit."

Mrs. Bennet looked at the floor, her cheeks flushing. "Oh, Mr. Bingley!"

"It is no trouble to host both of your daughters as Miss Bennet regains her health. Now, if you will excuse me."

"Yes, of course. You and your household have our deepest gratitude."

With that, Mr. Bingley quickly departed the room, presumably to have a discussion with his friend. Mrs. Bennet showered Elizabeth with a mix of overblown praise and unnecessary instructions mingled with admonitions before finally, to Elizabeth's relief, returning with Kitty and Lydia to the carriage. Before her departure, Mrs. Bennet handed Elizabeth a packet of letters. "From your father," she said in a low voice."

Elizabeth smiled with genuine pleasure and thanked her.

Holding the letters under her arm, Elizabeth made her way back to Jane's room. As she passed through the parlor, Miss Bingley confronted her.

Miss Bingley said, "You Bennets certainly know how to make an impression. While I did mention it, I suppose Miss Lydia could not be faulted for her lack of knowledge of the *depth* of animosity between Mr. Darcy and Mr. Wickham. I suppose…"

"My sister is very young," Elizabeth said. "Her words were not ill-meant."

"Young indeed, and yet out. Of course, it is done differently in the country."

"Perhaps if we had some hint as to the *reason* for the animosity between the two men, it might be easier to know which response would be more appropriate."

"Mr. Darcy keeps his own counsel," Miss Bingley said. "My!" She added, noting the packet Mrs. Bennet had handed Elizabeth before her departure. "You and your sister receive a significant amount of correspondence."

"Sometimes." Elizabeth curtsied. "Now I must see to Jane. Excuse me."

"Of course, you must. The dear woman. How difficult it is to be so ill!"

Miss Bingley fell into step with Elizabeth, and to her dismay, accompanied Elizabeth to Jane's sick bed.

17

Mr. Darcy stood in Mr. Bingley's library, staring sightlessly at the spines of dusty books standing like soldiers on the shelves.

Wickham!

It was as though the threads of fate conspired to put Mr. Darcy in constant misery. Nothing he did, and nowhere he fled, held any peace. Mr. Darcy, in his own mind at least, allowed himself to wish Mr. Wickham and his brother Reginald's fates had been switched. If anyone deserved the ignominy of being murdered by a cutthroat in a French alley, it was Wickham. But God's will was inexplicable and sometimes cruel. Maybe it would be best if Mr. Darcy returned to Pemberley. But with Miss Darcy absent, and only having the company of his own thoughts, Mr. Darcy feared he would fall into a bottle and dishonor himself.

Mr. Darcy's eyes blurred. What was he, a child, to be weeping at the slightest problem?

"Darcy!"

Of course, Bingley chose this moment to make himself known. Darcy blinked, imposing his will as best he could over his recalcitrant emotions. He kept his back to the door a moment longer, though it was impolite, and said, "Yes, Bingley."

Something of his discomfiture must have betrayed itself in his manner or tone because Mr. Bingley's footsteps slowed, and he placed a gentle hand on Darcy's shoulder. "Oh, Darcy, I have made a hash of things, haven't I?"

"You?" If anyone had made a hash of things, it was Mr. Darcy himself, despite his best efforts. It might be one of his truest areas of "accomplish-ment" as Miss Elizabeth might state it. "You have no reason to be ashamed. I am your guest, and it is not my place to say who you can and cannot invite into your home."

"Mr. Wickham can throw himself into the sea for all I care. From the rumors of his behavior in London and your own disapprobation, I realize the man has little to distinguish himself. But it might be of use if you were to share with me, as a friend, what he did to change your opinion of him. You used to admire him. There is truth to miss Bennet's words. Childhood bonds are often the strongest."

Discussion of Mr. Wickham, who Darcy despised, at least had the salubrious effect of pushing his mind from any thought of tears. And while the weight of his friend's hand comforted Mr. Darcy, he could not continue to converse with Bingley while facing a bookshelf. It only made Mr. Darcy ridiculous. He turned to face his friend and said, "It is not my own counsel I must keep. Mr. Wickham tried to take liberties and—" That was as close as Darcy could come to revealing how Wickham had seduced and almost ruined Georgiana.

Mr. Bingley grew pale; his eyes glittered, and his hand clenched into a fist. "The cad! I will stand as your second should you call him out."

"I cannot speak of these events. Any hint to the scandal would be more damaging than silence. You must understand."

Mr. Bingley took a breath. "Of course. You have my word as a gentleman. I will say nothing."

Mr. Darcy expelled a breath he had not realized he was even holding. "Thank you."

"I will not give Wickham leave to step foot at Netherfield Park. Of that you can be certain."

Bingley was a worthy friend. Darcy said, "You are beyond gold."

Bingley laughed. "You are unsettled to bestow such high praise upon me or anyone." He waved Darcy towards the chairs. "Sit. I keep whiskey behind those old farming manuals of my father's. After such heavy talk, I believe we could both use a taste."

Darcy sat, and Bingley rummaged around, as promised returning with a half-full bottle and two tumblers from the shelf. Bingley poured, and they sat in silence, allowing the drink to warm their palates and bellies.

Mr. Bingley was the first to break the silence. "Not to pry," he said, "but you and Miss Elizabeth —has the animosity eased between you?"

Had it? "I was merely attempting to appease Miss Bennet's wishes."

"You apologized! I cannot think of a time when you have apologized to a lady, excepting that one ball where you stomped on Miss Doherty's slipper."

Mr. Bingley took another drink. "Was your apology well received?"

"No."

Mr. Bingley, to Mr. Darcy's annoyance, laughed. "By chance, did you forget to use the words 'I am sorry' or 'I regret' when making your statement of apology?"

"I may have been remiss in the details."

"It was best to clear the air then, as your conversation with Miss Elizabeth was most amiable this morning."

"I may not be adept with the flowery words of apology, but I am attempting to make restitutions.

"Do not let me stop you. The Bennet sisters have an appeal, though none is as lovely as the eldest, Miss Jane Bennet, in my estimation."

Mr. Darcy considered warning Bingley about Jane, but he was as yet too close to the woman, and proximity would only increase the draw of his infatuation. Best to wait until Darcy and Bingley returned to London.

"I am trying to set things right between me and Miss Elizabeth," Mr. Darcy said. "There is no more meaning to it than that."

"Of course."

"She is in no means suitable for me as a wife, however charming one might find her."

"As you say." Mr. Bingley's lips twitched.

Bingley was determined to be amused. Mr. Darcy drank the final swallow from his glass. "I had intended to bring Miss Elizabeth some books, as she is fond of reading. Have you any of a mathematical nature?"

"Start there," Mr. Bingley said, waving towards a shelf to his left. "But if I have such volumes, I have not read them. My father, to his credit, drilled into me what was necessary so I could manage my inheritance. Beyond that…" Bingley shrugged.

Darcy thanked him. They finished their whiskey, and Bingley offered another clap on the shoulder before informing Darcy that he had been inside long enough and wished to go for a ride.

"Darcy," Mr. Bingley said before he left. "Bring the books to Miss Elizabeth yourself."

"Why would I do such a thing?"

"You are making an apology. Such things are best handled in person. And bring a deck of cards. They will surely enjoy the entertainment."

Mr. Darcy perused Mr. Bingley's bookshelf, and to his delight he found a small folio of mathematical theorems. He did not comprehend nor have interest in the contents, but Miss Elizabeth might, and in that way she might also recognize his attempt at restitution.

He chose that and two other volumes of a more narrative nature. After further consideration of Mr. Bingley's suggestions, gathered the books and a deck of cards in his arm and made his way to Miss Bennet's sick room. It could hardly be improper to deliver books to an ill woman and her sister.

When Mr. Darcy arrived, the door was ajar, and from inside the room, Mr. Darcy heard womanly laughter. Mr. Darcy's guts turned to ice. "Miss Bennet, it is good to see you smile." Was that Miss Bingley's voice? Blast Bingley and his suggestions! Darcy would have been better off to have sent his offerings with a servant.

Mr. Darcy hesitated and quietly—very quietly—stepped back from the door. But it was too late. Behind him, Mrs. Hurst exclaimed, "Why Mr. Darcy! Are those for Miss Bennet? Come! Come! The Bennet sisters will be most grateful for your kindness."

18

*E*lizabeth had little fondness for Miss Caroline Bingley, but her stories of London balls brought a light to Jane's countenance that Elizabeth grudgingly appreciated. Jane's illness still made her weak and inclined towards falling asleep, sometimes midway through speaking, but she was looking better as the day progressed. The treatments were helping, along with the honeyed porridge Mr. Darcy had sent. Despite her animosity towards him, Elizabeth appreciated his efforts.

However, when she heard Mrs. Hurst call out Mr. Darcy's name, and both entered the room, Elizabeth was unsure she was grateful enough to wish more time in his presence. In her experience, Mr. Darcy was a man best appreciated in his absence.

But she smiled anyway, standing to curtsy to him and thank him for all he had done for Jane.

"Done for Miss Bennet?" Miss Bingley asked with a note of incredulousness in her voice. "What has Mr. Darcy done?"

"My mother had some special remedies for colds," Mr. Darcy said. "When Reginald or Georgiana caught sick, I ensured the use of these remedies to speed my siblings' recovery."

Elizabeth was touched and frankly shocked that Mr. Darcy had thought to do something so kind. Perhaps she had misjudged him, at least to some extent.

"How thoughtful!" Miss Bingley exclaimed. "I had no idea you were so involved with the care of your younger siblings."

"My mother passed on when I was eleven, and my father... he grieved. I cared for my brother and sister until I was sent away for school."

Elizabeth had never considered a young Mr. Darcy tending to his siblings' illnesses and ailments. It was at odds with what the man had revealed of himself to this date, and Elizabeth found it, to her shame, rather charming. "Thank you," Elizabeth said. "For your remedies. Jane is recovering with much more ease."

He will ask for your hand in marriage. Twice.

Elizabeth pushed the fortune teller's words from her mind. Mr. Darcy's kindness to Jane was not the makings of a courtship.

Mr. Darcy was still stiff, but it seemed less reproachful, perhaps because he held three books and what appeared to be a deck of cards cradled in his right arm. "I had only intended to deliver these and not to interrupt Miss Bennet's rest." He crossed the room and placed the books on the nightstand.

Miss Bingley exclaimed, "Is that deck of cards? Why Mr. Darcy, you must stay and play with us."

Mr. Darcy said, "I do not wish to impose."

Jane said, "It is no imposition."

Elizabeth stared at her sister in shock. She was inviting Mr. Darcy to stay and play cards with them? Jane's lips curved upward, almost as though she was having a joke with herself. Maybe her fever had returned?

"If you would like," Mr. Darcy said, "then I am at your service."

A chair was brought for him, along with a tray table to place over Jane's lap, upon which they dealt the cards.

"But Commerce is so mercenary," Miss Bingley said. "Why not Loo?"

"Had we not enough of Loo last night?" Mrs. Hurst interjected. "I like Whist."

"We have one too many players," Elizabeth remarked, glancing at Mr. Darcy. Perhaps he would take the hint and find such entertainments beneath him.

But Jane cut that hope off at the knees. "No, Whist is perfect. Lizzie and I can share the same hand. I am like to fall asleep halfway through the game anyway and ruin everyone's fun." Jane yawned, almost to punctuate her point. If it had been anyone but Jane, Elizabeth might have suspected an ulterior motive. But Jane knew how odious Elizabeth found Mr. Darcy. She had been incredulous at Madame Godiva's intimation that Mr. Darcy would ask Elizabeth's hand in marriage. Surely, Jane wouldn't conspire to force them to spend *more* time in each other's presence!

After more negotiation, the group agreed to Whist. Miss Bingley maneuvered to have Mr. Darcy on her team, and Elizabeth, with some relish, turned all of her skills with probabilities and counting cards to trouncing them utterly.

It would have been easier without Mrs. Hurst, who chose her cards without the slightest hint of rationality. She was worse than Lydia! But as the game progressed, and Elizabeth, Jane, and Mrs. Hurst gleefully achieved five points to Mr. Darcy and Miss Bingley's three, Miss Bingley's countenance took on a decided frustration, her jaw taut and lips turned downward.

Jane, after the first few hands, leaned back against the pillows and fell asleep.

Mrs. Hurst said, "Fortune smiles on me when I am teamed with the Bennets. I believe I have never had such a string of good hands."

"I believe more than luck is playing into your fortunes today," Mr. Darcy said.

"Are they playing a trick on us?" Miss Caroline narrowed her eyes. "I had not thought to sit down with a Captain Sharp in sheep's clothing."

"I do not understand what you mean," Elizabeth said innocently. "Surely Mr. Darcy would not bring us a tampered deck to embarrass himself."

"Of course, Mr. Darcy would not stoop to anything improper. He is far too well bred for such tricks!"

"Certainly so," Elizabeth said dryly.

But Mr. Darcy surprised her. "If I tried anything of the sort, it would not be in the presence of such finely bred young ladies."

What did that mean?

Mr. Darcy added, "I assure you, Miss Elizabeth, no one is fooling anyone at this game. If anyone is winning it is fairly, through their skills and perhaps a hint of luck."

From that point, Mr. Darcy played significantly better. He and Miss Bingley gained another two points. Elizabeth, suspecting he too had memorized the order of the cards on the table and was now taking well-thought-out estimates of which remained, deliberately overlooked an opportunity to use a Trump take the next hand, instead throwing a seven of diamonds.

Mr. Darcy's eyebrows furrowed, and Elizabeth smothered her own smile. Oh! This was much more entertaining with a worthy opponent.

The next few games brought an even exchange of points. Both Elizabeth and Mr. Darcy were hampered by their partners, which added a certain degree of randomness to what had become a vicious exchange of estimated probabilities.

Miss Bingley exclaimed, "Trump!"

Miss Bingley laid down the eight of clubs Elizabeth had suspected was in her hand, and Elizabeth, knowing she had no more of that suit, designated it as Trump again and promptly took the following hand.

When they reached the agreed-upon ten points, it was well into the afternoon. The game ended with Elizabeth, Jane, and Mrs. Hurst squeaking out a win, largely due to the lead they had gained in the first few rounds.

Mrs. Hurst suggested, "Shall we play to fifteen?"

Miss Bingley, perhaps suspecting that her desired conquest was taking far too much interest in Elizabeth through the game, sighed and said, "No, let us do something else. Miss Elizabeth, you have such a lovely voice. Perhaps you can read to us? That small one," Miss Bingley pointed to the book of theorems on the table. "It seems short. What is it?"

"I should take my leave," Mr. Darcy said, standing abruptly.

To Elizabeth's surprise, she felt a pang of sadness that Mr. Darcy was leaving. He had been a fair match for her at cards, and few in her acquaintance, gentleman or lady, managed that. She wondered what it would be like to play him one on one. He would be a delight at Commerce, and then Elizabeth might determine if the sharpness of his mind matched that of his tongue.

Mr. Darcy, a delight? Had she caught some of her sister's fever?

In the interests of politeness, and because Mr. Darcy had managed, for over a full afternoon, to behave like a civilized human being, Elizabeth said, "I must convey my gratitude again on behalf of myself and my sister for your solicitude in her illness. And your agreement to visit and entertain us."

Mr. Darcy averted his gaze. Still formal, but softer somehow. "It was no trouble." He bowed.

Miss Bingley, seeing her prey make a move to escape, curtsied and said, "Yes, Miss Bennet needs her rest. We shall make certain to visit again before dinner."

"Just now?"

"Yes, Louisa," Miss Bingley shot her sister a sharp look.

Flustered, Mrs. Hurst stood. "Of course! Miss Bennet needs her rest."

When the three had left, Elizabeth breathed a grateful sigh of relief. Though the game was enjoyable, entertaining the sisters on her own seemed more a burden than a diversion.

Also, there was the business of ciphering and deciphering. Though Mr. Bennet's eyesight was not well enough to catch the subtle intricacies required to quickly decipher, he could write in a clear enough hand to develop encoding keys. Elizabeth looked over them, making certain his handwriting was legible enough, before putting them in a pile to return to Longbourn for mailing.

A pair of intercepted letters followed, in French, which Elizabeth over the course of the next hour cracked and, writing in her notes with the deciphering, also placed in the pile to return home.

Finally, at the bottom of the stack, was a letter addressed to her.

Elizabeth's heartbeat sped up as she noted the sender: Miss Georgiana Darcy.

She opened it. Miss Darcy wrote in an embellished hand.

Dear Miss Bennet,

After a terse greeting followed a page of manufactured Latin. Elizabeth smiled and set about deciphering Miss Darcy's words.

19
_____

*M*r. Bingley and Mrs. Hurst followed Darcy down the stairs into the parlor.

"My! You are ever so skilled at cards, Mr. Darcy. Not that I would ever accuse you of engaging in trickery. Merely a display of talent that was something to behold."

What had been something to behold was Miss Elizabeth's skill. Mr. Darcy kept that thought firmly to himself.

When Darcy was seventeen and Reginald fifteen, their cousin James Fitzpatrick, just before buying his commission, had instructed the brothers on how to count cards. Mr. Wickham had been absent on that occasion, and now that Darcy was older and had a better assessment of Wickham's character, he wondered if his cousin had held some inkling of Wickham's deficiencies and thus avoided him when possible.

It was likely the case. Until Wickham's betrayal, Darcy had counted him as a friend. Flawed at points, but Darcy was loyal to those he considered friends.

Reginald had been by far superior at the card counting and the many other small tricks James had shown them with the warning, "This will serve you in the hells, but be careful in proper company. One must choose his ground carefully, you understand."

Once realizing Miss Elizabeth intended to play with reckless abandon, Darcy had met on her ground and found himself thoroughly captivated.

Yes, Miss Elizabeth had been remarkable. She had taken care not only to ensure that she won a fair number of hands, but that Mrs. Hurst was equally favored by fortune. If Mr. Darcy had not learned and then drilled himself relentlessly until he achieved some mastery of the skill, he would not have recognized her machinations. More remark-able, when called to account, Miss Elizabeth had not backed down. Not that she was the sort to back down in anything as Mr. Darcy had come to understand and admire.

"It is as your sister said," Mr. Darcy finally responded. "Fortune smiles as she sees fit."

And how Miss Elizabeth had smiled, a subtle twitch of the lips that lit up her eyes as she noted her winnings, and even the occasional genuine laugh at one of his own comments during the game. Mr. Darcy was not the sort whose commentary elicited genuine mirth, at least not intentionally.

Miss Elizabeth was, of course, unsuitable as an object of infatuation, and Mr. Darcy would not allow himself to help such an undisciplined emotion besides. Still, he had enjoyed the game.

"Well, I enjoyed playing with her," Mrs. Hurst said, echoing his thoughts.

"Yes," Miss Bingley agreed. "It was an amusing diversion. Though I admit, I feel some concern with how Miss Elizabeth furrows her brow so when thinking. Such expressions lead to unattractive creases as one grows older."

Mr. Darcy had found the expression charming, in part because it revealed again the agile mind beneath the dark, silky tresses of her hair.

Not that Mr. Darcy had any good reason to think of Miss Elizabeth's tresses, silky or otherwise.

But as much as he wished to force the thought from his mind, a part of him could not help wondering if the feel of her hair was as smooth as it appeared.

"So how do you intend to amuse yourself, Mr. Darcy?" Miss Bingley asked, and then, without waiting for an answer, she continued, "The weather is fair, with only a few clouds, and we have an hour yet before we must change for dinner."

"I have correspondence I must review." Or so Mr. Darcy hoped. He had played cards for far longer than he had intended. Miss Elizabeth's presence had been an unexpected pleasure, and he feared had he stayed longer, his interest in her might strain the bonds of propriety. Darcy was not like Bingley to imagine himself in love with a country miss.

Mr. Darcy extricated himself from the sisters and made his way to retrieve his post. Seeing both a packet from his solicitor and a letter from his sister, he immediately closed himself off in Mr. Bingley's study.

Placing the correspondence on Mr. Bingley's desk, Mr. Darcy pulled open the bottom drawer where he knew Mr. Bingley stored a bottle of brandy and two glasses. Taking one, he poured the brandy and took a swallow. Bingley, generous in all things, would not begrudge Darcy the liquid courage.

Darcy opened the package from his solicitor first. His money had been well spent, if not, as yet, yielding conclusive results. Unsurprising. Gambling hells were often frequented by young men of status, and what happened within their walls was understood to remain between them.

Rumors of a bet of a large estate had abounded, along with the name Wickham, but of his opponent, an out-of-towner by the name of Smith, almost nothing was known. He was rumored to be a Northerner of indeterminate age. If he had won and conflicting rumors abounded, he had made no effort to claim his winnings.

Likely, he had lost. Mr. Wickham had soon after come into a sudden windfall, paying off his creditors and soon after buying a commission and leaving London altogether. From there, he had made a direct route to Hertfordshire, though why Wickham would choose such an out-of-the-way location to restart his life, Mr. Darcy had not the slightest inkling.

Maybe Wickham was attempting to reform himself?

Mr. Darcy doubted it. In fact, it would not

surprise him in the slightest if Mr. Wickham had once again lost whatever remained of his winnings in barracks and barroom gambling here in Hertfordshire.

The entire explanation given was confusing. According to the solicitor's notes, Mr. Wickham had played Mr. Smith more than once in various establishments in London. More often than not, his opponent had lost, and yet Mr. Smith had continued to play.

Mr. Darcy shook his head and pushed the correspondence aside. The problem with rumor and gossip was that it yielded only the most salacious aspect of truth. The reality of things was usually less interesting. Wickham had likely fleeced the country gentleman out of most of his fortune, or at least most of the fortune he had chosen to gamble. With his winnings, Wickham had paid off his creditors and fled for fear of this Mr. Smith discovering Wickham had played cards with what was not his.

And Bragg, in his careful reporting of events, must well have been too in his cups to comprehend the outcome of the game.

Perhaps Bragg was a fool but not a drunkard. On the other hand, had Wickham lost and been caught out in his lie, he'd have been sent to prison at the least. Or murdered in a duel. Or in an alley if the "gentleman" Wickham had wronged was more a man of action than honor.

It made sense Wickham would find some place out of the way to wait out his sins, and fate, capricious fate, had put Wickham in Hertfordshire and once again in Darcy's path.

Wickham would not have known of Darcy's intention to spend the autumn in Netherfield. Mr. Darcy had not expected to pass the season with Bingley, so it was bad luck, pure and simple, that had forced the two men to cross paths again.

Darcy took another drink of the brandy, a palate cleanser, and then opened his sister's letter. The address was from the country home of one of Georgiana's closest friends, Miss Emily Tremayne. It had delighted Darcy to give his permission for his sister to stay there.

Even before Wickham's betrayal, Darcy and Georgiana had not been close, though Darcy loved his sister with every fiber of his being. After, when Darcy had rescued Georgiana and her reputation from the clutches of his rapacious foster brother, Georgiana's shame and the hurt of Wickham's betrayal had strained her and Darcy's already fragile bond. Darcy feared he was not a comfort to her, and the fact he had erred so fantastically in his own judgment of Wickham's character had only made it worse.

Darcy was glad Georgiana had found someplace where she could grieve. And Mrs. Tremayne ran her estate with an iron hand. Neither young lady risked even the slightest blush of impropriety beneath her watchful gaze.

The letter began:

Dear Fitzwilliam,

Are you acquainted with a Miss Elizabeth Bennet? The lady has sent me the most unconventional piece of correspondence, and the shape of her words claim a familiarity with our brother that cannot help but give one pause.

He saw red. He had specifically insisted he did not want this letter shared with Georgiana until he had assessed the contents. And yet, Miss Elizabeth had written Georgiana without even so much as a by-your-leave.

Have you learned more about the circumstances of his passing?

What had Miss Elizabeth Bennet implied about Reginald in her letter to Georgiana? Mr. Darcy's fingers tightened on the leather letter, crumbling the paper's edges.

I admit to some large degree of foolishness in my past,

but I would pray as a punishment for this, you would not deny me our brother's words should this be the case, especially words of such import.

Yours sincerely,

Georgiana

Miss Elizabeth's words echoed in his mind at their first meeting: "This letter is not addressed to you."

Perhaps not, but he was Georgiana's brother and guardian. Miss Elizabeth Bennet had gone too far. He would have words with her, retrieve Georgiana's letter, and go to Georgiana at once to make amends.

20

*E*lizabeth read through her deciphering of the letter again.

Who are you to be so cruel as to imply my brother is alive?

Alive? Elizabeth had meant to imply no such thing.

Was Reginald Darcy the mysterious Lord Cunningham? But if he was, then Miss Darcy would already have known. Was it something about the butterflies? *Remember the butterflies?* Chrysalide?

Elizabeth's skin was cold, and a worm of shame burrowed itself into her gut. She had been so concerned with the second cipher, the first had made itself almost insignificant. But perhaps there was no second cipher. Or perhaps it did not matter.

No! The second cipher had meant what she had found. She had dismissed the first part as uninteresting, but Mr. Reginald Darcy had hidden meaning in those words. Meaning that Georgiana understood even as Elizabeth had not.

Like his brother, as Elizabeth was coming to learn, Mr. Reginald Darcy was a man of many layers.

The fortune teller's words brushed through her thoughts again. *A complicated man. Your fates are entwined.*

Entwined or no, Elizabeth had made things worse by contacting Miss Darcy.

"Lizzie? What is wrong?"

Jane was awake. Elizabeth looked up from Miss Darcy's letter and swallowed. "I have made a terrible mistake, Jane."

"Oh, Lizzie!" Jane said, "I believe Mr. Darcy may develop a fondness for you, if that helps."

Elizabeth blinked, confused. "Mr. Darcy? No! I mean, it is about Mr. Darcy, but not his opinion of me. I have erred with his letter."

"The code? I thought you were still working on it. Did you decipher it?"

And Elizabeth had lied to Jane as well. No

more. Elizabeth explained, "It was a cipher within a cipher, and I had thought if I wrote to Miss Darcy, she might offer insight on the second part. But instead—" Elizabeth sobbed.

Jane scooted over on the bed and tapped the space beside her. "Come here."

Elizabeth, bereft, sat next to her sister, who wrapped her arms around Elizabeth. "It cannot be so terrible."

And they were children again, and Elizabeth had run to her sister with a scraped knee and a bruised wrist after having fallen out of a tree. Except this wound was not the sort to be healed with rest and a kitchen salve. Elizabeth closed her eyes. Her lashes were wet with tears. "Miss Darcy believes her brother is still alive."

Elizabeth explained everything. The cipher, the cipher within a cipher, and all she had discovered. "So you understand why I thought I should contact Miss Darcy, as he intended the initial code for her."

"You think the Regent's life is in danger?"

"I thought so. But I was wrong about everything."

At that moment, an angry knock sounded on the door, and then before either Elizabeth or Jane could respond, Mr. Darcy flung it open and stalked in. He was flushed, his blue eyes flashing with a hotter and more intemperate rage that Elizabeth had ever witnessed in him. "What business have you writing to my sister?" he demanded.

"She told you?"

"Georgiana wrote of a Miss Elizabeth Bennet who was claiming impossible things about her brother. What did you say to her?"

"I told her only of the first cipher. Your brother intended it for her, and I thought she might know the identity of Lord Cunningham."

"There is no Lord Cunningham. I told you this."

As terrible as she felt about leading Miss Darcy to a false conclusion about her deceased brother, Elizabeth could not stop the flare of temper at Mr. Darcy's words. "The letter was not written to you," Elizabeth said. "It was intended for Miss Darcy, and so, as the intended recipient, I thought she could lend more insight."

"And did she?"

"No."

"I want Georgiana's letter returned. I had low expectations of your character from the moment your scheming mother tried to push you upon me in your father's study, but I tried to school my mind to a more charitable disposition. And now this! You intimate to my sister some form of slander from her brother. Because he was knifed in the dark and robbed? Is it because he was behind enemy lines? Do you call him a traitor!"

"I said no such thing!"

"You said something. Georgiana is inquiring into the circumstances of his death."

Miss Darcy had not told him. Elizabeth could not breathe. How could Georgiana Darcy have told Elizabeth about her hopes but not their oldest brother? So much silence between people who claimed to have the closest bond.

"What is it?"

Elizabeth said, "Miss Darcy thinks your brother still lives."

Mr. Darcy just stared.

"Read it for yourself." Elizabeth handed him the letter Miss Darcy had sent.

Mr. Darcy looked at the Latin and her translation of the cipher beneath. His hands shook, making the sound of the crinkling paper seem disproportionately loud. "What did you tell her?

"The same as I told you. No more. I used the

code of the first cipher, and she worked it out herself. It was intended for her."

"The first cipher?"

Elizabeth wished for a moment she could swallow her own tongue and choke if only to spare herself more mistakes. But it was too late for that. "Do you know why my father agreed to decipher your code?"

"It is his hobby. Codes and ciphers. That is as Mr. Bingley told me."

"It is more than a hobby. My father's skills are essential to the war effort. And they found your brother's body behind enemy lines. My father thought there might be something more to your brother's missive than mere last words to his only sister."

"And he thinks Georgiana was involved?"

"To some extent. She passed your brother's coded letters along to this Lord Cunningham, whoever he may be."

"I cannot believe Reggie was mixed up in such things. He should have known better!"

"Perhaps he did. Perhaps he trusted his sister because she was worthy of trust, more trust than you have given her."

Mr. Darcy looked up. "How dare you!"

"How dare you! You poisoned the trust between you and your sister, not I."

"What can you know? You are a meddling woman who oversteps herself every opportunity. Your father ought to keep a better watch on you, that you should steal his work and try to make your own way with it." Mr. Darcy loomed over Elizabeth, his expression a mask of energy and fury. He crumpled the letter in his hand and threw it onto the bed.

Now Elizabeth was furious. "It is you who meddles. Who do you think cracked your brother's cipher? My father's eyesight is failing, and I have been doing most of his deciphering work over the past year. And your sister understood the cipher I sent well enough to write her letter using the same code. An Ave Maria cipher, not that you have a care for that."

Elizabeth spread out Miss Darcy's letter and explained to him how one might go about deciphering the outer cipher, the Ave Maria, without the key. "I sent to your sister in code exactly the message I sent to you. You did not come to such a revelation, so it must have referred to something private between your brother and your sister. Butterflies are reborn. Maybe that is what your brother meant? I do not know. But even if it was your brother's intention to reassure your sister as to his safety, the letter is five months old. At least. He may have lived and since died. It is not for me to say. If you truly wish to understand, speak with your sister, as you should have done from the beginning.

"You overstep yourself. Get up. We are leaving for Longbourn."

Jane began to cough and Elizabeth, distracted, turned to her.

"Jane!" The weight of mistake upon mistake fell upon Elizabeth's shoulders. Jane had been doing so much better, and now she was worse again.

"What is this then about a second cipher?" Mr. Darcy asked.

Jane leaned forward so that her lips were almost at Elizabeth's ear. "Tell him," she whispered. "All of it."

Elizabeth had already broken her secrecy in telling Jane, but Jane was almost like a second piece of herself. To tell Mr. Darcy?

No. Elizabeth could not risk it. She had already broken too much trust. "I have told you all I can, Mr. Darcy."

"That is unacceptable. Who are you to keep such secrets? It is my sister's letter. If she is involved in something dangerous, I have a right to know. To protect her!"

"The danger is not to her."

"I will speak to your father then. If you will not tell me, then he will. And if he will not, then I will take the letter to my sister and demand answers."

"For her sake or your own?"

"Excuse me?"

To think, Elizabeth had begun to warm to this man. "It is you who meddles and you who interferes. With you, there is no way but your own."

Mr. Darcy's face was almost as red as it had been weeks before when he had witnessed Mr. Wickham's entry to the assembly hall. Mr. Darcy grabbed from the bed Miss Darcy's letter to Elizabeth. "You have no right to this."

"I see you make a habit then of stealing the correspondence of ladies in your acquaintance."

"Your father will return my sister's letter to me, and you will never write to her again."

As Mr. Darcy and Elizabeth were arguing, Miss Bingley, not being able to find Mr. Darcy at any other place in the premises, decided to remind Elizabeth that it was time to change for dinner. As she approached the door, she heard what sounded like a clear argument between a man and woman.

Entering the room, Miss Bingley's shock, and yes, curiosity, only sharpened. Mr. Darcy was standing far too close to Elizabeth holding what appeared to be a crumpled letter. Miss Bennet was awake and looking frankly overwhelmed by her sister and Mr. Darcy's angered tones.

"Mr. Darcy!" Miss Bingley blurted out, and all three others in the room stopped and stared.

Mr. Darcy glanced out the window and then back at Miss Bingley. "It is time to change for dinner," he said flatly.

Miss Elizabeth just blinked.

Mr. Darcy folded the letter. "Miss Elizabeth," he said with glorious coldness. "Tomorrow, in the morning, I will collect my sister's correspondence." He bowed and departed.

Miss Bingley, her curiosity overcoming her, asked, "Whatever was that about?"

But Miss Elizabeth ignored the question in its entirety, instead standing up from where she had been sitting on Miss Bennet's bed and gathering up the stack of correspondence, now organized into two distinct piles. She curtsied, "Miss Bingley."

After she had left, this Bingley turned to Miss Bennet, but the young woman lay with her back against the pillows, her eyes shut and mouth parted in a snore. Had she not been awake moments ago?

Now, her sleep seemed genuine. Miss Bingley, having no other option, gave a curtsy to the sleeping woman and said, "I must take my leave."

21

That evening, Jane was well enough to spend some moments in the parlor after dinner, and at her insistence, the pair were set to depart promptly the next day after morning service.

Mr. Bingley received this news with true sorrow, and tried to persuade Miss Bennet that leaving so soon would not be safe for her, as she was not yet fully recovered, but Jane was firm. Though Miss Jane Bennet did not spare Mr. Darcy a glance, he knew the reason for their hasty departure was himself. Miss Bennet would wish to keep a watchful eye over his visit to their home, which he resolved to take with her to speak with Mr. Bennet and Elizabeth together.

Reginald had always been prone to taking risks,

but for him to drag their sister into it was unforgivable. Georgiana was young and had almost sacrificed her virtue when she fell victim to Wickham's seduction. Certainly Reginald would not have trusted her with affairs of state!

It was more likely Miss Elizabeth had made a mistake and was now trying to cover for herself. And Georgiana, wanting so much for her brother's death to be a mistake, had fallen prey to false hope. It infuriated Darcy that Elizabeth had written his sister and thus caused her such pain. He should have just dragged Elizabeth back to Longbourn right then, no matter the hour or his own social obligations. But waiting a single night would make no difference, and after Mr. Darcy had retrieved his sister's letter, he could visit his sister at Mrs. Tremayne's with all due haste after.

They left the next day after the morning service. Though the departure was at first agreeable, Miss Bingley grimaced when Mr. Darcy declared that he would accompany the two ladies with a maid in their borrowed carriage to Longbourn as he had important business with the master of the house.

As the carriage approached, it became clear the household was in disarray. A buggy, which Mr. Darcy recognized as belonging to Mr. Jones, was parked outside the main entrance. Perhaps another of the Bennet sisters had caught ill.

But upon entering the main house, Miss Lydia met them with in the parlor with dire news. She ran to Jane and threw her arms around her oldest sister's waist.

"Lydia, what is wrong?"

"Papa." Lydia shook her head.

"Was it an apoplexy?" Elizabeth said, her hands shaking and face pale.

"No. We were robbed." Lydia sobbed against her sister. "Papa must have awakened and went to his study in the middle of the night, and—" Lydia's breath caught and she let out another sob.

"Is Papa alive?"

"He lives, but he has not awakened yet."

Mrs. Bennet looked over at Mr. Darcy and said, "Thank you, Mr. Darcy, for seeing our daughters safely home. We will not trouble you further."

Darcy, at a loss, stared.

Elizabeth said, "Mr. Darcy needs his sister's letter," and with no further words dashed into the house.

"Lizzie!" Mrs. Bennet ran after, and Mr. Darcy followed, feeling very much like an imposter.

Had Elizabeth the presence of mind to notice

Mr. Darcy, she would have insisted he remain in the parlor. But she was far more concerned for her father and the tragedy that had befallen them.

Robbed?

Would not a thief have availed himself of the silver candlesticks in the dining room, or any number of the small, yet valuable keepsakes in the hallway? Elizabeth's eyes blurred with tears as she ran. The thief had been remarkably inept. Or at the least, uninterested in ordinary valuables.

Elizabeth was reminded of Mr. Dowding's sudden apoplexy. He'd had no history of such episodes. And now, just after Mr. Bennet had taken over Mr. Dowding's encoding work, Mr. Bennet was assaulted and "robbed."

When Elizabeth entered the study, the room was a mess. Papers had been moved about and tossed carelessly. At a glance, many of her and her father's notes were missing. Fortunately for England, Mr. Bennet had sent his most recent and clearly written work to Elizabeth at Netherfield Park, which meant whatever the thief made away with would not endanger the war effort. But any comfort Elizabeth might've taken from these facts was wiped away by the pale, still form of her father propped up and yet unconscious, on the library couch against the study wall.

Mrs. Bennet sat beside him on a chair, holding his hand. She was uncharacteristically silent, her face drawn and almost without color. He had a gash on his right temple which had been cleaned and stitched.

Elizabeth said, "How long has Papa been like this?"

"I found him this morning," Mrs. Bennet said. "I went to call him for morning services, believing once again he had forgotten the time—" Mrs. Bennet swallowed. "And then, he was collapsed! On the floor by his desk. I thought he had died! I screamed and Mary came."

Mary sat on the floor beside her mother. Though books surrounded her, she stared down at her hands. Kitty was balanced on the thick arm of the couch, running her fingers over her father's thinning hair.

Elizabeth took her mother's free hand. They were not always at ease with each other, but in this time of grief, Mrs. Bennet took comfort from her daughter's touch.

"Oh Lizzie! What if he does not wake?" Mrs.

Bennet hugged her arms to her chest, head bowed, shoulders shaking.

The door opened again, and Jane and Lydia entered. Jane, taking one look at the group, asked, "Should Papa not be moved to his bed?"

"Mr. Jones suggested the same, but all the stairs —" Mrs. Bennet sobbed again. "He tried to help us but with his leg..."

"If you have another set of hands, I can carry him," Mr. Darcy offered.

Elizabeth had forgotten his presence. Mr. Darcy stood at the edge of the room, his hands behind his back. Elizabeth did not like the idea him manhandling her father, but leaving Mr. Bennet here for a long period was also not ideal. His neck developed a very painful spasm on the occasions when he fell asleep in his study; it would be far easier for him to recover in comfort in his own bed.

Jane said, "If you please, Mr. Darcy, but I will call Mr. Avery from the stable."

"Billy already went to his mother's?" Elizabeth asked. Mr. Avery was elderly and had a limp from being kicked by a tenant's mule a few years ago. He had breathing attacks when pushed to excessive efforts. His son Bill did the heavy lifting in the stable at his father's direction. Unfortunately for the

Bennets, the younger Avery joined his mother every Sunday for services and to help around her house.

"Last night."

Elizabeth said, "I will take father's feet." Elizabeth might be a woman, but she was young and in good health.

"Is Mr. Avery out?"

"He is older and cannot breathe well when he tries to lift things," Elizabeth explained.

With Elizabeth and Kitty's help, they got Mr. Bennet up the stairs into his bed with no sign of further injury.

"Who would do such a thing?" Mrs. Bennet whispered as Jane settled their father on the bed of pillows.

What if her father died? Her throat closed. Their mother was always opining about the possibility, but Elizabeth had never considered it imminent. Mr. Bennet, aside from his eyesight, was in excellent health, and Mrs. Bennet was so prone to exaggeration only a fraction of her dire prophesies came to any effect.

But anyone, no matter how healthy, could succumb from a blow to the head. If Mr. Bennet did not wake, everything was lost. Their home, Elizabeth's work, and most importantly, her beloved father who accepted and understood her in ways no one else could match.

It was as though Mr. Bennet and Jane formed between foundations, with Elizabeth making the third post of a tripod that kept her life firm and grounded. Without him, how could she stand?

Mr. Jones advised them to feed Mr. Bennet small amounts of broth and, when he woke—if he woke—to ensure that he did not sleep for more than two hours at a time before waking him again.

"Mr. Bennet has a hard head," Mr. Jones said. "I felt no cracking, though whoever knocked him out did it right firmly. He may not remember the incident." Mrs. Bennet nodded.

"You can send for a physician from town, but they won't tell you much different. A blow to the head will settle up on its own." Or it wouldn't, but Mr. Jones did not need to say that out loud. "I don't hold with bloodletting for leeches for this kind of trouble." Mr. Jones gave them some draughts for the pain and to strengthen his blood and then left.

Mr. Darcy asked, "Has a constable been called?"

"Yes. He came after morning services. The window to the study was open. It must have been left unlatched. I am always reminding Mr. Bennet to latch it before dinner, but he often forgets. Especially with Lizzie away."

"So it is only you ladies here?"

"And Mr. Avery."

"Who is not well enough to help carry an unconscious man up a flight of stairs."

It was a testament to Mrs. Bennet's discomfiture that she did not immediately beg Mr. Darcy for help, instead explaining, "I have sent for my brother in London."

"Your brother will be of little use to you tonight, should this villain return. I shall stay."

Elizabeth's shock at the offer was such that it overcame her grief and fear. "You? Mr. Darcy? Why?"

"I know of my duty," Mr. Darcy said. "This miscreant likely came in through the study and stumbled upon your father, clubbing him and then making away with what he could. Now, sensing you undefended, he may wish to return to the scene of his crime and glean for himself greater treasures."

Ordinarily, Elizabeth would have found herself in a doubt of such a theory. A household, once robbed, would be on guard against a second attempt. It would be easier for an ordinary thief to try his luck elsewhere, preferably in another village.

But nothing about this theft was ordinary. Longbourn was not a wealthy estate, and it was well known to be entailed. Mr. Bennet's income went to uphold the expenses of a wife and five unwed daughters. A thief would have been better served to rob the Lucases, or another, wealthier family. But considering that the thief had focused his attentions on Mr. Bennet's notes, his goals had not been for monetary gain, but instead to pilfer her father's work, it was likely the thief would try again.

At the same time, the last person Elizabeth wished to have stay as their guest was Mr. Fitzwilliam Darcy. But before Elizabeth could raise an objection, Mrs. Bennet said, "Thank you, Mr. Darcy. We will have a guest room prepared for you. You have our very deepest and most heartfelt gratitude."

22

─────────

*E*lizabeth and her sisters took turns giving Mr. Bennet sips of broth through the rest of the day. Mr. Bennet stirred after a few hours, opening his eyes and speaking, though his words were garbled and it was clear after a few moments he was not aware of his surroundings.

The second time he awoke, after dinner, he was more sensible. "Lizzie!" he called out, and Elizabeth leaned closer to the bed, putting a hand on her father's forearm. "Papa?"

Mrs. Bennet, who had sat fast by his side, took his hand. "My dear Mr. Bennet. By all that is good and holy, you have awakened at last!"

Mr. Bennet said, "Amelia? Are you here? Is it time for services already?"

"Do you remember, Mr. Bennet?"

"Remember, I must remember." Mr. Bennet's voice trailed off. After a long silence, he said something about an Alberti Cipher. "Take down these numbers Lizzie, exactly as…" He mumbled, but Elizabeth could not make out his words.

Mrs. Bennet shook her head. "He is on again about codes."

Elizabeth said, "It must be because he was in the study when it happened."

"Foolish man! What code could be so important to have him shuffling about in the middle of the night?" Mrs. Bennet closed her eyes. "When Mr. Bennet and I were courting, he would slip me love notes in code. We danced, and he would press it into my hand at the start of the dance or slip it into my sleeve when handing me a glass of punch. The rascal! Mr. Gardner would translate them for me, and I would pretend that I had understood them from the beginning. It seemed a harmless ruse. And now…" Mrs. Bennet's voice hitched. She swallowed. "He should never have been awake."

Elizabeth felt torn in two, caught between worry for her father and the pain she heard in her mother's voice.

The evening progressed. Mary curled up like a

child around the Bible she clutched to her chest at the foot of her father's bed. Kitty and Jane sat in chairs brought up from the dining room across from Elizabeth and her mother. Kitty embroidered a cushion until her eyes drooped and she swayed, waking in time to catch herself before she fell from the chair.

Lydia sat closest to Mary. She stared down at her hands, tugging at the fingers of her mitts, glancing at her father and swallowing at the sight of his injury.

As the hour grew later, Lydia's glances split between her father and the clock on the wall. Lydia's head dropped forward, her chin resting on her chest. A the clock chimed once at half eleven Kitty startled, her eyes flying open, "Papa! Is he—"

"I should take Kitty to bed," Lydia said.

"And yourself," Jane said. None had the heart to move Mary.

Elizabeth was tired too, and Jane, though she tried to hide it, had not yet recovered from her illness. She did her best to smother her coughs, knowing how much the sound of coughing troubled their father,.

"Jane," Elizabeth said. "You should lie down a while. It will do no good for Papa to recover only to have you bedridden. Should anything change, I promise on my heart I will wake you."

"I should stay—" Jane began, but Elizabeth shook her head.

"Rest a while. For me."

Eventually, Jane also did as she was bid and followed her sisters from the room.

At some point after the midnight chimes, outside Mr. Darcy shouted, "You devil!"

Elizabeth jumped to her feet.

"Lizzie!" Mrs. Bennet tried to grab her but Elizabeth was already running. The sound had come from near the servants' entrance. Elizabeth dashed down the stairs and grabbed a poker from the fireplace in the kitchen.

A gunshot sounded and someone screamed. Elizabeth's guts turned to ice. Her heart beat hard and painful. Poker in hand, Elizabeth shoved open the servants' door. Mr. Darcy knelt, his back and a part of his arm visible as he stared down the sight of the rifle at a figure fleeing in the distance.

Elizabeth saw that Lydia was on the ground, struggling with her skirt twisting between her legs to stand. "Stop!" she shouted as Mr. Darcy fired the second shot.

23

As in all things, Mr. Darcy took very seriously his duty to protect the Bennet household. He first ensured the delivery of prompt meals to Mr. Bennet's sickbed, also taking care that the remedies he had asked for Jane at Netherfield Park were sent in her own home.

"My, Mr. Darcy, you are a kind and generous young man," the cook said.

The generosity of the cook's praise made Mr. Darcy uncomfortable, and he demurred, falling back on the excuse of duty even as he recognized his making special efforts to see the Bennet ladies' comfort was a step beyond what duty required.

Mr. Darcy also received instructions from the housekeeper about where to find the family's rifle.

The gun was dusty and showed signs of long disuse. Though Mr. Darcy was not an adept shot like his cousin, he well understood the basics of using and maintaining a firearm. He disassembled, thoroughly cleaned, and that afternoon went out on the grounds to practice firing the rifle to ensure it worked.

According to the staff, a constable had been called that morning. It was presumed the miscreant had entered through the unlatched study window and proceeded, likely as a prank, to wreak havoc through the room. Mr. Bennet, as was his occasional habit, had been unfortunate enough to visit his study and get bludgeoned by the startled miscreant before he took his leave.

A simple theory for what appeared to Mr. Darcy to be an odd crime. Why vandalize a study and ignore the obvious valuables in the rest of the house?

Whatever the villain's reasoning, should he return, Mr. Darcy would make certain that no harm came to the Bennet ladies. As furious as he had been about Miss Elizabeth's overstep regarding Georgiana, he would never have wished on Miss Elizabeth the crushing pain and worry her father's injury had caused.

It was with that thought in mind he made himself nap for two hours before sunset and then awakened to begin patrols.

Darcy's cousin, now Col. Fitzpatrick, had taught both Darcy brothers the basics of stealth in enemy territory. Darcy put those lessons to good use that night.

Just after midnight, as he made a circuit of the lower floors, he heard whispers.

"You should not be here. Did you hear what happened?"

It was one of the younger Bennet sisters, though which one, Darcy did not know them well enough to guess from only a whisper. From his location, the angle was too poor to note either her or the other's face. Mr. Darcy crept closer, hoping to glimpse the sister and who she was talking to.

"What happened?"

"My father." A hitch of breath. "I left the door open, but you never came."

"I got called on patrol. Mr. White was ill and—"

"We were robbed!" The young woman's voice grew louder at that word. "A robber entered our home and beat my father..."

A sharp intake of breath. "Miss Lydia, my love. I am—"

"I know you have no fault in this, George."

George? Mr. Darcy came close enough to see the partial silhouette of a man in dark trousers and coat, and he recognized the profile, fair hair and voice Darcy had known since childhood. Wickham. "You devil!"

The man started, and without pausing to explain himself, shoved through the servants' entrance and tore off a mad dash. Darcy followed, grasping the stock of the rifle and drawing it into a firing position as he ran outside onto the estate grounds. Wickham was moving as if the devil himself was after him. Mr. Darcy felt like the devil, all fire and rage as he dropped to his knees and, looking along the barrel sights, positioned himself to fire.

Miss Lydia crashed into Mr. Darcy's side, and the gun went off. "No," Miss Lydia cried, "pray, do not hurt him!"

Mr. Darcy shoved Lydia away. She grabbed at his arm again, and it took more precious time to extricate himself. By the time he drew the gun to fire again, Mr. Wickham, in the crescent moon darkness, was a vague silhouette. He dashed down a hill, the faint halo of his fair hair the only thing marking him from the shadows. Then he was gone.

"You fool!" Mr. Darcy said, turning on Lydia. The gun was still in his hand and Lydia took a step back, wringing her hands, her face pale.

Mr. Darcy forced himself to breathe. His heart was pounding, and the smell of powder filled the air.

"Was that Mr. Wickham?" Miss Elizabeth stood in front of the servants' door. She was still in her day dress. With her dark curls displaced from their pins and framing her face, her eyes glittering and cheeks—even in the darkness—in full color, appeared the perfect mix of a warrior and lady as she swung a fireplace poker over her shoulder. "Why in the devil was Mr. Wickham here?"

"Mr. Wickham was not the thief," Lydia insisted. "He means to court me plainly, but he has duties and you, *you* would not understand."

Mr. Darcy lowered the rifle. "Mr. Wickham had designs upon your sister's virtue. And she on his, such that remains," he explained. Miss Lydia was too caught in Wickham's thrall, but Miss Elizabeth was a sensible young woman.

"Lydia, is it true about Mr. Wickham? Was he here?"

"It was only because Mr. Wickham gave the signal, and I knew Mr. Darcy might see him and hurt him and I needed to warn him."

Mr. Darcy wiped his sleeve over his forehead. He was sweating, and the lingering remains of his rage mingled with his current annoyance, leaving him thoroughly spent. But he could not, in good conscience, allow Lydia to walk the same painful road that almost destroyed his own sister. Mr. Darcy said, "Wickham does not love you. He is using you for some purpose of his own. That is his character."

Lydia, eyes wide and face red with obvious temper, stomped her foot on the grass and said, "You are an…! Odious! You are an odious man!"

Lydia tried to storm past her sister back into the house, but Miss Elizabeth barred her way. "You will not see him again."

"You cannot stop me for marrying him. We are in love."

"You have been acquainted for barely a fortnight."

"Not everyone is as hard-hearted as you, Lizzie."

"Hard-hearted?" Miss Elizabeth's expression froze for a second, and Darcy felt a sudden sympathy. He was often called hard-hearted simply for doing his own duty.

Miss Elizabeth's tone was harsh as she said, "You care nothing for your family and how your behavior might affect us. I know you have no care for me, but what about Jane? If word of you entertaining strange men becomes part of the common gossip, it ruins Jane's prospects. And Kitty's. And Mary's, no matter how hard she strives for virtue in her every action and thought."

Lydia took a step back. "Lizzie. I did not mean to hurt Jane or Papa—"

"Go inside. Now! And if I see Mr. Wickham skulking about our grounds again, be assured, my response will be exactly as Mr. Darcy's was, if not with truer aim."

Miss Elizabeth stepped aside and Lydia, her face wet with tears, dashed into the house.

When the door had fallen shut behind her, Miss Elizabeth turned. "Mr. Darcy, I know I have no right to it, but I can only ask your discretion. Please, I beg of you, do not speak of what you witnessed tonight between my sister and Mr. Wickham. Please."

Darcy, struck mute by the incredible woman before him, managed a nod.

Miss Elizabeth blinked rapidly and swallowed, hard. Dear heavens, was she about to cry? What should he do? A small touch or gesture of affection was acceptable between family members, but not acquaintances. Darcy and Georgiana had cried in each other's arms at the news of Reginald's death. Darcy could not offer Miss Elizabeth an embrace even if such a gesture from him would be welcome.

Miss Elizabeth said, "Lydia is a fool. I keep praying that age will bring her wisdom, but it seems she only grows older."

"I will not speak of what happened tonight. You have my word. Miss Lydia is not the only young woman who has been led astray by Mr. Wickham's charms. Do not be too harsh with her. You must protect her. Even if it is from herself."

Miss Elizabeth rested the tip of the fire poker on the ground. "I have often made a pretense at the study of character, and I believe my assessments are often accurate than not. But in your case…" She bit her bottom lip, a gesture that called more tension than was proper to her mouth. "I have misjudged you, Mr. Darcy. You are a good man."

Mr. Darcy swallowed. His skin was flush and his heart pounded again, almost as rapidly as if he were chasing down a villain, except what he felt was not anger. It was something far worse, something he could not allow himself, especially not with Miss Elizabeth Bennet.

Mr. Darcy bowed. "Allow me to continue my rounds," he said.

"Yes. Please. And thank you. I pray we have no more trouble tonight."

24

---

*E*lizabeth stayed up the rest of the night at her father's bedside. Had her father been well, she still would not have slept. Too much had changed. Mr. Darcy's actions in protecting their home had sparked some awareness in the core of her being, and Elizabeth had been unable to wrest her eyes from him as he fired the second shot.

Mrs. Bennet had been circumspect in following Mr. Jones's instructions and attempted to wake Mr. Bennet every few hours, though with limited success.

An hour after dawn, Mr. Bennet sat straight up in his bed and shouted, "Thief!"

Mrs. Bennet, who had dozed off with her head

on the edge of the bed at her husband's side, woke immediately, "Mr. Bennet! My dear Mr. Bennet!"

Mr. Bennet turned his head towards his wife's voice and winced. "Amelia? Did you catch him?"

"You remember?"

Elizabeth, now awake, added, "Papa, tell us everything."

Mr. Bennet blinked. "I woke, there was an error with the encoding, and I went to correct my notes in the study. I was inside the room when I sensed… a change in atmosphere… And then—to the devil with my eyes! It was a thief, and I swung at him with my cane, but he was too fast. He struck me and I remember no more."

Elizabeth took her father's hand. "Mr. Jones said it was likely you might remember nothing at all. So it is good you remember something."

"If only I had seen him. What business did a thief have in my study?"

Mrs. Bennet stood and put her palms on her husband's shoulders, gently pushing him back towards the pillows. "Rest," she said. "You have had a very trying day and night, so trying, and our entire household is in such disarray with your convalescence. I felt my heart might break when I discovered you bleeding into the oriental carpet.

My brother's gift, it is ruined now! You must be more careful! To be wandering around at any time of the day or night—" As Mrs. Bennet spoke, her voice took on a higher pitch until Mr. Bennet closed his eyes and groaned.

"Mother," Elizabeth said, "I believe with his head he cannot countenance loud voices."

"Yes, of course," Mrs. Bennet said in a whisper. "Be quiet, Lizzie. We must not disturb your father's recovery."

Mary stirred. Her eyes opened, and the brightness of her smile made her beautiful. "Papa," she breathed. "I spent the night praying for you. You are well, tell me you are well!"

"Were you there the entire night?" Mr. Bennet asked gently.

Mary nodded.

"I am well," Mr. Bennet reassured her. "Very well." They embraced.

Mr. Bennet said, "You should go to your room now and sleep."

"Are you hungry, Papa? You must be. Mother has been feeding you broth, but broth can only sustain a person for so long."

Mr. Bennet patted his belly. He nodded his head and then winced. "Perhaps some toast?"

"Yes, Papa!" Mary nodded sleepily and cradling her Bible, she left for the kitchen.

When she was gone, Mr. Bennet asked, "How long was I insensible? I pray this robber did not return?"

"Oh, we were frightened, very frightened, but Mr. Darcy stayed the night, and——"

"Mr. Darcy? Why Mr. Darcy?" Mr. Bennet blinked. "Where is Jane? Is she still convalescing at Netherfield?"

"We returned yesterday after morning services. Mr. Darcy accompanied us." Elizabeth did not wish to explain about the letter and her role in upsetting Mr. Darcy to the point he now demanded its return. Not until her father was improved.

"I see," Mr. Bennet said suspiciously. "Very gentlemanly of him I suppose."

"Very gentlemanly!" Mrs. Bennet agreed with enthusiasm. "Why, he must have cleaned and repaired your old rifle because he had no trouble firing it last night."

"The miscreant came back? I hope Mr. Darcy wounded him!"

"There was some commotion," Mrs. Bennet said, "but Lizzie said it was a false alarm."

"False alarm? Mr. Darcy is quick on the trigger then."

"He is a very conscientious young man," Mrs. Bennet said.

Elizabeth hated lying to her family, but the truth would only upset her mother and infuriate her father, neither of whom could handle such dire emotions at this juncture.

If, as Mr. Darcy had intimated, Mr. Wickham had attempted to seduce his sister in the same way he was practicing his charms upon Lydia, then Mr. Darcy would say nothing. Lydia, not wishing to have her freedoms curtailed, would also be silent. And hopefully Mr. Wickham, not wishing to face rifle shot again, would make himself scarce.

It was an imperfect solution, but the best Elizabeth could manage. Lydia would not change her ways even if they sent her away to school. At least under Elizabeth's watchful eye, she could, through time if nothing else, be returned to the path of virtue. Or at least a less damaging form of ill virtue.

"I would like to speak with Mr. Darcy, to offer my thanks," Mr. Bennet said.

"I will see——" Mrs. Bennet started to stand.

"Mr. Darcy is asleep," Elizabeth said. "I will

have Mrs. Hill send him in when he has woken again."

"Yes. Yes," Mr. Bennet said. "That is for the best." He yawned.

The door to the bedroom opened again, and the rest of the Bennet daughters returned with a tray containing toast, honeyed porridge, and tea.

"Papa, you are awake!" Jane said and sneezed.

"And you should return to bed, Jane," Mr. Bennet ordered. "You are still ill."

"The joy in seeing you alert has erased all thoughts of my illness," Jane said. "I have chamomile tea and you must drink another of Mr. Jones's draughts."

"How healthful," Mr. Bennet said dryly.

"You are well," Lydia said in all sincerity. Her eyes were shining, and her joy and relief seemed genuine. "Mary told me you had awakened. I was so worried." She ran to her father's side and they shared a quick embrace. "Mr. Jones's draughts taste vile, but you must drink it all."

"I suppose I must." Mr. Bennet took a bite of the toast before tackling the medicine. He grimaced at the taste and followed it with a gulp of tea.

"Good," Jane said, taking up her chair at her father's side. "It will help with your pain."

"And the porridge?"

"From Mr. Darcy. It is quite heartening. One of his mother's remedies."

"Mr. Darcy has made himself a part of this household in a short time," Mr. Bennet said. He glanced at Elizabeth. "It is remarkable."

Elizabeth averted her gaze.

The family spent a pleasant morning together, and Mr. Bennet even managed to get up and walk around a bit before his headache became too severe and he had to lie down again.

At half one, Mr. Darcy visited. Elizabeth had fallen asleep in Jane's chair at their father's side, and when Mr. Darcy spoke, the fear of what he might reveal pushed the cobwebs of sleep from Elizabeth mind.

"Mr. Darcy," Elizabeth said, blinking and rubbing her curled-up fingers under her eyes. "Our father wishes to thank you for your kindness to all of us."

"Yes, Lizzie. And it pleases me to express this gratitude myself."

"Yes, Papa, of course," Elizabeth said and sat back on the chair, her gaze fixed on Mr. Darcy who, as was his wont, revealed little emotion in his own expression.

Mr. Darcy bowed. "Mr. Bennet, it was my duty and my honor to ensure the safety of your family to the best of my ability. And I am very pleased to see your returning to health."

"As am I. It is the mark of a true gentleman to extend himself to assist those in need. I do not have enough words to thank you."

"Such words are not needed."

Elizabeth looked upon Mr. Darcy with admiration. Admiration! He had gone beyond what any would consider duty in the protecting of her family.

"My wife informs me there was a commotion last night."

"Nothing of consequence."

"Well, I assure you I have been working with diligence to decipher your sister's letter. It seemed to me an initial code might hide a second cipher with greater meaning, and that is the path we have been exploring, right Lizzie?"

Elizabeth nodded, pushing down a stab of anger at her father claiming credit for her own work and ideas. Guilt and fear quickly followed the anger. Would Mr. Darcy reveal Elizabeth's writing to Miss Georgiana on her own?

"I thank you, Mr. Bennet. But as I had explained to your daughter, the reason I returned with her and Miss Bennet yesterday was to retrieve my sister's letter. It was, in fact, intended for her, and I realize that my taking it without asking her consent may have been an overstep."

It was as though the chair had been yanked out from beneath Elizabeth, and she was falling towards a short and ignominious end. Had Mr. Darcy admitted an error? Was he being kind?

If Elizabeth had not received Mr. Darcy's promise last night to protect Lydia's reputation from herself, she would have believed it. But looking beyond his previous insults, his behavior since that disastrous night in Jane's sickroom had been solicitous. Kind.

Mr. Darcy could have revealed to Mr. Bingley about how Elizabeth had taken it upon herself to write Miss Darcy without asking a by-your-leave. He had not. Instead, despite his anger, he had listened to Elizabeth's own criticisms. The warmth Elizabeth had felt toward Mr. Darcy since the first bowl of porridge and treatment for Jane, just two days ago, had grown. Now Elizabeth could not deny her growing attraction.

Mr. Darcy will ask your hand in marriage.

The statement did not seem so ridiculous, or so unwanted, now.

Perhaps at the next ball, Elizabeth would accept Mr. Darcy's invitation to dance. If he attempted again to offer it.

Elizabeth was getting ahead of herself. Mr. Darcy was just being considerate of her father's health. And while Mr. Darcy had ceased offering her insults at almost every turn, a lack of insult did not imply a growing admiration on his part. Maybe, if Mr. Darcy stayed another night, then maybe Elizabeth could gain insight into his intentions. Mr. Bennet was not well enough at this point to fight off a second robbery attempt.

Or a third? Mr. Wickham would have known the latch was open the previous night, and if he was looking for Mr. Bennet's newest work, he would have realized it was not in the papers he stole.

Elizabeth palms were sweaty, and she clutched her skirts to dry them. Had they let her father's attacker get away?

Mr. Bennet blinked and cocked his head, wincing at the pain caused by the gesture. "What day is it?"

"It is Monday, Father," Mary responded, a hint of fear in her tone. "Yesterday the services. You were attacked on Saturday while we were sleeping."

"Yes. Monday. Mr. Darcy. I must again offer my

thanks and assure you that there will be no need of your protection this evening."

"No need!" Mrs. Bennet interjected. "My dear Mr. Bennet, while your improvement relieves me and all of us, if the commotion last night was not an animal..." Mr. Darcy had suggested no cause for the commotion, but Elizabeth was for her mother's general habit of embellishment. "Then I am uncertain Billy alone will be enough to send such a miscreant on his heels. Mr. Darcy must be the first person to have fired your rifle in a decade."

"Be that as it may, we are expecting another, young gentleman guest."

"We are!"

"He will arrive for dinner."

"And you are only informing us now! Why I must speak with the cook immediately, and who is this gentleman caller? Jane?"

Jane shook her head.

"Mr. Collins's letter is somewhere in my papers. I admit, I had first thought it an amusement to extend the hand of invitation to my cousin, and then the situation was quite forced from my mind——"

"Mr. Collins!"

"Yes. We will need to have rooms readied for

him, and it would be improper, and frankly unnecessary to have a second gentleman stay on for our protection, especially one who is not a direct relation. Mr. Darcy, I hesitate to ask for you to depart with such haste, though you are most welcome to stay for dinner—"

"I do not wish to impose."

"It is no imposition," Elizabeth blurted out.

Mr. Darcy stared at her a moment too long. Finally, he said, "I cannot convey to you my gratitude for your hospitality and kindness, but my presence would only serve as a distraction and perhaps viewed as improper. Your cousin, Mr. Collins, should be adequate for protecting your home." Mr. Darcy's gaze then rested on Elizabeth, warming her skin and making her heart flutter. "But I must again convey my appreciation for your hospitality. I only wish we had occasion to enjoy each other's company under better circumstances."

"I will see to it Mr. Darcy gets his sister's letter," Elizabeth said, standing. "Mother?"

"I will send a maid. Mary, come with us."

"You have your notes?" Mr. Bennet said.

"Yes."

Elizabeth, Mr. Darcy, Mary, and Mrs. Bennet walked together down the stairs to the study. Mrs.

Bennet chattered on about preparations for their impeding guest, Mr. Collins, who her husband had invited to stay a week "without even a hint of warning, and how are we to arrange a proper menu?"

After the maid arrived, Mary, Mr. Darcy, and Elizabeth entered the study. Mary asked, "Mr. Darcy, are you certain it was only an animal last night?"

Mary grabbed at her skirts and avoided Mr. Darcy's gaze. Though Mrs. Bennet had given all four of her daughters "lessons" on how to use one's eyes to capture a man's interest, Mary often avoided meeting anyone's gaze, even those in her own family. Especially when she was nervous or uncomfortable.

"You have no reason to fear or concern yourself," Mr. Darcy said. "And with your cousin arriving, the ladies of this house will not be undefended."

"Mother thinks Mr. Collins would rather see our father pass sooner than later so he then inherits our estate," Mary said. "Not that I would imply Mr. Collins capable of or interested in doing away with anyone. I have never met the man. None of us have."

"Mary!" Elizabeth admonished her sister,

though it was of little use. Mary was truthful to a fault. "Mr. Collins is a parson and well established enough he need not speed up any of our relatives' passing."

"Yes, of course. If he is a man of God, he certainly would not engage in any behavior so horrific."

Elizabeth was not so certain religiosity precluded evil intent, but her father was no fool. He would not have invited the man to guest with them if he felt Mr. Collins would put the Bennet family in danger. Their father likely wanted Mr. Collings to have the best impression of the family in case the worst happened and they had to throw themselves upon their cousin's charity. Elizabeth, not one to throw herself on charity, had long ago resolved she would take work as a governess first. But hopefully her future held brighter prospects.

The day before, Elizabeth's attention had been on her father and not the mess the thief had left in the study, but entering this afternoon, the sheer weight of the destruction was obvious. Books had been thrown from the shelves and papers were scattered everywhere.

Elizabeth's stomach roiled as she approached the desk. The drawers were open.

"Perhaps we should straighten up before Papa returns," Mary suggested. She began stacking some books which had been thrown to the floor on her father's desk as Elizabeth walked around to the front.

Mr. Bennet had sent her notes about the letter to his contact to the prime minister's office but kept the original in case Mr. Darcy asked for its return. An ordinary thief would have had no interest in such a letter, but as Elizabeth looked over what had been stolen—notes and what looked like several of her father's journals—Elizabeth now knew this was, as she has only suspected before, no ordinary thief.

Mr. Darcy's letter was also gone.

"Mr. Darcy," Elizabeth began. She took a breath. She recognized no point in prolonging the inevitable. "Your sister's letter. They stole it."

Elizabeth could only be glad that the translation, which she had written on a separate sheet of paper, was now safely in the care of the prime minister.

"Are you certain?" Mr. Darcy came around the desk. Elizabeth was struck by his scent. Sandalwood and something else that made her want to breathe him in again.

Elizabeth pushed such inappropriate thoughts

on her mind and explained, "I put your sister's letter in this drawer. The lock has been broken, and everything was stolen."

Mr. Darcy stared down at the empty drawer. Elizabeth expected him to shout, blaming Elizabeth for the letter's disappearance, but he only clenched his fist. He shoved the drawer closed.

"I am so sorry," Elizabeth said.

"You did not steal it. I must go."

Just like that? Elizabeth said, "I can write out his note from memory." She looked at it often enough. "It may not be perfect, but it will be something to offer your sister."

"No. I will make amends to Georgiana."

Make amends? Mr. Darcy did not act as though he thought the letter was missing. Elizabeth remembered Mr. Darcy, rifle in hand, firing at Mr. Wickham. Mr. Darcy wore the same expression of cold focus now.

"Mr.—?" Glancing at Mary, on the opposite side of the room stacking books into a pile, Elizabeth whispered, "Our late-night visitor?"

Elizabeth should have suspected Mr. Wickham. She had been so surprised to see him with Lydia, and so certain that no matter Lydia's faults, she would not put their father in danger. But Lydia could be manipulated.

Mr. Darcy said. "I will return your father's items to you, if I can."

But if it was Wickham, then he had to be involved in the plot to assassinate the Regent. The only ones besides Mr. Bennet and Jane who knew about it were the ones involved. And Mr. Wickham had not acted like an assassin last night. A scared rake, but not an assassin.

Elizabeth said, "I will come with you."

Mary looked up. "Where, Lizzie?"

"I will go," Mr. Darcy said. "This is not a situation for a young lady."

"What situation? Lydia believes she is in love with Mr. Wickham. I have told her to be cautious. She has done nothing... unseemly, has she?"

"Mary, this is not your business," Elizabeth said.

"Good day, Miss Elizabeth, Miss Mary. Please pass my regards to your father," Mr. Darcy said. "I will need our carriage. You will soon have company, and it is best if I take my leave."

Elizabeth glared at Mr. Darcy, but she would not continue the conversation in Mary's presence. Mr. Darcy and Lydia might be capable of keeping a secret, but their Mary was not. And if Mary got involved, it would only put her life, and the lives of Elizabeth's entire family, in danger. Not to mention the increasing threat to Lydia's virtue. Mr. Darcy had said Mr. Wickham seduced with an ulterior motive. Had his ulterior motive been to find an entry into their home?

Elizabeth said, "Please, be careful. If something were to happen to you, it would upset me." Elizabeth's cheeks warmed. "It would upset us all."

Mr. Darcy bowed again. "I understand."

After Mr. Darcy had taken his leave, Mary walked to Elizabeth's side and in a low whisper, asked, "Are you and Mr. Darcy engaging in a secret courtship?"

"No!" Elizabeth grabbed a book Mary had piled up on her father's desk. "Help me with this, Mary. We should tidy Father's study before Mr. Collins arrives. We ought to put our best foot forward, yes?"

25

_____

When Mr. Wickham was honest with himself, which was rarely, he admitted himself to be a rake with an unhealthy enjoyment of cards. But whatever his faults, none included a death wish, or worse, the desire to marry a young twit with no fortune of her own.

So getting caught in a compromising position with Miss Lydia and nearly shot down by Mr. Darcy, Wickham recognized the need for a swift departure from Netherfield.

Had his cover been blown, Mr. Smith gave Mr. Wickham instructions on how to give his leave and go to an arranged meeting point in London. Wickham followed these instructions. Only when he was outbound on a stagecoach, teeth clacking, and clutching a single bag with the incomplete notes he had stolen from Mr. Bennet's study, and the town of Meryton was far behind him did he allow himself a moment to relax.

Mr. Smith would not be pleased with Mr. Wickham's performance. Wickham had intended to take his time with his assignment, seducing one or perhaps more of the Bennet girls and having them pilfer the documents, but Mr. Smith had written a week ago with an increased sense of urgency, and Wickham had been forced to take a more direct approach.

Still, it would have been fine if the old man had stayed asleep. Luck cut Mr. Wickham at every opportunity. It was only his quick feet and skills at seduction that had saved his life when Mr. Darcy had started shooting. Wickham rode, drinking liberally from a flask of cognac he kept in the inner pocket of his coat for thinking. He would need some form of insurance on Mr. Smith to protect himself when Mr. Bennet's papers proved not to Mr. Smith's satisfaction.

The address Wickham had been directed to send his stolen letters differed from the arranged meeting point that Mr. Smith and Mr. Wickham had agreed. Perhaps he might learn more of his "benefactor" there and that information could provide him with the insurance he sought.

Wickham would start there.

When Wickham reached London, the sun had set, and it was well past time to find a room in a respectable inn. Fortunately, Wickham did not require a respectable inn. The address listed on the post was in a shabby area, a three-story boarding-house with wafer squares of glass covered by dark curtains. Mr. Wickham approached the door and rang for entry. A servant in threadbare clothing opened the door and beckoned Mr. Wickham inside.

"We've only got one room for let and it's in the back," he said.

"I was given an excellent reference about this place by Mr. Smith," Mr. Wickham said.

"Aldous Smith! Friendly man, Mr. Smith. Always getting letters and packages."

The servant led Mr. Wickham to a sitting room, and a few minutes later, the landlady came down to meet him. She was attractive, if long in the tooth, with the faintest hints of crow's feet blossoming from the corners of her eyes. "Mrs. Finch," the servant said, "this here is Mr. Wickham. He wants to let the second floor back."

"We were given no notice of your arrival," Mrs. Finch said. "It is good fortune we have a room. Your references?"

"Mr. Aldous Smith recommended this establishment," Mr. Wickham said. He was still in his regimentals, and Mrs. Finch gave him a long look up and down, her tongue darting between her lips as she nodded. "Mr. Smith. A fine man. Will you be going with him to the Regent's ball?"

Regent's ball! That must have cost Mr. Smith a pretty penny. Mr. Wickham wondered what business Mr. Smith had with the Ton. Their previous conversation made it clear Mr. Smith despised all nobility. He had felt Mr. Wickham of the court, and to some degree Mr. Wickham was, though his problem was more that they denied him the privilege of noble status rather than animosity towards the concept of nobility itself.

Though Mrs. Finch was dressed respectably, with a shawl covering the front of her dress and ample décolletage, it took no real effort for Mr. Wickham to begin a flirtation. "I am very fortunate then. When far from home, it is heartening to receive a kind welcome. Your smile, my lady, warms my heart."

Mrs. Finch laughed, bringing her hand briefly

over her mouth. "I am no lady," Mrs. Finch said. "And my husband, God rest his soul, is long passed, leaving me alone to run this establishment as best I can."

Mr. Wickham gave the widow credit. She had managed in two sentences to reveal her unattached status and her interest. While Wickham had no desire to settle down and run a semi-respectable boardinghouse, a night with an experienced widow would not be unwelcome.

"Is Mr. Smith in?"

"No. He said he would be out until late this evening. We lock our doors at nine, but Mr. Smith is always so kind and so punctual with his weekly rents I said I would wait up for him. He often spends the evening at Dobson's alehouse."

After a brief inquiry, Mrs. Finch gave Mr. Wickham directions to the establishment. "Or perhaps we can have tea and wait up together," she added, but Mr. Wickham, more interested in insurance than a pleasant evening, demurred. "Perhaps another night. I had hoped to meet with Mr. Smith. It is one of my primary reasons for visiting London."

Mr. Wickham paid Mrs. Dobson for a week of lodgings, and after taking his bag up to the room, which was small and smelled of tobacco smoke, he placed his bag next to the bed. He changed from his regimentals into a plain jacket and waistcoat, shoved the papers for Mr. Smith into his coat, and left.

It was only a few blocks to Dobson's. Though the neighborhood of Mrs. Finch's boardinghouse was at the very edge of respectable, Wickham still got the distinct impression he was being watched and assessed by the cut of his coat and shine on his Hessians that even the manure-stained streets had not, as yet, marred.

Wickham reached the alehouse and walked past it, glancing in the open doorway to catch a glimpse of Mr. Smith. But it was too crowded. He would need to go inside, preferably with a group. It took ten minutes for a group of young men, students by their dress and manners, to approach. Wickham made introductions. His brief stint at education in the law was enough to allow him to present himself as a student from a different university, and as they entered, he made certain to put himself as close to the center of the group as possible.

Dobson's was crowded with a mix of poor students and laborers, many in shirtsleeves as the press of bodies and corner fire, along with liquor and a haze of tobacco, made the bar overly warm despite the cooler temperatures outside. Most of the students' talk centered on classes and excitement at having finished the first round of exams. Wickham seated himself against the wall, using the group as cover to look over the bar.

"What are you reading, Brierley?" one student asked Mr. Wickham, using the false name Wickham had given them.

"Law," Wickham said.

"I have heard Professor Gouldsmith is a bear."

Mr. Wickham nodded and said, "I will buy the next round!" in hope the offer of free ale distracted all from asking more questions about his bona fides.

From his corner, Mr. Wickham looked over the rest of the tavern. Finally, fortune smiled on him. An older gentleman with a tuft of grayish-brown hair atop his head, reminiscent of a squirrel's tail, stepped inside. He jerked his head this way and that and then started towards the table at the opposite end of the room. The bar itself partially obstructed Mr. Wickham's view, but Wickham noted a packet under the older man's arm.

Wickham stood, and begging a moment to relieve himself, crossed the room towards the facilities to get a better glimpse of where the man was walking. It was Mr. Smith. He had altered his hair and mustache, but his frame and manner were the same. Mr. Smith smiled at the squirrel-haired man who sat across the small table from him.

Wickham, nervous that Mr. Smith might spot him, sat down beside a passed-out drunk as Mr. Smith and his companion talked. After finishing an ale, Mr. Smith's companion handed the package over and left.

Mr. Smith stayed a few more minutes, gathered his things, and pushed through the crowd to the door. Wickham followed. His palms sweated as he clutched the packet beneath his coat. Instead of returning to the boardinghouse as Mr. Wickham had expected, Smith appeared to be going elsewhere.

The neighborhood worsened as they walked, and while Wickham had confidence in his ability to win a fistfight should things come to that, he recognized the cut of his clothing and fabric made him stand out. Mr. Smith, who was more plainly dressed, appeared to take no notice of his surroundings. He fiddled with the packet.

Wickham shivered and glanced behind him. A knife from a stranger could kill him as quickly as a shot from Darcy, and Wickham knew better than to let down his guard. Not in a place such as this.

The air took on a distinct smell of refuse and rotting fish. A woman with the front of her dress cut low enough to show the upper crust of her nipples called out, "Sir!" Her lips and cheeks were rouged, and, seeing she had Wickham's attention, she shifted her skirt up to reveal the arc of her calf.

A small child squatted at the woman's feet. The little girl sucked her thumb and scratched at the dirty ground with her other hand. Dark hair, like her mother's, hung around her face in stringy waves.

Mr. Wickham averted his gaze. He was not desperate enough to risk the pox in pursuit of his pleasures even if he'd had the slightest interest of copulating within the watchful gaze of a hungry child.

When he looked back towards Mr. Smith, the man had turned between two buildings. Wickham took a moment to gather his courage and followed again.

The alley was dark and smelled of garbage. A persistent drip from the above rooftops hit the ground with a steady *tap-tap-tap*.

Crates were stacked farther down the alley, and

to Mr. Wickham's left, an open, rotting barrel over-flowed with filmy rainwater.

"Smith?" Wickham called out. What business did Mr. Smith have here?

No response. It was near pitch with only a dim light falling from the window above, where someone had set a lantern.

"Why are you following me, Mr. Wickham?" Mr. Smith's came voice came from farther down the alley.

Though Wickham had followed Smith hoping to secure some form of insurance, now, so far out of his own element, it relieved Wickham to have an ally of sorts, and he strode towards Mr. Smith. "It was bad luck," Wickham said. "I broke in and took what you asked, but——"

"Do you have the papers?"

"I had hoped to meet and discuss them."

"How did you find me here? You spoke with Mrs. Finch?"

"She is fond of you," Mr. Wickham said.

"This was not our arrangement."

"I had thought it faster to go to the address on the package," Mr. Wickham offered as an excuse.

Mr. Smith stepped out from behind the crates. "If you had wished to meet with me, you would have begged my attention in the bar. You wished to spy on me."

Wickham glanced back to the mouth of the alley. "You cannot fault me for wanting insurance," Mr. Wickham said with an overly bright smile that was likely wasted in the darkness.

Mr. Smith sighed. "No, I suppose I cannot. You have a package beneath your coat. Is that the correspondence I requested?"

As Wickham reached into his jacket, he heard something move. Perhaps it was fear of his surroundings, or perhaps luck had favored Mr. Wickham for once, but he saw the movement in time to leap back as Mr. Smith lunged at him. He wore an ornate, silver ring. A thin silver needle protruded from the center, glinting in the dim lantern light from above.

Wickham bolted for the mouth of the alley. He clutched the package to his chest as he ran, his boots pounding and squishing on the refuse-stained stone. He turned at the alley's mouth and kept running. His heart pounded in his ears. It hadn't been a knife. Definitely a ring with a needle. A poison? Wickham had no intention of finding out. He would do what he should have done in the first place: take what funds he had left and run north for Scotland.

Wickham was winded and his chest hurting from exertion when a man stepped in front of him. "Mr. Wickham?" The man had the dress of a gentleman secretary.

Wickham dared to look behind him. Mr. Smith leaned against a nearby building, his arms crossed, the ring glinting on his index finger.

The other man said, "Mr. George Wickham is it? Your foster brother, Mr. Fitzwilliam Darcy, has some questions for you."

A half hour ago, Mr. Wickham would have run from this man. But given a choice between Darcy, who at least would not attempt to murder Wickham in the presence of the law, and Mr. Smith, who would not relent until Wickham was dead, Darcy offered the preferable fate.

"Yes," Mr. Wickham said, towards Darcy's hired copper. "We have much to discuss. Now. Away from here."

26

*M*r. Bennet improved over the first two days of Mr. Collins's visit. Mr. Collins, to Elizabeth's dismay, did not. It became apparent to Elizabeth that Mr. Collins had eyes for her, and worse, Mrs. Bennet heartily approved the match.

Elizabeth was ready to rip both his and her hair out.

"A walk is, of course, to the greatest degree, a most healthful exercise, Miss Elizabeth. But you cannot mean once again to take us from the delicate paths—" Mr. Collins paused to catch his breath. "Of this estate's most—" Mr. Collins gasped again, and though Elizabeth would rather have left him, she was not quite so ill-mannered as to abandon a cousin who had so "kindly" insisted upon accompanying her, for her own safety, as though she needed his accompaniment in the early morning hours on the land she had explored since she was a child, and yet…

"Mr. Collins, if you are tired and wish to return to the house…?"

"No!" Mr. Collins took another breath. "No, Miss Elizabeth, I would not be so crass as to abandon you here—" He gasped. "On your own, without company or a chaperone."

Considering Mr. Collins, in his gazes and increasingly embellished compliments of Elizabeth's imagined character, was making his intentions to attempt a courtship well known, Elizabeth doubted his ability or interest in chaperoning. It served his own self-image to pretend he, who got winded after a mile walk, would somehow be able to protect her. It was infuriating. Unfortunately, without spurning him, which her family could not afford, she would instead have to cut her walk short and return to hide in her father's study, as she had since yesterday when Mr. Bennet had risen from his bed.

"It is best we return home," Elizabeth said.

"Do not—" Mr. Collins wiped his sleeve over

his forehead. "I pray, cut short your morning exertions on my behalf," Mr. Collins said. The longing look he cast over his shoulder to the main house undercut his gallantry.

"It is no trouble," Elizabeth lied. Though Elizabeth hardly set a brisk pace returning home, by the time they reached the main door where Mr. Collins, in his overblown sense of propriety insisted they enter, he looked near collapse.

Mr. Collins caught his breath and bowed, "I thank you, Miss Elizabeth, for the pleasure of your most amicable company. I did so enjoy our walk, and pray I may again be allowed another such extensive tour of these lands."

"Mr. Collins," Elizabeth said with a curtsy. "I must make certain my father does not overexert himself at his work."

"You, Miss Elizabeth Bennet, are the portrait of filial duty. A married woman, of course, would enjoy many benefits and freedoms, and not be chained to a study and her father's correspondence."

Elizabeth wished she could smack him. "Mr. Collins, I must go."

Mr. Collins, taken aback for a moment, his eyes widening, gave her a second, hurried bow. "Of course. It was my pleasure to accompany you this fine morning, Miss Elizabeth."

"Thank you." Elizabeth could not bring herself to lie, even in the interest of politeness, as Mr. Collins would take even the slightest cordiality as encouragement.

Elizabeth opened the door to her father's study. Mr. Bennet called out, "Lizzie, is that you?"

"Yes, Papa." Elizabeth pulled the door shut behind her. She took a step into the room before noting her father had company. "Mr. Darcy!"

A flutter of gladness like a butterfly's wings rose in her chest. Mr. Darcy with his tall frame, lean muscle, and fluid grace would not expire after walking a mile. Mr. Darcy also would not attempt to win her over with hollow platitudes. This was followed by the more troubling thought that Mr. Darcy would not attempt to win her over at all. And though Elizabeth was delighted to see him, she could not help but wonder why he was here. "Has your sister written?" she ventured.

"Mr. Darcy was discussing with me an odd request from Mr. Wickham concerning your sister Lydia."

It was like the ground fell out from underneath Elizabeth in that moment. Mr. Darcy promised to keep the clandestine meeting between Mr. Wickham and Lydia secret. Elizabeth had trusted him. And yet, now, he and her father were discussing the pair. Lydia. Wickham. "Mr. Darcy! What did you—?"

"I have no explanation why Mr. Wickham would insist on speaking only to your daughter Lydia."

"He what?" Elizabeth was confused.

"As I was informing your father, Miss Bennet, Mr. Wickham was tracked down by an investigator I hired to a seedier portion of London. He was carrying stolen correspondence from your father's home, and now he insists only on speaking to Miss Lydia Bennet concerning information of great import. His words. He has also made other outrageous claims of a disturbing nature."

"What claims?" Elizabeth asked.

"The ravings of a desperate man who has overstepped himself one too many times," Mr. Darcy said. "I had only felt it important to share Mr. Wickham's statements, as relayed by my solicitor, because his actions concerned you and your household. I would not put your daughter, any of your daughters, in harm's way."

"Please, Mr. Darcy," Elizabeth insisted, "share with us exactly what Mr. Wickham said."

Mr. Bennet gave a curt nod. "Please, Mr. Darcy. It will ease our concerns to know the full situation."

"So be it," Mr. Darcy said. "Mr. Wickham claims an attempt was made on his life. It is possible there is truth to his claim, considering the neighborhood where he was found, but he insists the threat is not a cutpurse but an assailant of a less usual nature. Further, the method of his assault, which again I must caution you is likely an exaggeration, was by means of a ring with some manner of pin inside."

"A needle?" Elizabeth breath caught.

"I suppose. Mr. Wickham claims it held a poison, but Mr. Wickham will say anything to avoid the consequences of his own actions."

A needle. A ball. A prince.

Elizabeth did not believe in fortune tellers, but she recognized not everything was within her ability to measure or understand. The hidden cipher had intimated a threat against the Regent, and now, a man who used a needle to kill.

"Lydia must not speak with Mr. Wickham alone," Elizabeth said.

"Of course we cannot involve your sister," Mr. Darcy said with a curt wave of his hand.

"We must. But she cannot speak to Mr. Wickham alone. I will go with you to hear his words. I believe they are connected to the situation your brother intimated about in his second cipher."

"The one you refuse to tell me anything about."

"You told Mr. Darcy of the second cipher?" Mr. Bennet flushed. "How could you reveal such a thing? You have put all of our lives at risk!"

"She told me nothing except a second cipher existed," Mr. Darcy said. "And Mr. Wickham had no way of knowing what Miss Elizabeth spoke of at her sister's sickbed. He must have been sent by another to steal your notes."

Elizabeth said, "Papa, we must speak to Mr. Wickham and find out what he knows. What point is there in remaining here and pretending at a false safety if Bonaparte destroys all we love?"

"Lizzie…" Mr. Bennet's voice held the undertone of pleading. "If anyone should go, it is I."

"No. You are only just recovering from Mr. Wickham's attack. You cannot tolerate jostling, and your vision still goes black at points." Elizabeth had thought Mr. Wickham was a feckless seducer, but she had underestimated him. Just as she had underestimated Mr. Darcy. "Lydia and I will go to London with Mr. Darcy to speak with Mr. Wickham," Elizabeth said. "Please, give us your blessing, Papa."

"You would go whether or not I gave my blessing."

"Papa!"

Mr. Bennet shook his head. "I have raised you to think for yourself, Lizzie. Whether that was in error hardly matters now. You have my blessing. Take Mrs. Hill. My wife can do without her for a few days, and nobody will doubt her ability to protect any lady's virtue." Mr. Bennet turned to Mr. Darcy. "It is only because you have been honorable in protecting this house I feel comfortable giving consent for you to take my daughters to London. I expect you to return them both safe and well."

"You have my word, sir," Mr. Darcy said.

"Then you may as well tell Mr. Darcy the rest, Lizzie. If nothing else so he knows which questions are of the greatest import."

Elizabeth went through what she had discovered in the second cipher, ending with, "If the king or the Prince Regent is killed, it will put our government and thus the war effort into disarray. Perhaps even opening us to a usurper or an invasion."

Mr. Darcy said, "My brother. I tried not to doubt him for where and how his body was discovered. I feared he had betrayed us, but instead... I hardly knew him. He was my brother, and I hardly knew him."

Elizabeth wished she could put a hand on Mr. Darcy's to comfort him. His expression was brittle and so sad. "Your brother lived with honor," Elizabeth said. "His work for us may have been irregular, but he did it with honor."

Mr. Darcy nodded. He took a breath, pulling his shoulders back. "Yes. Reggie was always honorable, even in his tricks."

Mr. Bennet said, "Go now, get Lydia. I will tell your mother what has transpired after you are all on your way. My wife's brother has a home in town. Make certain to deliver my daughters there to overnight when your business with Mr. Wickham is finished."

27

"*L*ondon! And Mr. Wickham insisted I was the only one with whom he could share his pain. Is that not romantic, Lizzie?" Lydia asked for the twentieth time since she had learned of Mr. Wickham's request to see her and only her.

Mr. Darcy sat across from the two women, his gaze fixed out the window. Mrs. Hill sat beside him in one of Mrs. Bennet's castoff frocks, bright blue with raised hem and brought in at the waist to fit her shorter, slighter frame. Mrs. Hill's hair had gone almost to gray. She wore muslin gloves and had, since taking her place in the carriage, knitted, her needles tapping a steady *click-click* at they rode.

"It is not romantic," Elizabeth muttered.

"Mr. Wickham and I are destined to wed. It is as Mme. Godiva said. You do not speak so critically of Mme. Godiva as you had before. Perhaps Mary is right and you are having a secret courtsh—"

"Quiet!" Elizabeth said, grabbing her sister tightly by the wrist. "Not one more word." She glanced at Mr. Darcy, who thankfully appeared indifferent to Lydia and Elizabeth's conversation. "Mr. Wickham robbed us. How can you persist in this infatuation?

"You cannot be certain Mr. Wickham was responsible."

"He was found in London with our father's papers. The papers that were stolen from Papa's study. You cannot think those papers came to Mr. Wickham by chance?"

"Perhaps he discovered the thief later. And perhaps the thief is the man who attempted to murder Mr. Wickham."

"And perhaps Mr. Wickham is a lost Russian prince, and perhaps all he wishes is to take you back to his kingdom in the snow. You will eat borscht and drink honey wine every night."

"Now you are fooling with me. You dislike Mr. Wickham. Both you and Mr. Darcy dislike him."

"Both I and Mr. Darcy have good reason to

dislike Mr. Wickham. Lydia, will you at least consider the possibility he may not be the fair-haired man of Mme. Godiva's vision?"

Mrs. Hill looked up from her knitting. "Emily, she is a good sort."

"Emily?"

"Mme. Godiva, my apologies. She has a kind heart. She helped Billy and his mom with their eggs from the market last Sunday."

"Exactly. Mrs. Hill is right," Lydia said, bringing her gloved hand, in a fist, up to her collar-bone. "Mme. Godiva is a good woman. And her visions have truth in them. Why, I believe though Jane will not speak of it directly, Mme. Godiva told her Mr. Bingley and she were meant to fall in love."

"Mr. Bingley often falls in love," Mr. Darcy said, his gaze still focused on the growing sprawl of London through the carriage window.

Elizabeth's stomach lurched. Mr. Bingley had said it himself. He was as content with the country as the city, happy wherever his feet took him. Elizabeth had feared at the time his heart was inconsistent. Now Mr. Darcy confirmed her worst fears. "Mr. Bingley is fickle then?" Elizabeth ventured to ask.

"Not so much fickle as quickly infatuated." Mr.

Darcy shifted in his seat. "I have helped him through many a loss."

"He was spurned?" It was hard to imagine any woman casting Mr. Bingley aside, but if his previous courtships had ended because the woman was feckless, then Jane had nothing to fear. Jane loved with her whole heart, and she would stay true to Mr. Bingley. So long as Mr. Bingley was honest in his approbation for Jane, then everything would work out for the best."

Though it was better Jane occupy herself with securing Mr. Bingley's regard, Elizabeth wished her sister had joined them for this trip. Jane was the best at talking sense into Lydia. Elizabeth had no such skills. The harder she pushed, the more Lydia rebelled.

Now, Lydia seemed ready to forgive Wickham for bludgeoning their father and outright theft. It was infuriating. If she could have gotten Mr. Wickham to speak without involving Lydia, she would have. As it was, Elizabeth and Mr. Darcy both, as well as Mrs. Hill, were forced to suffer through Lydia's increasingly fanciful imaginings of love.

But was Elizabeth any better? She too had been swayed by Mme. Godiva's words. *A needle. A ball. A prince.* Elizabeth glanced across the wagon Mr. Darcy again. The fluttering butterflies in her chest had descended to her stomach. The carriage was warm, which justified the heat in her cheeks and her neck. The same cold features Elizabeth had initially dismissed now compelled her. Would they ever have a chance at a second dance?

A needle. A prince. A ball.

He will ask your hand in marriage.

Elizabeth shook her head. She was not traveling to London for balls or princes, and certainly not to woo Mr. Darcy, if any such a thing were possible. While Elizabeth, like a ninny, admired Mr. Darcy, he would not even look at her. And how could she blame him for his current disinterest? Mr. Darcy had every good reason to wish never to see Mr. Wickham again, and yet faced with all reasonable evidence, Lydia continued to sing the blackguard's praises.

Mr. Darcy must think Elizabeth's entire family mad.

Upon leaving Netherfield, Mr. Bingley had insisted both Elizabeth and Jane take the books Mr. Darcy had lent in Jane's sick room. Now, Elizabeth read the small folio of theorems Mr. Darcy had chosen for her. The equations were not related to coding, but instead a pure mathematics that predicted the movement of the planets. Mercury. Venus. Mars.

Elizabeth, not being well-versed in physics, had only skimmed the surface of what the author, a Russian, had put forth. The text was in Cyrillic, which Elizabeth could not read. Still, the nights after Mr. Darcy had left, Elizabeth had flipped through the pages, her finger tracing the author's neatly organized equations. She felt a closeness to these numbers.

"Are you still reading that dull book?" Lydia asked, peering over Elizabeth's shoulder. "It is not even in English?"

"Mathematics is universal," Elizabeth said.

Mr. Darcy looked up and rested his gaze on the front cover of the book Elizabeth held. "You are enjoying it?"

"I cannot claim to understand everything the author has written, but reading it offers a new perspective."

"Does it?" Mr. Darcy shook his head. "I fear I did not understand it at all."

"Understanding comes with time. And companionship."

"Whatever are you on about, Lizzie?" Lydia squinted at the book. "It looks like gibberish to me.

Elizabeth forced a laugh. "Some equations are an acquired taste."

Mr. Darcy's eyes widened.

Lydia sighed. "Well, I doubt I shall ever acquire it. I cannot wait until we reach London. Mrs. Hill, can you hand me my bag? I have a pillow to finish embroidering."

Two hours later, they arrived at Mr. Darcy's London townhouse. The sun was setting. A mist hung in the air, but it thankfully was not the yellowish-green encompassing fog that sometimes descended upon the city.

For a young woman used to the country, London had always held for Elizabeth an impression of both energy and a sense of overcrowding. She was grateful Mr. Darcy's townhouse was in a quiet area. The oppressive scent of horse dung, while still present, was not so strong here. And the houses were orderly and well maintained.

Mr. Darcy alighted first. He held out his arm for Mrs. Hill, Lydia, and then Elizabeth. Elizabeth caught a whiff of Mr. Darcy's scent as she rested her gloved hands on his forearm for just long enough to maintain propriety before continuing after her sister to the house.

Elizabeth clutched her shawl around her shoulders. As she walked, the damp air muffled the sound of her footsteps on the cobbles. The house was grand, four stories in height, and immaculately kept. They passed through a small courtyard to the main door. A butler opened it, took their outer wrappings, and led them up a flight of stairs to the drawing room.

Mr. Darcy and his butler Mr. Pritchard spoke briefly, asking after Mr. Darcy's guests. Elizabeth explained her and Lydia's luggage was to go ahead to the Gardiners, her aunt and uncle, who were prepared to receive them after this meeting.

Lydia, in the interim, made excited remarks about the decorations. "My, that is a lovely painting!" she said, pointing to a seascape hung above a flickering wax candle on the mantle. "Is it Brighton? I so wish to visit Brighton!"

"My sister painted it," Mr. Darcy said.

The painting was small but vivid, drafted with an exacting eye, and yet there was something charming to the brush strokes. The ocean seemed almost playful, waves capped with white foam like cake icing.

"It is lovely," Elizabeth said.

"Where is Mr. Wickham?" Lydia asked.

Mr. Darcy said. "We will speak with him in the library.

Elizabeth, though tired and thirsty from their long ride, was eager to speak with Mr. Wickham and find out all he knew. But before she could ask to meet with Wickham, a second man came into the room. "Mr. Darcy? Which of these ladies is Miss Lydia Bennet?"

"I am," Lydia said, stepping forward. "Mr. Wickham asked for me."

Mr. Darcy made introductions. "My solicitor, Mr. Hart..."

After exchanging courtesies, Lydia asked, "How is he?"

"As well as can be expected. He refuses to open the curtains of the guest room where he is installed. Mr. Pritchard was concerned he might run, but I think he is too frightened."

"But not of me?" Darcy asked.

"He muttered something about the devil you know."

Elizabeth said, "We would like to speak with Mr. Wickham as soon as possible."

"And you are Miss Lydia's sister?"

"Yes."

Mr. Darcy said, "Miss Bennet has a practical mind and a familiarity with Mr. Wickham's machinations. As such, it was necessary she joined us."

A practical mind? It was almost a compliment from Mr. Darcy, but best not to put much stock in it. He probably meant she was not a ninny who was easily seduced.

A housemaid entered, carrying a tray with bread, sliced meat, and tea.

Elizabeth stomach growled.

Mr. Darcy said, "Eat. Mr. Wickham can wait a few minutes longer."

Lydia looked prepared to argue the point, but then her stomach rumbled too, and she took some food. After eating, they followed Mr. Darcy to his library.

The curtains were shut. Wax candles gave the room a warm air. Elizabeth was struck by Mr. Darcy's wealth to use so many candles and not one paraffin lantern.

"Where is Mr. Wickham?" Lydia asked, looking around the room.

"Mr. Pritchard will bring him down."

The solicitor handed Mr. Darcy a thick packet of papers.

"Miss Bennet," Mr. Darcy said, beckoning Elizabeth over. "Is this your father's handwriting?"

Elizabeth flipped through the first few sheets. Many were in her own handwriting, and Elizabeth said, "These were from my father's study."

"Let me see them," Lydia asked. Elizabeth handed over a pair of the more innocuous pages. Lydia looked over them, and her lips tightened.

"They also found this with Mr. Wickham," Mr. Hart said, and Elizabeth recognized Miss Darcy's letter. "He carried it in his breast pocket."

Mr. Darcy's face flushed a vivid red, the same color as when he had spotted Mr. Wickham at the Meryton assembly. He put the letter in his pocket.

Mr. Wickham was brought in. He wore a simple gray jacket and rumpled cravat. Though he flashed Lydia a dazzling smile, Elizabeth recognized a deep tension within the man. He glanced first at Mr. Darcy and then Elizabeth, who was holding the stolen papers from her father's study.

Lydia said, "Mr. Wickham, please tell us you had nothing to do with our father's injury. I cannot believe you would be so cruel, and to lie to me about it.

"I never meant to hurt you in any way, Miss Lydia," Mr. Wickham said.

"Well, you did hurt her," Elizabeth cut in. "You hurt her and us when you took these papers from my father's study."

"Your father should not have been there. You cannot understand the danger I am in. We are in. I meant no harm."

"And you clubbed my father upon the side of the head with, what was it, the paperweight our uncle sent us from Germany when we were children?"

"Miss Lydia," Mr. Wickham said, ignoring Elizabeth. "I asked you here because you are the only one who would believe me. I know I have wronged you, and for that I can only beg your forgiveness. But there are larger forces at play. Forces I've only begun to recognize and understand. We are in great danger."

"Tell us what you know," Mr. Darcy ordered.

"I am here for Miss Lydia's ease. I have wronged her, and her family, and it is with Miss Lydia I must make amends."

"Oh, Mr. Wickham!"

Lydia could not be such a fool as to fall for these inane protestations! Elizabeth squeezed her eyes shut. Of course she would. Lydia had always been shallow, and Mr. Wickham appealed to her vanity. They were of a kind.

"Then tell Miss Lydia what you know," Mr. Darcy said, tapping his two index fingers together. "If you must play this game."

"It is no game. I made a mistake and found myself involved with a treacherous fellow."

"You made a pretense of gambling Pemberley, our childhood home and my inherited estate, and now you suffer the consequences."

"I was manipulated by a master. A murderer, and I believe an agent of the French."

"Is he the one who paid your debts and assured your posting in Hertfordshire?" Mr. Darcy asked.

Which meant Mr. Wickham had intended, all along, to what—insinuate himself somehow in their independent household and steal her and her father's work? He had made good headway with Lydia, so why had he acted so rashly in breaking into their home and assaulting their father?

"You meant to seduce me. Or Lydia. Why?"

"I had no intention of hurting you. I simply wanted a chance at a life. Mr. Darcy is unforgiving, and I am subject, I admit, to certain weaknesses. But when I realized what I had been asked to take and what it meant, I knew I had to stop him."

How dare Mr. Wickham try to put himself forward as the hero! Elizabeth said, "After robbing our home, attacking our father, and getting chased off by Mr. Darcy."

"I went to confront Mr. Smith, and I followed him, hoping to get some idea of his associates. I thought if I could prove myself in this one instance as the brave man I have always wished to be, then I would make myself worthy of love." His eyes were shining as he sat, back erect, his gaze only for Lydia, the gullible fool. "But Mr. Smith instead attempted to take my life. He is a dangerous man. One who you all must take care to protect yourselves from."

Lydia clapped her hands together. "Mr. Wickham, you are worthy of love. You were brave to confront him, and risk your own life, for the sake of us!"

Elizabeth doubted Mr. Wickham had done any such thing for anyone other than himself. But he did seem afraid.

"This Mr. Smith, what did he reveal to you of his plans?"

"He addressed none of it directly," Mr. Wickham said. "I had only wished to warn you, to warn Miss Lydia."

"If he said nothing, then you are of no use to us," Mr. Darcy said. He waved to his butler. "Have a constable called."

"No!" Mr. Wickham jumped to his feet, his gaze darting to the door. "They will kill me. He will send someone to kill me."

"If you know nothing," Elizabeth said, "then why would this Mr. Smith, or anyone, wish to kill you?"

Mr. Wickham threaded his fingers through his hair at the base of his temple. "I know because he has tried. He used a ring, a silver ring, heavy and old. When he grabbed for me, a needle sprang from the bottom. He leapt at me with a murderous guise, his teeth bared and eyes of a monster. The needle, it must have been poisoned."

"A needle?" Elizabeth's breath caught. "Are you certain?"

"As sure as my life. It was by God's grace I escaped that alley and found my way to your man, Darcy."

"Where is Mr. Smith now?" Elizabeth asked.

Mr. Wickham gave the address of the boarding house. "The landlady was Mrs. Finch."

Mr. Hart went pale. "Are you certain that is her name?"

"Yes. He will have fled from there, knowing I knew where he was staying."

"Mrs. Finch passed on. It was in this morning's paper."

A sick certainty settled in Elizabeth's stomach. "Was it apoplexy?" she asked.

"Yes."

Elizabeth had no doubt should they go to the place, whatever records the landlady had kept of Mr. Smith's references and payments would be missing.

Mr. Wickham, at the least, had the grace to look ill. "Why would he kill her? She had done nothing to him." He lowered his head, covering his mouth and nose with his hands. His shoulders shook as he took two deep breaths.

"He plans to hurt the Regent. Is that what he told you?"

Mr. Wickham gave a start. He looked up, eyes wide, and lowered his hands. "Mr. Smith said nothing of his plans but..." Wickham breathed in through his teeth and shook his head. "Smith had an invitation for the Regent's ball. Oh Lord, that's why he killed her!"

"The autumn masque!" Lydia exclaimed. "It has been all over the London papers for weeks.

Only the most esteemed and beautiful and wealthy will attend. How could someone as despicable as this man you speak of get a ticket?"

"Money," Mr. Hart said. "It is open to all who can pay."

"Can you identify this Mr. Smith?" Elizabeth asked.

"No. He wears disguises. And if he sees me, he will kill me for certain. You have what I know. Take it to the constables, or Miss Bennet can write to her father's friends at the minister's office."

"The ball is in two days," Lydia said. "Do you think they can cancel it in time, Lizzie?"

Elizabeth shook her head. "Even if my father were here, all we have as proof is Mr. Darcy's letter and the word of a liar. Perhaps if we had more time, but..."

"The Regent has guards," Mr. Wickham said. "We must put our trust in the Almighty that no harm will come to him. God Save the King."

"Mr. Wickham," Lydia pleaded. "Surely you can do something. You have seen the ring. You can identify it. And if this Mr. Smith plans to kill Prince George, then he would have to get close to him. You have said you wish to become a better man. I am begging you to try."

Lydia might be a fool and a ninny, but her words were true, and for a painful moment, Elizabeth allowed herself to hope her sister's tearful blue eyes and trembling lips might sway the blackguard. Lydia took three steps to Wickham and looked up at him. "I know you wish to reform yourself and become the man you were meant to be. Please, Mr. Wickham, help us. Do it for our love!"

Mr. Wickham was silent. Elizabeth's hand clenched, and though she was smaller and weaker, and had never, despite many temptations, hit a man, her fury was such she did not care about pain or propriety. Mr. Wickham, in his cowardice, betrayed their country and her sister. But Elizabeth had no means to force him to develop courage or a conscience.

Rings were common, especially at a costumed ball where everyone would glitter with real and imagined finery. Even with Mr. Wickham there to help identify Mr. Smith, more likely than not they would fail. Without Mr. Wickham, what did they have? Just a ring among hundreds of rings.

"Do what you want with him," Elizabeth said. Maybe she could find one of her father's contacts and convince him, somehow, of the threat they faced.

Lydia sobbed.

Mr. Darcy said, "If that is your answer, Mr. Wickham, we will call for a constable and have you sent for trial. A public announcement will be made, and we shall see what happens from that point."

Mr. Darcy was brilliant! A public announcement would put Mr. Wickham in the spotlight. If Mr. Smith wanted him dead, he would make an attempt at the jail. The color drained from Mr. Wickham's face as he recognized the true threat in Mr. Darcy's words.

Mr. Darcy added, "We shall also make certain to publish your confession. It may be seen as the ravings of a desperate man flailing to escape justice, but if there is truth in your words, there will, at the least, be a record of what you witnessed."

Lydia, bereft, had begun crying in earnest, her nose an unattractive red and her eyes puffing up. Mr. Wickham reached for her.

"Miss Lydia. Dear Miss Lydia, do not cry. Fear freezes a man's soul, but love revitalizes it. Your words, your sincere faith in me, give me strength. I will help you. Help us."

Lydia lifted her chin, and she wiped her nose with her sleeve as she smiled. "Mr. Wickham! I knew it! I told Lizzie you love me and love is the strongest of all forces. We shall go together, and I will stand at your side, and you will have nothing to fear."

"Then it is agreed," Mr. Darcy said in a far more measured tone. "We shall all attend."

The momentary relief Elizabeth had felt at Mr. Wickham's agreement was overwhelmed by the realization that neither she nor Lydia had money to spare for a ticket to the ball nor any costume. Elizabeth said, "Lydia, we must leave this to Mr. Darcy and Mr. Wickham. We cannot impose upon Mr. Darcy to fund us. While our uncle will wish to help, making the attempt will unduly strain him. We shall have to trust our presence, in spirit, is enough to bolster these men in their endeavors."

"Lizzie—!" Lydia started.

Mr. Wickham, his expression grave, said, "Without Miss Lydia at my side, I do not know if I will be strong enough to do what must be done."

Mr. Wickham, the cad, would do anything to avoid his own duties.

Mr. Darcy said, "I will see to your tickets and dress, Miss Bennet. Miss Lydia."

"You will!" Lydia jumped to her feet and hopped once on her toes. "You are the most wonderful man! Lizzie may not find you in any way worthy of approbation, but you have made me the happiest woman in all of London!"

"Lydia!"

But Lydia was too occupied with chattering at Mr. Wickham, who occasionally responded with a nod or a meaningless syllable. Elizabeth had never been more embarrassed in her entire life. "Mr. Darcy—"

Mr. Darcy bowed. "Miss Bennet, I must see to our preparations. The carriage will take you and your sister to your uncle's, and I will send word for when your fitting is scheduled."

28

Mr. Darcy could not keep his eyes from Miss Elizabeth. Her dress and sheer presence stood in contrast to Mr. Darcy's dark suit and white half-mask that only covered his eyes. She wore her glorious dark hair up in an intricate weave of braids and curls. Laurel leaves nestled in her hair and she wore pearls from her ears and her neck.

The cut was not improper though it revealed the twin rise of her décolletage. Draped in the Grecian style, the dress highlighted the slimness of Miss Elizabeth's waist and curve of her hips. Her mask's expression, white and framed at the edges with filigree gold and black felt, was severe, a contrast to Miss Elizabeth's expressive countenance.

Miss Elizabeth held the mask in her right hand and took Mr. Darcy's arm with her left to alight from the carriage.

Lydia's words, "Lizzie may not find you in any way worthy of approbation," rang in Mr. Darcy's mind. To think, just a fortnight past, Mr. Darcy had been fearful of attracting her romantic attention. Now, he regretted his cold behavior.

Miss Elizabeth smiled up at Mr. Darcy through long lashes and his chest clenched as he struggled to maintain a neutral expression. She held him in no approbation, and he would not force himself upon her, neither in word nor deed. They were here for a purpose, and it was not each other.

Wickham followed next, draped in a black domino that covered his body and head. He held to his face a white mask that made him look very much like a ghost. If Mr. Wickham dressed to be ignored, Miss Lydia, who stepped out next, strove to be seen. She wore a wide hooped skirt supporting multiple layers of pink, blue, and green, all trimmed with gold lace. Lydia's hair styling was elaborate, with pearls braided into her fair tresses. A locket rested above the curve of her breasts, which for modesty, were covered by a lace shawl.

"Am I not the picture of a Russian doll?" Lydia

asked, resting her fingers on Mr. Wickham's forearm.

Wickham stared down at her, his gaze settling too long on the locket or more the cream skin beneath. His voice was muffled as he said, "You are, my lady, the very bloom of youth and beauty."

Lydia giggled and brought the mask over her face.

Mrs. Hill, dressed as a country matron with puffed sleeves and feathers in her hair, followed behind the ladies. Having a housekeeper chaperone Miss Elizabeth and Miss Lydia to this event was already straining all bounds of propriety. If the cause was anything less than the kingdom, Mr. Darcy would have refused. As it was, he wished he could knock some sense into Wickham. He hated how his once-foster brother pulled the strings of Miss Lydia's heart as though she was the doll she pretended to be and not a sadly misled young girl.

After they finished this, Mr. Darcy resolved to pay Mr. Wickham whatever he required to go on his way and leave the Bennet family alone. No matter how Miss Lydia supported Wickham's vanity, he would cast her aside for a large enough sum. Mr. Darcy hated paying it, but better to pay than to cause Miss Elizabeth and her family more pain.

The masquerade ball was held in the King's Theater. Mr. Darcy, Mr. Wickham, Mrs. Hill and the Bennet sisters joined the line to be announced into the ball. The air outside was chilly and damp, and Miss Elizabeth clutched her red velvet shawl around her shoulders.

Mr. Darcy was grateful they were soon allowed entry.

Though the theater generally showed opera and other musical performances, tonight the benches had been pushed aside to make room for tables of food and drink and to leave space for the attendees to mingle with each other before dancing.

The decorations thoroughly captivated Miss Lydia. She peered up at the private boxes and exclaimed, "They have gold frames! I had read so, but to see it in person... How grand!"

Though Miss Elizabeth was more reserved in her reactions, she too, holding her mask in her right hand, looked about, her lips slightly parted. "So many candles," she breathed. "It is remarkable."

Mr. Darcy took a step closer to her side. "Perhaps you should ask your sister where she expects the Regent might enter."

"He is not here?"

"It is but half eleven," Mr. Darcy said. Though

Mr. Darcy did not keep up with the habits of royalty, his aunt did and Lady Catherine had sharp words for those who kept late hours. "Sadly," she often remarked, "such things cannot be helped at court."

"But there are already so many people," Miss Elizabeth said.

Darcy looked back towards the end of the line, and then ahead of them again. Miss Elizabeth, for all of her brilliance, was still a young lady from the country. She would not realize how well attended a city ball might be, especially one hosted by the Regent.

Finally, they reached the head of the line and were announced as a party. Mr. Fitzwilliam Darcy, Miss Elizabeth Bennet, Mr. George Wickham, Miss Lydia Bennet, and Mrs. Mary Hill.

As Miss Elizabeth started down the stairs, she stumbled. She reached out, and Mr. Darcy steadied her. The firm grip of her hand on his arm sent shivers through him. Her mask was too severe, but the woman behind it captivated Darcy, an infatuation he now could not help but acknowledge.

"Excuse me, Mr. Darcy," she said as they descended the stairs.

"No trouble."

"Darcy!"

Mr. Darcy froze, looking towards the voice. A man in priestly vestments, his face chubby and his belly exaggerated by padding beneath his robes, waved to Mr. Darcy as he strode over.

"Mr. Bragg," Darcy said, and his school chum grinned.

"Formal as always, Darcy." Bragg grinned. "I heard them call out your name. This young lady, Miss Bennet, is not your sister."

Still on Wickham's arm, Lydia giggled. "No, Lizzie is *my* sister."

Mr. Wickham kept his head bowed and the domino over his face. Mr. Bragg cocked his head at Wickham and pursed his lips. He glanced back at Darcy and Miss Elizabeth.

Mr. Darcy walked a fine line, having Miss Elizabeth on his arm with no stated promises between them. It was the worst luck his college acquaintance had seen him. He made quick introductions, and then before Bragg could engage any of the others in conversation, said, "If you will excuse us for a moment, Miss Bennet, Miss Lydia," Mr. Darcy said. He bowed.

"Darcy—!"

"Your shipping project..." he whispered in Bragg's ear.

Mr. Bragg brightened. "I had thought you disinterested!" he said. "Come." He talked rapidly about Chinese porcelain. Darcy kept his gaze fixed on Wickham, lest the man try to run. Though as tightly as Miss Lydia clung to him, Darcy doubted the man would make a clean escape.

"Darcy, you have not heard a word, have you?"

"I… Perhaps if you were to explain it again?"

"Over a cigar and whiskey away from the ladies." Mr. Bragg laughed. "She is lovely. I never thought I would see the day when you showed special interest in a lady. Are congratulations in order?"

Miss Elizabeth held him in no approbation, but she was under his protection. He could not let a feckless dreamer like Mr. Bragg attempt to court her. Mr. Darcy ventured, "Miss Bennet is chaperoned. Any agreements are between myself and Miss Bennet, you understand."

"Not yet then." Mr. Bragg held a hand out between himself and Mr. Darcy. "Far be it from me to put my nose where it does not belong. But I would not wait so long to make my intentions known if I were in your place. I have never heard of the Bennet family, but any woman who can meet your exacting standards must be a paragon."

Were his standards so high? His own father and Lady Catherine had admonished him to seek a lady worthy of his station. Miss Elizabeth was not a woman of his station, but Mr. Darcy was tired of living for other people's expectations. "Miss Bennet is unique. One might say remarkable."

"Then do not let her get away." Mr. Bragg leaned in. "It is well known the Regent is a romantic. Should she be inclined to accept your proposal, I suspect it would delight Prince George to offer support for your union."

"I will handle affairs between myself and Miss Bennet in the proper manner," Mr. Darcy said firmly.

"Yes. You have always been the sort for a proper manner." Bragg patted Darcy's arm. "Do not despair. She must have an inkling. A man believes his heart a mystery, but a lady always knows."

Had Miss Bennet an inkling of his feelings for her? Her remarks about the folio of theorems he had gifted her seemed to hold a hidden meaning, but Darcy had not allowed himself to hope. Not in the wake of Miss Lydia's statement that Miss Elizabeth had no interest in him. And he had not made the best impression at first. He had not wished to, and whatever feelings he had, the eccentric ways that so compelled him also made Miss Elizabeth an unsuitable wife.

Mr. Darcy stared out over the assembled lords and ladies, men and women of wealth and good lineage, and imagined any of them on his arm. His stomach twisted. Then there was Miss Bingley who had all the trappings of accomplishment. He felt ill.

"Nervous? This lady is someone of note to make Mr. Darcy nervous. Fear not. Show her what is in your heart, and all will be well."

Mask after mask. Customer costume, all hiding the truth beneath. Was that not an accurate statement for all of their lives?

Mr. Bragg mercifully caught sight of a young, elaborately coiffed milkmaid and said, "The next set will begin soon. If fortune smiles, her dance card is not yet filled." He nodded to Darcy and said, "I wish you the best, Darcy. Be bold. The moment is yours, but only if you take it." Mr. Bragg made his way back into the crowd.

Darcy stood a moment longer. Be bold. Perhaps Bragg had the right of it. Miss Elizabeth did not appear to be close with her sister Lydia. Further, Miss Elizabeth had no issues with speaking her mind. If Mr. Darcy asked, she would tell him plainly what she thought of his suit. In the worst case, he would know how she felt.

A shiver passed over Mr. Darcy. The hair on his arms rose, and the back of his neck tingled. Was someone watching him?

Mr. Darcy glanced around. A man dressed as a jester in wine red, gold, and blue, caught his attention. He wore a white mask with rouged cheeks and exaggerated eyebrows and lips. His fingers glinted with a medley of gold and silver rings glittering with jewels, though whether they were paste or real Mr. Darcy had no way of knowing.

Mr. Darcy tried to catch his gaze, and the jester took a step back, raising two gloved fingers to his cheek. Reginald had done the same thing when startled.

It was impossible. Reginald was dead, and the gesture of raising two fingers to one's cheek was common enough. If Reginald were alive, he and the man would be of a height. And then there was the issue of the rings. Logic told Darcy to ignore the signs. His brother was dead, and many men and women at this ball wore rings.

And yet...

Hope and fear twisted together in a horrifying

knot in Darcy's gut. His skin was cold. He would make a fool of himself, but if he did not attempt to speak with the jester, Darcy would always wonder. He called out, "Reggie!"

The jester froze. It was only for a second. The jester shook his head, but as Darcy moved towards him, the jester backed away until he pushed himself into a group of other costumed men who called after him for his rudeness.

Mr. Darcy gave chase.

"Mr. Darcy!" Miss Elizabeth shouted from behind him.

Darcy's heart pounded in his ears. The joy at the possibility of his brother being alive was overwhelmed by a more salient and terrifying fact. If his brother was alive, what was he doing here? Why had he lied to his family? Was he in the employ of the man who had attempted to kill Mr. Wickham and planned to kill Prince George?

29

"Is this not the most wondrous theater, Lizzie?" Lydia went on. "After we have gained the favor of the Regent, perhaps he might show us his box. I have read each of the boxes has a statue in the center, and they are gilded on the inside and out."

Elizabeth listened with half an ear to her sister while keeping a sharp eye on Mr. Darcy. The costumed priest seemed jovial enough. Elizabeth was not yet adept in reading Mr. Darcy's expressions, but she sensed a definite discomfort as the man whispered something and clapped Mr. Darcy in a most personal way on the shoulder.

"When the Regent arrives, I believe they will announce him, though cannot know whether he will come to the common entrance or another door. Oh! This is so exciting!"

"We are not here to gawk but to protect the Regent's life," Elizabeth whispered harshly.

"Yes. Yes. I know. But the Regent has not arrived, so there is no need to be grim and somber for the sport of it. Leave that to Mr. Darcy."

"Considering all Mr. Darcy has done to help us, his seriousness is both well warranted and appreciated."

Mr. Darcy's friend walked away, but instead of returning to them, Mr. Darcy stared out over the ball. Whatever the other man had said had upset Mr. Darcy, and Elizabeth wished she were allowed the familiarity to offer comfort. Then, he shouted something and set off at a brisk walk into the crowd.

He had seen something? The poisoner? If so, he would not face that danger alone. Elizabeth, forgetting propriety, grabbed Lydia's hand. "Come!"

"Miss Lydia!" Mr. Wickham shouted and grabbed Lydia, pulling her from Elizabeth. Elizabeth, afraid of losing sight of Mr. Darcy, let go of her sister and pushed into the crowd. Mr. Darcy's costume, by virtue of not truly being a costume but instead formal attire in black and white with only a simple white mask over his eyes, was at least easy to keep track of. But a group of revelers, dressed in exaggerated Eastern garb—red turbans and shawls for the ladies and similar headwear in gold and blue on the gentlemen—stepped between Elizabeth and Mr. Darcy. By the time Elizabeth elbowed her way through the group, Mr. Darcy was gone.

Elizabeth, panicked, looked back the way she had come, but with the press of people, she could see neither her sister nor Mr. Wickham.

So many people. Her heart pounded.

"Miss?"

Elizabeth turned towards the voice, dropping into a curtsy. It was the false priest Mr. Darcy had been speaking with earlier.

"Miss Bennet is it?"

"Yes. You are a friend of Mr. Darcy's? Have you seen him?"

"Earlier. Mr. Darcy is a good man."

It spoke well of a man when his friends gave approbation in his absence. Elizabeth said, "I know."

"Will you accept his proposal?"

"Excuse me?" Was that what he and Mr. Darcy had been discussing? Mr. Darcy intended to propose! Here? *He will ask your hand in marriage.* Elizabeth shook her head. "Who are you to ask such a thing?"

"If not, tell me now. I will speak with him to spare him the embarrassment of his asking."

"Any conversations concerning matrimony are between me and Mr. Darcy, sir."

"My apologies," the man said. He ran his hand over his overly stiff hair. "Please forget I asked. My curiosity gets the better of me. It is one of my greatest failings."

Elizabeth felt a moment of sympathy for the man. She admired Mr. Darcy, and to her shock, she realized she would not reject a courtship. But to speak of proposals so soon? Until recently, she had despised Mr. Darcy. And with the Regent's life in danger, it was neither the time nor place to ask nor answer such questions. Mr. Darcy could not intend to propose, no matter what he had told his friend.

"My sister," Elizabeth lied, waving towards the punch table. "Excuse me."

"Yes." The man bowed. "My apologies."

Elizabeth fled. When she reached the tables, an older woman holding a mask in her hand grimaced at the selection. She complained to her companion, "The Regent in attendance, and no shellfish!"

At the next table was negus. Elizabeth took a glass and looked back the way she came. Mr. Darcy's priest friend was gone, thank all that was holy.

"Miss. I have no intention to be forward, but are you lost?"

Everyone at the ball was formally introduced, else politeness would forbid anyone from asking all but their closest acquaintances to dance. Still, Elizabeth was struck again by how forward the people were in London. This was the second young gentleman to approach her in minutes! Perhaps it was the masks.

"I am waiting for my sister," she responded, shortly.

This young man was dressed as a jester. He wore a brightly colored mask over his eyes, and his hair was hidden by a large piebald hat. From the top arced five points with alternating silver and gold balls sewn to the end of each.

Unlike Elizabeth's mask which only had holes for the eyes, the jester's had a slit between the lips. Instead of being held in place, it was secured to his face by a pair of ties that hooked over the ears. When he spoke, the mask muffled his voice, and Elizabeth had to lean in to make out his words.

"And the young gentleman you entered with? Mr. Fitzwilliam Darcy?"

"I had no idea Mr. Darcy was so popular in London," Elizabeth said. "Why, everyone I meet seems to be his friend!" Elizabeth tried not to betray her apprehension as she raised the glass of punch to her lips, taking a sip.

"We were close as children. He is reserved in his temperament, but no one has a truer heart."

"Who are you?" Elizabeth demanded. "Mr. Darcy often keeps his own counsel, and he has made no mention of you."

The jester stepped closer to Elizabeth. "Forgive me," he said. " I have not spoken with Fitz for over a year, and it seems in that time he has made some significant changes."

Changes? Elizabeth recognized she ought to send this young gentleman on his way, but her curiosity was sparked. "Mr. Darcy and I have been acquainted for but a short time."

"That is surprising. He seems quite comfortable with you."

He did?

"To be frank, I have never seen him show a special interest in any young lady. He had his usual boyhood fancies, but even in those, he spoke and comported himself with restraint. Our aunt influenced him too well when he was young."

Our aunt? This jester was a relative of Mr. Darcy? Or perhaps the jester was related to the mysterious Lord Cunningham? Elizabeth said, "You have the advantage of me. You speak of Mr. Darcy's childhood, but he has never spoken of you. What is your name, sir?"

"My lady Artemis, I would not presume to strip your mask. Please allow me the same favor."

"Yet you ask questions of and intimate a blood relationship to Mr. Darcy, my..." What was he to her? Someone who stirred her emotions too much for propriety, who defended her and kept her secrets even as he sometimes drove her to murderous rage.

"Interesting. Mr. Darcy has not made his intentions known?"

"What has he told you of his intentions?"

"Nothing. We have not spoken in almost a year, as I have said."

"He has no intentions." Enough with this conversation, spinning and spinning but going nowhere. Elizabeth lowered the mask from her face. "My name is Elizabeth Bennet. Either do me the courtesy of an introduction or leave, sir."

To Elizabeth's shock, the jester laughed. His

mask muffled the sound, but his shoulders shook and the sound of his mirth was more than evident. "Now I understand. You are a match for him. Fitz must be in fits!" The jester slipped a finger beneath his mask to wipe his eyes.

This jester had to be telling the truth about being related to Mr. Darcy. How else could he incite Elizabeth to such an immediate rage? "That is a jest, sir, not an introduction."

"Raghnall. My friends call me Raghnall."

Scottish was not the preferred language for codes, though Elizabeth had deciphered a few in that language. She recognized the name. Raghnall. Reginald. Reginald Darcy. Impossible. He was dead, except...

"Mr. Darcy," Elizabeth said.

Reginald Darcy froze. "He told you."

Elizabeth saw red. To blazes with this man, to lie and cause such pain to his family. And now, to treat the entire affair as a joke. "They believe you dead."

"Georgie knows the truth."

"It has been near half a year. They mourned. They still mourn."

"Georgiana keeps her own counsel, and Fitz, he will pick up and move onward as he always does—"

"You believed a letter about butterflies and plots would be enough assuage your sister's fears, and that your brother would pick up and carry on with no harm from your 'passing'? You are the worst. You broke their hearts!"

"Butterflies? She told you? My sister would never—!" Reginald took a step towards her. "Miss Bennet—"

"Stay away from her!" From her left, Mr. Darcy's voice cut over the sound of the other revelers. She expected him to be red with fury, but he was pale, and his hands shook. "Miss Elizabeth, please, look at his fingers. Do not let him touch you."

Elizabeth looked. Reginald Darcy wore rings on every finger, a mix of gold and silver, all glittering with paste jewels.

"Fitz, what are you on about?" Reginald looked at his brother. "I would never come between you and the lady you've chosen. She has spirit. I like her."

"Reggie, I cannot protect you from your actions."

"I never asked that of you, Fitz. You have always taken too much on yourself."

"Your brother cannot be Mr. Smith," Elizabeth

said. "Mr. Wickham would have known him."

"Reggie...." Mr. Darcy's voice cracked.

"Mr. Smith?" Ignoring his brother, Reginald turned back to Elizabeth. "Smith is a common name."

"The letter you sent to your sister, was it a warning?"

"I cannot speak of this here. Miss Bennet, you have an astute mind. If you have read my letter, then you know why I am here. This is but one of Chrysalide's butterflies. A poisonous one."

Chrysalide on our shores.

"You know of his plans."

"What plans?" Mr. Darcy interjected. "Elizabeth, you need to step away from my brother."

"It was the cipher within the cipher," Elizabeth tried to explain. "But none of this explains what you did to your family."

"If the French knew I was alive, they would know I had warned the crown, and then we would have no chance to stop them. Please, I know I have done little to earn your trust, but you must believe me."

"Announcing the Prince Regent," the master of ceremonies' voice boomed over the gathering. As he spoke, the ballroom hushed. "George the Fourth."

Elizabeth looked at the staircase. The Regent was not there.

From the stage, the musicians played the first bars of "God Save the King."

"Oh!" Someone gasped and pointed towards the stage. The dancers had been cleared away, and flanked by a pair of guards, the Regent stepped into the center. He leaned on an ornate cane, limping from what appeared a recent injury. Even so, his carriage was erect, and he managed a smooth bow. He was dressed in full regimentals, bright red and glittering with gold braid and jewels. A thin mask of bright red covered his eyes. The mask was the same color as his elaborate uniform.

"Excuse me," Reginald bowed.

A ring. A needle. A prince.

Elizabeth grabbed Reginald's arm. "Stop."

Reginald looked back at Elizabeth. "Miss Bennet, unhand me. It is a matter of life or death."

"Take off your rings," Elizabeth said. "Give them to Mr. Darcy."

"What is this?"

"A matter of life or death. Please. For your brother's sake if not mine."

"If you insist." Reginald held out his free hand. "Darcy, come here and take these."

Elizabeth's heart pounded. If Elizabeth was wrong, and Reginald was working for Mr. Smith... What if Reginald triggered the poison ring? Would Reginald murder his own brother? Elizabeth wanted to believe in Reginald, and her heart bled for Mr. Darcy. Bad enough when his brother was dead. Darcy could mourn a dead brother. But a living traitor?

Mr. Darcy pulled the rings off, one by one.

"Now, if you are satisfied, time is short. There are guards in the boxes, but as soon as the Regent begins to mingle with the crowd, which he will even with his twisted ankle as our prince loves a party, he will be vulnerable. We cannot trust anyone."

"Mr. Smith has a ring with a poison needle inside," Elizabeth told him. "He will have to get close."

"It is unfortunate my brother has snatched you up, Miss Bennet, else I would certainly begin a courtship." With that, Mr. Reginald Darcy twisted his wrist with a sudden jerk, and Elizabeth lost her grip. Tapping two fingers to the side of his temple in a mock wave, he bowed and slipped into the flow of masked revelers making their way towards the stage.

30

---

*R*eginald, alive. And Miss Elizabeth…

A painful longing burst out of Darcy's every pore. Was this love? Mr. Darcy had never given much thought to love beyond the familial, which he was obligated to protect. Mr. Bingley stepped in and out of love like dipping buff naked into a series of cool ponds in the dead of summer. Mr. Darcy had never felt the urge to stand naked in spirit before anyone. It was too risky, and Darcy abhorred unnecessary risks.

For the entirety of his life, Mr. Darcy had devoted himself to tempering the emotional fits of others, and now he was caught in one himself. He should have been relieved his brother was not a traitor to the crown. Instead, heart-clenching terror lingered. If Reginald had been the traitor he appeared, he could have killed Miss Elizabeth. Her observations, her jests, her quick wit and even her tempers, in a few moments, gone.

Reginald bowed and made his way towards the Regent, and Miss Elizabeth made to follow. How could she?

Though it was well outside the bounds of proper behavior, he grabbed her wrist. "No."

"Unhand me!"

So Miss Elizabeth could throw herself into danger?

Mr. Darcy had made efforts all of his life to protect those he loved. He could not fail her. But he had already failed. He had covered for Mr. Wickham's flaws to spare his father. Because of that, Georgiana had been blinded to Wickham's faults with near-disastrous consequences.

Darcy had tried to protect Georgiana by hiding their brother's "last words" and instead hidden from her the fact Reginald lived, and worse, hidden from this Lord Cunningham the plot they now faced. His own brother, stifled by Mr. Darcy's admonitions towards proper behavior, had gone abroad and now was what—a spy for their own forces?

Miss Elizabeth struggled to escape his grasp.

All of Mr. Darcy's efforts had driven those he loved further away. He could not make the same mistake with Miss Elizabeth. His admiration for her was far outside the bounds of propriety, and he was glad of it. He could not hide her away and pretend he was keeping her safe by doing so.

Mr. Darcy said, "Not without me. It is not proper, and that is not safe, but if you will have me, I will stand at your side."

Miss Elizabeth stopped. It seemed all the tension went out of her and she looked back at him, her eyes wide. "You will?"

"Yes. Forever. If you will have me."

"Is this a proposal?"

"I—" A proposal. In public. Mr. Darcy wondered how he could be so brave and so foolish. "Yes."

A glorious smile blossomed over Miss Elizabeth's face and Mr. Darcy could not breathe. The Regent, the ball, everything faded until there was only Miss Elizabeth Bennet. She said, "Ask me again."

"Are you accepting?" She had to accept. If not, the shards of Mr. Darcy's broken heart would slice him to pieces.

Miss Elizabeth said, "Of course I am accepting, but you must ask me twice."

How could Mr. Darcy resist this wonderful, brilliant, and mad woman with whom, against all rationality, he had fallen in love?

"Will you be my wife?"

"Yes."

To the devil with proper behavior. Mr. Darcy pulled her close, using his free hand to cradle the back of her head, and then, in full view of everyone, he kissed her.

Someone gasped.

Elizabeth pressed herself to his chest and the heat of her lips sent shivers through him. Now, she could not change her mind. Or demand a third proposal, which frankly, after the first two, he would not manage.

Applause rang out around them.

"Congratulations, Darcy." It was Bragg, and when he clapped Mr. Darcy on the back as though they were brothers, Mr. Darcy couldn't even find the will to slight him. "Good man! I knew you would not make a liar out of me! And you have caught his attention."

Mr. Bragg gestured towards the stage, and a low

murmur set up through the group surrounding them.

"A proposal!" The Regent's voice, amplified by his placement on the stage and the shape of the amphitheater, carried out over the revelers.

"I said the Regent was a romantic," Bragg whispered to Darcy. "I hope you listen when I send out a letter about this new project. It promises to make both you and your fiancée that much wealthier."

Bragg was a gossip who had his thumb in every scheme, but as the others around them parted to allow Miss Elizabeth and Darcy a path towards the stage, he could not doubt Bragg had the right of this.

Miss Elizabeth clutched his arm, and Mr. Darcy felt her shaking. She held the mask up to her face again.

Mr. Darcy, wanting to reassure her, whispered, "It will be quick."

Or at least so he hoped. Their plan had been to stop the assassin, if there was an assassin, but Mr. Darcy had not considered how getting close enough to protect the Regent might expose himself and Miss Elizabeth.

Mr. Darcy and Miss Elizabeth were presented to the Regent. She gave a profound curtsy, her gaze lowered and her knees nearly touching the floor in her genuflection. Mr. Darcy gave an equally low and respectful bow.

The Prince Regent was flanked on either side by four bodyguards, each soberly dressed with the only gestures to costume a half mask, much like Darcy's, that covered their eyes.

"Your Royal Highness," Elizabeth and Darcy said in unison.

The Regent was quite handsome, tall and fair-haired, though this close it was clear that fine tailoring and a tight corset hid a tendency towards fat. Mr. Darcy had seen older gentleman, and a few notorious rakes, employ the same obfuscations, though Darcy's own father had turned his nose down on such tricks. "A regular habit of exercise and restraint from gluttony will earn the respect of your tenants and save you a fortune in tailoring," Mr. Darcy's father often advised.

Mr. Darcy's father had not raised his son to be a fool however, and Darcy kept such admonitions to himself.

One of the bodyguards whispered in the Regent's ear, and the Regent addressed them, "My felicitations, Mr. Darcy. Miss Bennet."

"Thank you, your Royal Highness," Miss Elizabeth said. Mr. Darcy had never heard her so subdued.

"I can see you are well suited to each other," the Prince Regent said. Though the Regent's breath smelled of wine, his expression was measured and his manner charming as he spoke. The Regent glanced down at his ankle. "I alas overstepped myself was it one...no...two weeks ago, showing off my Highland Fling..." He sighed, and said, "Mr. Darcy, Miss. Bennet, if you would do the honor of leading the next dance in my stead."

"It would be my honor, your Royal Highness," Mr. Darcy said.

"Yes, your Royal Highness," Miss Elizabeth said, curtsying again. "Thank you.

Mr. Darcy held out his arm, and the musicians began warming up their instruments. Elizabeth smiled at Darcy, and then her face lost all color. Though there was a wide berth of space around the Regent, other partygoers were coming and going. Mr. Darcy noted his brother, still in jester costume, standing a few feet off, speaking with another man in an elaborate turban and mask.

One of the bodyguards moved.

Miss Elizabeth threw herself forward, appearing

to trip on her skirt as she flailed her hands towards one of the bodyguards.

The guard wore a heavy, silver ring.

"Miss," the Prince Regent swayed on his cane as he stepped towards Miss Elizabeth. That movement, along with Miss Elizabeth's distraction, made the false bodyguard hesitate, and Reginald grabbed him. He slipped his arm around the bodyguard's waist and did something to the guard's wrist. The man grunted, and the ring fell. Before any of the other guards could hamper Reginald's movements, he said something to them, and they closed around the Regent while Reginald led the false bodyguard way.

The entire thing happened so quickly, Mr. Darcy doubted anyone else besides himself and Miss Elizabeth had even noticed.

"Miss Elizabeth," Mr. Darcy steadied his fiancée. She had adroitly regained her balance. "Thank you," she murmured. "I am ashamed to be so clumsy."

One of the other guards whispered something to the Regent, and the prince nodded. Had they told him of the attempt on his life? If so, the news did not affect the Regent's good mood. He announced, "Mr. Darcy and Miss Bennet will lead us in the next dance."

Mr. Darcy and Miss Elizabeth took their places at the center of the floor.

She rested her hand in his and said, "Your brother saved him."

"*You* saved him."

"It was us. We saved him." The first bars of the minuet began, and Darcy and Elizabeth were swept up in the dance.

EPILOGUE

They left the King's Theatre just before dawn. Elizabeth had danced until her feet hurt. As she and Mr. Darcy were engaged, she could now sit beside him in the carriage. She reveled in the warmth of his thigh against hers, and her heart fluttered as he smiled at her.

They were not fortunate enough to have the carriage to themselves. Lydia and Wickham sat across from her with Mrs. Hill between them, her eyes shut and head nodding to the side as the carriage rumbled through the streets.

"You are so lucky," Lydia said. "To be honored by the Prince. And to have a proposal. To Mr. Darcy! I never guessed he would be so dashing!

When Mr. Wickham asks for my hand, can you prevail upon the Prince to bless our union as well?"

Mr. Wickham said, "Let us not get ahead of ourselves, Miss Lydia."

If only Mr. Wickham would disappear from Lydia's life from this day. Elizabeth had no desire to call Wickham her brother. And though she and her sister were not close, Lydia did not deserve the pain a life married to Wickham would bring. She might not see past his fair hair and handsome features, but Elizabeth did.

Mr. Darcy squeezed Elizabeth's hand. She glanced up at him, and he gave a brief nod. He had some plan for Wickham. Elizabeth closed her eyes, grateful to have him at her side.

Forever.

Lydia said, "Perhaps we can have a double wedding! Would that not be lovely, Mr. Wickham?"

"No," Mr. Darcy and Elizabeth said at the same time.

Lydia looked hurt. Elizabeth, who despite everything loved her sister, said, "I do not wish for you to share your special day with me or anyone."

"Yes, I suppose that is most sensible. After you practically collapsed on the Regent, I am certain he will not attend your wedding in any case."

Elizabeth winced. No matter how hard she tried, she could only understand her sister but so well. Maybe Jane could persuade Lydia to set her infatuation with Wickham aside.

"I think Elizabeth comported herself most properly," Mr. Darcy said. Elizabeth smiled at Mr. Darcy's... Fitzwilliam's... use of her given name.

Elizabeth had known she must marry, and she wished to marry for love, but she had always feared she must sacrifice one for the other. Now, somehow, she had found both.

Though she was breathless at the speed of things, Elizabeth's new future thrilled her. She would have to tell her family, and prepare for a wedding, and there was still Chrysalide. Even if his assassin had been dispatched, as Reginald Darcy had said, Mr. Smith was but one of his butterflies. Chrysalide was still on their shores, a cocoon spawning further menace.

Elizabeth would have to find a way to continue with her father and his work. Her work. Their work. The threats to England would not end with her wedding.

Elizabeth could only pray Mr. Darcy understood that.

Alighting from the carriage at her uncle's home, Elizabeth took Mr. Darcy's arm.

"We must return to Longbourn tomorrow, so I may ask your father's permission for your hand."

"Do not look so nervous, Fitzwilliam," Elizabeth said, trying out the sounds of her husband's given name for the first time. "Once my parents have overcome their shock, they will both delight in welcoming you to our family. I should also like to meet your sister in person. And I pray your brother will return from the dead once more to attend our nuptials. It is the least he can do, as he is the one who brought us together."

Mr. Darcy stopped in front of the Gardiners' door. Lydia and Mrs. Hill had already entered the house. Wickham remained in the carriage.

Elizabeth, suddenly shy, turned to Mr. Darcy. She held the mask at her side. Mr. Darcy had removed his in the carriage, and they stood together without pretense.

"Thank you, Mr. Darcy," Elizabeth said. "I had always wished to marry for love, but love was a cipher that seemed beyond me. You gave me the key. I could not understand at first, but you are what I was searching for."

Mr. Darcy shook his head. "It is you, not I, who

is key. I did not understand or believe in love, but you unlocked my heart. I am the luckiest man in all of England."

He placed his hand over hers and together, as the sun rose through the London fog, they kissed.

The End.

Thank you for reading! I hope you loved reading this book as much as I loved writing it!

If so, I hope you keep your eye out for next book in this series will be titled Mr. Darcy's Enigma. Elizabeth and Mr. Darcy plan their wedding in the midst of family opposition and espionage. It's going to be a wild ride! You can get notified of when *Mr. Darcy's Enigma* is out and also get access to free chapters of the book when **you sign up for my newsletter at violetkingauthor.com.**

Also, if you have a moment to leave a review on this book, that would be an amazing gift. We all read reviews when deciding whether to give a new author a try. Just a sentence or two letting others know how you felt about the book makes a huge difference for whether authors like me can keep writing books. So if you have 2-3 minutes, drop over to wherever you bought this book and let people know what you think of it.

Lastly, if you are interested in learning more about the resources I used to bring this book to life, check out the author's note in the next chapter.

All the best,

Violet

AUTHOR'S NOTE

Mr. Darcy's Cipher was born from the words, "Spies and Prejudice," and from there, I knew I had to write this series.

Much of this book came down to the question: 'how do you write a character who is smarter than you?'

Miss Elizabeth Bennet is much smarter than Ms. Violet King. To write her brilliance, I had to learn A LOT about codes and even attempt a "new to me" form of math to give Miss Bennet the tools she needed to crack the codes and save the Prince Regent.

If you are interested in learning more about the Affine Cipher what's the heck is going on with that triple equals sign, here are some resources on ciphers and modular math, both of which I had to figure out well enough to explain in this book.

Modular Math via the *Khan Academy*: https://www.khanacademy.org/computing/comput er-science/cryptography/modarithmetic/a/what-is-modular-arithmetic

And when that breaks your brain, check out the *Wikipedia* article: https://en.wikipedia.org/wiki/Modular_arithmetic

In addition, it would have been impossible for me to write this book without the amazing, free code cracking resource at https://www.dcode.fr/tools-list#substitution_cipher.

This is a French website but they have an English translated version (which I pointed you to), thank heavens! With the tools on this site, you can create and crack codes without breaking your own brain against them. As someone who is actually pretty terrible at puzzles and puns, I found this resource invaluable both for trying out new codes and also as a jumping off point for more research.

Besides codes and ciphers, for this book, I also spent serious time researching British and French spy craft in the Napoleonic Wars.

Friends and Enemies: The Underground War between Great Britain and France, 1793-1802 - Chapter One – Aims, Acquisition, Analysis and Action: https://www.napoleon-series.org/research/government/british/Espionage/c_espionageChapter1.html

English Secret Agents and Sprawling Continental Espionage--Not 007, but 1812: An interview with historical fiction author M.M. Bennetts http://riftwatcher.blogspot.com/2011/12/english-secret-agents-and-sprawling.html

Unfortunately, one of the other sites I bookmarked on this subject appears to have lost their web hosting, but these are good places to start looking if you're interested in learning more on the topic.

The main thing I gained from this research is that, especially on the British side, espionage was a scattered process. The British Army, Navy and Prime Minister's office all had their own spies. These offices did not communicate well (or often at all) with each other. This gave me plenty of room to take liberties regarding Mr. Bennet's contacts, and of course, Mr. Smith and Chrysalides are pure figments of my imagination.

In addition to the espionage, I discovered some

nifty historical events that were woven into my imagined storyline. For example, I based the Regent's ball off of a real costume ball that took place in the King's Theatre where the Prince Regent attended.

You can read more about this event and costumed Regency Balls at *18th Century Masquerade Balls:*

https://georgianera.wordpress.com/2015/03/19/1 8th-century-masquerade-balls/

In addition, in November 1811, the Prince Regent did sprain his ankle while demonstrating his Highland Fling.

These little bits of history were a delight to learn, and I loved being able to put them into this story.

I hope you enjoyed reading this book as much as I loved writing it! There will be a sequel, Mr. Darcy's Enigma, where Elizabeth and Mr. Darcy face challenges to their relationship while still working to foil Chrysalide's ultimate plan.

Elizabeth and Georgiana will meet, and we will see more of Mr. Reginald Darcy as well. Mr. Darcy's Enigma is being written under the working concept: A Wedding with Espionage. If you are interested in being notified of when Mr. Darcy's Enigma is out, and also getting access to free chapters of the book as I'm writing it, take a moment and sign up for my newsletter at violetkingauthor.com.

ABOUT THE AUTHOR

Violet King is a Pennsylvania native who loves reading and writing Regency romance. She had some Pride and Prejudice plot bunnies that wouldn't leave her be, so she started writing her first JAFF in 2018. Her first book, Mr. Darcy's Cipher, is inspired by her interest in history and the desire to write about a smart, savvy heroine who saves her country while falling in love.

Violet's other interests include drawing and painting, trying specialty teas (she lived in Japan for a few years and is especially picky about Jasmines and Greens,) cuddling her cats, karaoke, and reading, reading, reading! You can learn more about her books and sign up for her newsletter at violetkingauthor.com.

www.ingramcontent.com/pod-product-compliance
Lightning Source LLC
Chambersburg PA
CBHW032136270626
47172CB00008B/65